PENGUIN TWENTIETH-CENTURY CLASSICS

NAUSEA

Jean-Paul Sartre – one of the best-known and most discussed modern French writers and thinkers – was born in Paris in 1905. He was educated in Paris and later taught in schools at Le Havre and Laon. In 1934 he spent a year at the French Institute in Berlin where he rapidly gained a thorough knowledge of modern German philosophy. He then taught at the Lycée Condorcet in Paris. Sartre played an active role in the Resistance during the war and afterwards left the teaching profession to spend most of his time writing and editing the magazine *Les Temps modernes*.

Sartre was a Marxist and the founder of French existentialism but he will perhaps be remembered more as a man of passion, a fighter for what he believed in rather than as an idealist. After he died in 1980 *The Times* wrote, 'His death removes from the world literary, philosophical and political scene one of the most brilliant as well as one of the most original thinkers of the twentieth century ... The most openly political of all great French writers, his sometimes intolerant and always violent passion for freedom and justice made him as hated and as loved in his own day as Rousseau, Voltaire and Zola were in theirs.' George Steiner also wrote of him, 'The importance of the man will not only prove to reside in works like *Nausea* which is a masterpiece, but in the example of trying to live rationally, day in day out. It is the type of being he was that will influence men more than the specific declarations he made.'

Sartre's philosophical works, such as *L'Être et le néant* (1943), have had a profound effect on modern thought; and he also expounded his philosophical and political ideas through his novels and plays. His plays include *Huis clos* (1944), *Les Mouches* (1943), *Les mains sales* (1948), *Nekrassov* (1955) and *Les Séquestrés d'Altona*, in which he put forward his own view on the need for literature to take sides which had caused so much controversy when *Qu'est-ce que la littérature?* was published in 1947. Of his novels the trilogy *Les Chemins de la liberté* (published in Penguin as *The Age of Reason*, *The Reprieve* and *Iron in the Soul*) is perhaps most famous. Sartre's other works published in England include *Words* (1964), reminiscences of his childhood, *Baudelaire* (1964), *Saint Genet, Actor and Martyr* (1964) and *Situations*, a volume of essays (1965). His *Literary and Philosophical Essays* were published in 1968. Several of Sartre's novels and plays have been published in Penguin.

It was
like God lay down
let the moss suckle, the mist
shroud

JEAN-PAUL SARTRE

Nausea

There is a
magical
dissociation
between
word and
idea.

TRANSLATED FROM THE FRENCH
BY ROBERT BALDICK

The Peatman
David Deans
or "Would you
fancy some
sex?" - Andrew
(40 yr. old
pimp)

The disgust, nausea, pain at times
reminds you of your own
existence.

PENGUIN BOOKS

I revel in the
absurd

PENGUIN BOOKS

Published by the Penguin Group
Penguin Books Ltd, 27 Wrights Lane, London W8 5TZ, England
Penguin Putnam Inc., 375 Hudson Street, New York, New York 10014, USA
Penguin Books Australia Ltd, Ringwood, Victoria, Australia
Penguin Books Canada Ltd, 10 Alcorn Avenue, Toronto, Ontario, Canada M4V 3B2
Penguin Books (NZ) Ltd, 182–190 Wairau Road, Auckland 10, New Zealand

Penguin Books Ltd, Registered Offices: Harmondsworth, Middlesex, England

La Nausée first published by Librairie Gallimard 1938
First English translation *The Diary of Antoine Roquentin*,
published by John Lehmann Ltd 1949
This translation published by Penguin Books 1963
29 30

Printed in England by Clays Ltd, St Ives plc
Set in Linotype Granjon

TO THE BEAVER

'He is a fellow without any collective significance, barely an individual.'

L. F. Céline, *The Church*

Editors' Note

THESE notebooks were found among Antoine Roquentin's papers. We are publishing them without any alteration.

The first page is undated, but we have good reason to believe that it was written a few weeks before the diary itself was started. In that case it would have been written about the beginning of January 1932, at the latest.

At that time, Antoine Roquentin, after travelling in Central Europe, North Africa, and the Far East, had been living for three years at Bouville, where he was completing his historical research on the Marquis de Rollebon.

THE EDITORS

Undated Sheet

THE best thing would be to write down everything that happens from day to day. To keep a diary in order to understand. To neglect no nuances or little details, even if they seem unimportant, and above all to classify them. I must say how I see this table, the street, people, my packet of tobacco, since *these* are the things which have changed. I must fix the exact extent and nature of this change.

For example, there is a cardboard box which contains my bottle of ink. I ought to try to say how I saw it *before* and how I —* it now. Well, it's a parallelepiped rectangle standing out against – that's silly, there's nothing I can say about it. That's what I must avoid: I mustn't put strangeness where there's nothing. I think that is the danger of keeping a diary: you exaggerate everything, you are on the look-out, and you continually stretch the truth. On the other hand, it is certain that from one moment to the next – and precisely in connexion with this box or any other object – I may recapture this impression of the day before yesterday. I must always be prepared, or else it might slip through my fingers again. I must never —† anything but note down carefully and in the greatest detail everything that happens.

Naturally I can no longer write anything definite about that business on Saturday and the day before yesterday – I am already too far away from it; all that I can say is that in neither case was there anything people would ordinarily call an event. On Saturday the children were playing ducks and drakes, and I wanted to throw a pebble into the sea like them. At that moment I stopped, dropped the pebble and

* A word is missing here.

† A word has been crossed out here (possibly 'force' or 'forge'), and another word has been written above it which is illegible.

walked away. I imagine I must have looked rather bewildered, because the children laughed behind my back.

So much for the exterior. What happened inside me didn't leave any clear traces. There was something which I saw and which disgusted me, but I no longer know whether I was looking at the sea or at the pebble. It was a flat pebble, completely dry on one side, wet and muddy on the other. I held it by the edges, with my fingers wide apart to avoid getting them dirty.

The day before yesterday, it was much more complicated. There was also that series of coincidences and misunderstandings which I can't explain to myself. But I'm not going to amuse myself by putting all that down on paper. Anyhow, it's certain that I was frightened or experienced some other feeling of that sort. If only I knew what I was frightened of, I should already have made considerable progress.

The odd thing is that I am not at all prepared to consider myself insane, and indeed I can see quite clearly that I am not: all these changes concern objects. At least, that is what I'd like to be sure about.

10.30 *

Perhaps it was a slight attack of insanity after all. There is no longer any trace of it left. The peculiar feelings I had the other week strike me as quite ridiculous today: I can no longer enter into them. This evening I am quite at ease, with my feet firmly on the ground. This is my room, which faces north-east. Down below is the rue des Mutilés and the shunting yard of the new station. From my window I can see the red and white flame of the Rendez-vous des Cheminots at

* Obviously in the evening. The following paragraph is much later than the preceding ones. We are inclined to think that it was written the following day at the earliest.

the corner of the boulevard Victor-Noir. The Paris train has just come in. People are coming out of the old station and dispersing in the streets. I can hear footsteps and voices. A lot of people are waiting for the last tram. They must make a sad little group around the gas lamp just under my window. Well, they will have to wait a few minutes more: the tram won't come before a quarter to eleven. I only hope no commercial travellers are going to come tonight: I do so want to sleep and have so much sleep to catch up on. One good night, just one, and all this business would be swept away.

A quarter to eleven: there's nothing more to fear – if they were coming, they would be here already. Unless it's the day for the gentleman from Rouen. He comes every week, and they keep No. 2 for him, the first-floor room with a bidet. He may still turn up; he often drinks a beer at the Rendez-vous des Cheminots before going to bed. He doesn't make too much noise. He is quite short and very neat, with a waxed black moustache and a wig. Here he is now.

Well, when I heard him coming upstairs, it gave me quite a thrill, it was so reassuring: what is there to fear from such a regular world? I think I am cured.

And here comes tram No. 7, *Abattoirs – Grands Bassins*. It arrives with a great clanking noise. It moves off again. Now, loaded with suitcases and sleeping children, it's heading towards the Grands Bassins, towards the factories in the black east. It's the last tram but one; the last one will go by in an hour.

I'm going to bed. I'm cured, and I'm going to give up writing down my impressions, like a little girl, in a nice new notebook.

There's only one case in which it might be interesting to keep a diary: that would be if *

* The text of the undated sheet ends here.

Diary

Monday, 29 January 1932

SOMETHING has happened to me: I can't doubt that any more. It came as an illness does, not like an ordinary certainty, not like anything obvious. It installed itself cunningly, little by little; I felt a little strange, a little awkward, and that was all. Once it was established, it didn't move any more, it lay low and I was able to persuade myself that there was nothing wrong with me, that it was a false alarm. And now it has started blossoming.

I don't think the profession of historian fits a man for psychological analysis. In our work, we have to deal only with simple feelings to which we give generic names such as Ambition and Interest. Yet if I had an iota of self-knowledge, now is the time when I ought to use it.

There is something new, for example, about my hands, a certain way of picking up my pipe or my fork. Or else it is the fork which now has a certain way of getting itself picked up, I don't know. Just now, when I was on the point of coming into my room, I stopped short because I felt in my hand a cold object which attracted my attention by means of a sort of personality. I opened my hand and looked: I was simply holding the doorknob. This morning, at the library, when the Autodidact * came to say good-morning

* Ogier P—, who will often be mentioned in this diary. He was a bailiff's clerk. Roquentin had made his acquaintance in 1930 at the Bouville library.

to me, it took me ten seconds to recognize him. I saw an unknown face which was barely a face. And then there was his hand, like a fat maggot in my hand. I let go of it straight away and the arm fell back limply.

In the streets too there are a great many suspicious noises to be heard.

So a change *has* taken place in the course of these last few weeks. But where? It's an abstract change which settles on nothing. Is it I who has changed? If it isn't I, then it's this room, this town, this nature; I must choose.

I think it's I who has changed: that's the simplest solution, also the most unpleasant. But I have to admit that I am subject to these sudden transformations. The thing is that I very rarely think; consequently a host of little metamorphoses accumulate in me without my noticing it, and then, one fine day, a positive revolution takes place. That is what has given my life this halting, incoherent aspect. When I left France, for example, there were a lot of people who said I had gone off on a sudden impulse. And when I returned unexpectedly after six years of travelling, they might well have spoken of a sudden impulse once more. I can see myself again with Mercier in the office of that French official who resigned last year after the Pétrou business. Mercier was going to Bengal with an archaeological expedition. I had always wanted to go to Bengal, and he urged me to go with him. At present, I wonder why. I imagine that he didn't feel too sure of Portal and that he was counting on me to keep an eye on him. I could see no reason to refuse. And even if, at the time, I had guessed at that little scheme with regard to Portal, that would have been another reason for accepting enthusiastically. Well, I was paralysed, I couldn't say a word. I was staring at a little Khmer statuette on a card-table next to a telephone. I felt as if I were full of lymph or warm milk.

With an angelic patience which concealed a slight irritation, Mercier was saying to me:

'You see, I have to be certain from the official point of view. I know that you'll end up by saying yes, so you might as well accept straight away.'

He has a reddish-black beard, heavily scented. At every movement of his head I got a whiff of perfume. And then, all of a sudden, I awoke from a sleep which had lasted six years.

The statue struck me as stupid and unattractive and I felt that I was terribly bored. I couldn't understand why I was in Indo-China. What was I doing there? Why was I talking to those people? Why was I dressed so oddly? My passion was dead. For years it had submerged me and swept me along; now I felt empty. But that wasn't the worst of it: installed in front of me with a sort of indolence there was a voluminous, insipid idea. I don't know exactly what it was, but it sickened me so much that I couldn't look at it. All that was mixed up for me with the perfume of Mercier's beard.

I pulled myself together, convulsed with anger against him, and answered curtly:

'Thank you, but I think I've done enough travelling: I must go back to France now.'

Two days later I took the boat for Marseille.

If I am not mistaken, and if all the signs which are piling up are indications of a fresh upheaval in my life, well then, I am frightened. It isn't that my life is rich or weighty or precious, but I'm afraid of what is going to be born and take hold of me and carry me off – I wonder where? Shall I have to go away again, leaving everything behind – my research, my book? Shall I awake in a few months, a few years, exhausted, disappointed, in the midst of fresh ruins? I should like to understand myself properly before it is too late.

Tuesday, 30 January

Nothing new.

I worked from nine till one in the library. I organized Chapter XII and everything concerning Rollebon's stay in Russia up to the death of Paul I. That is all finished now. I shan't touch it again until the final revision.

It is half past one. I am at the Café Mably, eating a sandwich, and everything is more or less normal. In any case, everything is always normal in cafés and especially in the Café Mably, because of the manager, Monsieur Fasquelle, who has a vulgar expression in his eyes which is very straightforward and reassuring. It will soon be time for his afternoon nap and his eyes are already pink, but his manner is still lively and decisive. He is walking around among the tables and speaking confidentially to the customers:

'Is everything all right, Monsieur?'

I smile at seeing him so lively: when his establishment empties, his head empties too. Between two and four the café is deserted, and then Monsieur Fasquelle takes a few dazed steps, the waiters turn out the lights, and he slips into unconsciousness: when this man is alone, he falls asleep.

There are still about a score of customers left, bachelors, small-time engineers, and office workers. They lunch hurriedly in boarding houses which they call their 'messes', and, since they need a little luxury, they come here after their meal, to drink a cup of coffee and play poker dice; they make a little noise, but a vague noise which doesn't bother me. In order to exist, they too have to join with others.

I for my part live alone, entirely alone. I never speak to anybody, I receive nothing, I give nothing. The Autodidact doesn't count. Admittedly there is Françoise, the woman who runs the Rendez-vous des Cheminots. But do I speak to her? Sometimes, after dinner, when she brings me a beer, I ask her:

In order to exist I must only know of myself separate from others

'Have you got time this evening?'

She never says no and I follow her into one of the big bedrooms on the first floor, which she rents by the hour or by the day. I don't pay her: we make love on an *au pair* basis. She enjoys it (she has to have a man a day and she has many more besides me) and I purge myself in this way of a certain melancholy whose cause I know only too well. But we barely exchange a few words. What would be the use? Every man for himself; besides, as far as she's concerned, I remain first and foremost a customer in her café. Taking off her dress, she says to me:

'I say, have you ever heard of an apéritif called Bricot? Because there are two customers who've asked for it this week. The girl didn't know it and she came to ask me. They were commercial travellers, and they must have drunk it in Paris. But I don't like to buy anything without knowing it. If you don't mind, I'll keep my stockings on.'

In the past – even long after she had left me – I used to think about Anny. Now, I don't think about anybody any more; I don't even bother to look for words. It flows through me, more or less quickly, and I don't fix anything, I just let it go. Most of the time, because of their failure to fasten on to words, my thoughts remain misty and nebulous. They assume vague, amusing shapes and are then swallowed up: I promptly forget them.

These young people amaze me; drinking their coffee, they tell clear, plausible stories. If you ask them what they did yesterday, they don't get flustered; they tell you all about it in a few words. If I were in their place, I'd start stammering. It's true that for a long time now nobody has bothered how I spend my time. When you live alone, you even forget what it is to tell a story: plausibility disappears at the same time as friends. You let events flow by too: you suddenly see people appear who speak and then go away; you plunge into

17

stories of which you can't make head or tail: you'd make a terrible witness. But on the other hand, everything improbable, everything which nobody would ever believe in a café, comes your way. For example, on Saturday, about four in the afternoon, on the short wooden pavement of the station yard, a little woman in sky-blue was running backwards, laughing and waving a handkerchief. At the same time, a Negro in a cream-coloured raincoat, with yellow shoes and a green hat, was turning the corner of the street, whistling. Still going backwards, the woman bumped into him, underneath a lantern which hangs from the fence and which is lit at night. So there, at one and the same time, you had that fence which smells so strongly of wet wood, that lantern, and that little blonde in a Negro's arms, under a fiery-coloured sky. If there had been four or five of us, I suppose we would have noticed the collision, all those soft colours, the beautiful blue coat which looked like an eiderdown, the light-coloured raincoat, and the red panes of the lantern; we would have laughed at the stupefaction which appeared on those two childlike faces.

It is unusual for a man on his own to feel like laughing: the whole scene came alive for me with a significance which was strong and even fierce, but pure. Then it broke up, and nothing remained but the lantern, the fence, and the sky: it was still quite beautiful. An hour later, the lantern was lit, the wind was blowing, the sky was dark: nothing at all was left.

There is nothing very new about all that; I have never rejected these harmless emotions; far from it. In order to feel them, it is sufficient to be a little isolated, just enough to get rid of plausibility at the right moment. But I remained close to people, on the surface of solitude, quite determined, in case of emergency, to take refuge in their midst: so far I was an amateur at heart.

Now, there are objects everywhere like this glass of beer, here on the table. When I see it, I feel like saying: 'Pax, I'm not playing any more.' I realize perfectly well that I have gone too far. I don't suppose you can 'make allowances' for solitude. That doesn't mean that I look under my bed before going to sleep or that I'm afraid of seeing the door of my room open suddenly in the middle of the night. All the same, I am ill at ease: for half an hour I have been avoiding *looking* at this glass of beer. I look above, below, right and left: but the glass *itself* I don't want to see. And I know very well that all the bachelors around me can't help me in any way: it is too late, and I can no longer take refuge among them. They would come and slap me on the back and say to me: 'Well, what's special about that glass of beer? It's just like all the others. It's bevelled, and it has a handle and a little coat of arms with a spade on it, and on the coat of arms is written *Spatenbräu*.' I know all that, but I know that there's something else. Almost nothing. But I can no longer explain what I see. To anybody. There it is: I am gently slipping into the water's depths, towards fear.

I am alone in the midst of these happy, reasonable voices. All these characters spend their time explaining themselves, and happily recognizing that they hold the same opinions. Good God, how important they consider it to think the same things all together. It's enough to see their expressions when one of those fishy-eyed men who look as if they are turned in upon themselves and with whom no agreement is possible passes among them. When I was eight years old and used to play in the Luxembourg Gardens, there was one who came and sat in a sentry-box, against the railing which runs along the rue Auguste-Comte. He didn't speak, but every now and then he would stretch his leg out and look at his foot with a terrified expression. This foot wore a boot, but the other foot was in a slipper. The keeper told my uncle that the man was a former schoolmaster. He had been retired because he had turned up to read out the marks at the end of term dressed as an academician. We were terribly afraid of him because we sensed that he was alone. One day he smiled at Robert, holding his arms out to him from a distance: Robert nearly fainted. It wasn't the fellow's poverty-stricken appearance which frightened us, nor the tumour he had on his neck which rubbed against the edge of his collar: but we felt that he was shaping crab-like or lobster-like thoughts in his head. And it terrified us to think that somebody could have lobster-like thoughts about the sentry-box, about our hoops, about the bushes.

Is it that which awaits me then? For the first time it disturbs me to be alone. I should like to talk to somebody about what is happening to me before it is too late, before I start frightening little boys. I wish Anny were here.

It's odd: I have just filled up ten pages and I haven't told the truth, at least, not the whole truth. When I wrote under the date: 'Nothing new', it was with a bad conscience: as a matter of fact there was a little incident, with nothing shameful or extraordinary about it, which refused to come out. 'Nothing new'. I admire the way we can lie, putting reason on our side. Obviously, nothing new has happened in a manner of speaking. This morning, at a quarter past eight, as I was leaving the Hôtel Printania to go to the library, I tried to pick up a piece of paper lying on the ground and didn't succeed. That's all, and it isn't even an event. Yes, but, to tell the whole truth, it made a profound impression on me: it occurred to me that I was no longer free. At the library, I tried unsuccessfully to get rid of that idea. I attempted to escape from it at the Café Mably. I hoped that it would disappear in the bright light. But it stayed there inside me, heavy and painful. It is that idea which has dictated the preceding pages to me.

Why didn't I mention it? It must have been out of pride, and then, too, a little out of awkwardness. I am not accustomed to telling myself what happens to me, so I find it hard to remember the exact succession of events, and I can't make out what is important. But now that's over and done with: I have re-read what I wrote in the Café Mably and it made me feel ashamed; I want no secrets, no spiritual condition, nothing ineffable; I am neither a virgin nor a priest, to play at having an inner life.

There's nothing much to say: I couldn't manage to pick up the piece of paper, that's all.

I am very fond of picking up chestnuts, old rags, and especially pieces of paper. I find it pleasant to pick them up, to close my hand over them; for two pins I would put them to my mouth as children do. Anny used to fly into a rage when I picked up by one corner pieces of paper which were heavy and rich-looking but probably soiled with excrement. In summer or early autumn, you can find in gardens pieces of newspapers baked by the sun, as dry and brittle as dead leaves, and so yellow you might think they had been dipped in picric acid. Other pieces of paper, in winter, are pulped, crumpled, stained; they return to the earth. Others which are new and even shiny, white and palpitating, are as sedate as swans, but the earth has already ensnared them from below. They twist and tear themselves away from the mud, but only to fall a little farther on, this time for good. All these pieces of paper are worth picking up. Sometimes I simply feel them, looking at them closely; at other times I tear them to hear the long crackling noise they make, or else, if they are very wet, I set fire to them, something which is not easy to do; then I wipe the muddy palms of my hands on a wall or a tree trunk.

So, today, I was looking at the fawn-coloured boots of a cavalry officer who was coming out of the barracks. As I followed them with my eyes, I saw a piece of paper lying beside a puddle. I thought that the officer was going to crush the paper into the mud with his heel, but no: with a single step he strode over paper and puddle. I went up to it: it was a lined page, probably torn out of a school note-book. The rain had drenched and twisted it, and it was covered with blisters and swellings, like a burnt hand. The red line of the margin had blurred into a pink smear; the ink had run in places. The bottom of the page was hidden by a crust of mud. I bent down, already looking forward to touching this fresh and tender pulp which would roll into grey balls in my fingers . . . I couldn't do it.

I stayed in a bent position for a moment, I read: 'Dictation: The White Owl', then I straightened up, empty-handed. I am no longer free, I can no longer do what I want.

Objects ought not to *touch*, since they are not alive. You use them, you put them back in place, you live among them: they are useful, nothing more. But they touch me, it's un-bearable. I am afraid of entering in contact with them, just as if they were living animals.

Now I see; I remember better what I felt the other day on the sea-shore when I was holding that pebble. It was a sort of sweet disgust. How unpleasant it was! And it came from the pebble, I'm sure of that, it passed from the pebble into my hands. Yes, that's it, that's exactly it: a sort of nausea in the hands.

Thursday morning, at the library

Earlier this morning, coming down the hotel stairs, I heard Lucie complaining for the hundredth time to the *patronne*, while polishing the steps. The *patronne* was speaking with difficulty and in short sentences, because she hadn't put her false teeth in yet; she was almost naked, in a pink dressing-gown and Turkish slippers. Lucie was dirty as usual; every now and then she stopped rubbing and sat back on her heels to look at the *patronne*. She spoke without pausing, with a serious expression.

'I'd be much happier if he went with other women,' she said; 'it wouldn't make any difference to me, so long as it didn't do him any harm.'

She was talking about her husband: at the age of about forty this swarthy little woman had bought herself, with her savings, a good-looking young man, a fitter at the Lecointe works. Her married life is anything but happy. Her husband doesn't beat her, isn't unfaithful to her: he drinks, he comes home drunk every night. He's in a bad way; in three months I have seen him turn yellow and melt away. Lucie thinks it's the drink. My opinion is that he's got tuberculosis.

'You've got to get on top of it,' said Lucie.

It's gnawing away at her, I'm sure of that, but slowly, patiently: she gets on top of it, incapable either of consoling herself or of abandoning herself to her unhappiness. She thinks about it a little bit, a very little bit, now and then; she cadges a scrap of it. Especially when she is with people, because they console her and also because it comforts her a little to talk about it in a calm voice, as if she were giving advice. When she is alone in the rooms, I hear her humming to prevent herself from thinking. But she is morose all day long, suddenly weary and sullen.

'It's there,' she says, touching her throat, 'it won't go down.'

She suffers like a miser. She must be miserly too with her pleasures. I wonder if sometimes she doesn't wish she could be free of this monotonous suffering, of these grumblings which start up again as soon as she stops singing, if she doesn't long to suffer once for all, to drown herself in despair. But in any case, that would be impossible for her: she is too set in her ways.

Thursday afternoon

Monsieur de Rollebon was extremely ugly. Queen Marie Antoinette was fond of calling him her 'dear monkey'. Yet he had all the women of the Court, not by clowning like Voisenon the baboon, but by a magnetism which drove his beautiful victims to the worst excesses of passion. He schemed and plotted, played a somewhat suspicious part in the affair of the Necklace, and disappeared in 1790, after being in close connexion with Mirabeau-Tonneau and Nerciat. He turned up again in Russia, where he helped to assassinate Paul I, and from there he travelled to the most distant lands, to the Indies, China, Turkestan. He smuggled, plotted, spied. In 1813 he returned to Paris. By 1816 he had become all-powerful: he was the sole confidant of the Duchesse d'Angoulême. That capricious old woman, obsessed by horrible childhood memories, used to calm down and smile when she saw him. Through her, he ruled the roost at Court. In March 1820 he married Mademoiselle de Roquelaure, a very beautiful girl of eighteen. Monsieur de Rollebon was seventy; he enjoyed the supreme honours, was at the zenith of his life. Seven months later, accused of treason, he was arrested and thrown into a dungeon where he died after five years of imprisonment, without ever having been brought to trial.

It is with a certain melancholy that I have re-read this note by Germain Berger.* It was through these few lines that I first came to know Monsieur de Rollebon. How attractive he seemed to me, and how I loved him straight away, on

* Germain Berger: *Mirabeau-Tonneau et ses amis*, page 406, note 2, Champion, 1906 (Editors' footnote).

the basis of these few words! It is for his sake, for the sake of that little fellow, that I am here. When I returned from my travels, I could just as well have settled in Paris or in Marseille. But most of the documents concerning the Marquis's long stays in France are in the Municipal Library of Bouville. Rollebon was the squire of Marommes. Before the war, you could still find one of his descendants in that little town, an architect called Rollebon-Campouyré, who, on his death in 1912, left an important legacy to the Bouville library: some letters of the Marquis, a fragment of a diary, and papers of all sorts. I haven't gone through it all yet.

I am happy to have found these notes again. It is ten years since I last read them. My writing has changed, or so it seems to me: I used to write in a smaller hand. How I loved Monsieur de Rollebon that year! I remember one evening – a Tuesday evening: I had worked all day long in the Mazarine; I had just realized, from his correspondence of 1789–90, the masterly way in which he duped Nerciat. It was dark, I was going down the avenue du Maine, and on the corner of the rue de la Gaîté I bought some chestnuts. How happy I was! I laughed all by myself at the thought of the face Nerciat must have made when he came back from Germany. The Marquis's face is like this ink: it has grown much paler since I started taking an interest in him.

In the first place, as from 1801, I can't understand his behaviour any more. This isn't for lack of documents: letters, fragments of memoirs, secret reports, police records. On the contrary, I have almost too many of these. What is lacking in all this testimony is firmness and consistency. True, they don't contradict one another, but they don't agree with one another either; they don't seem to concern the same person. And yet other historians are working on documents of the same sort. How do they do it? Is it that I am more scrupulous or less intelligent? In any case, put like that, the question leaves me completely cold. At bottom, what am I looking for? I don't know. For a long time, Rollebon the man has interested me more than the book to be written. But now, the man ... the man is beginning to bore me. It is the book to which I am growing attached, and I feel an ever-increasing compulsion to write it – the older I get, you might say.

Obviously it is possible to agree that Rollebon took an active part in the assassination of Paul I, and that he then accepted an important espionage mission to the Orient on behalf of the Tsar and consistently betrayed Alexander for Napoleon's benefit. At the same time he may have carried on an active correspondence with the Comte d'Artois and sent him unimportant information in order to convince him of his loyalty: none of all that is improbable, and Fouché, at the same period, was playing a much more complex and dangerous game. Possibly the Marquis also trafficked in rifles with the Asiatic principalities for his own profit.

Well, yes: he may have done all that, but there's no proof that he did: I am beginning to believe that nothing can ever be proved. These are reasonable hypotheses which take the facts into account: but I am only too well aware that they come from me, that they are simply a way of unifying my own knowledge. Not a single glimmer comes from Rollebon's direction. Slow, lazy, sulky, the facts adapt themselves at a pinch to the order I wish to give them, but it remains outside of them. I have the impression of doing a work of pure imagination. And even so, I am certain that characters in a novel would appear more realistic, or in any case would be more amusing.

Friday

Three o'clock. Three o'clock is always too late or too early for anything you want to do. A peculiar moment in the afternoon. Today it is intolerable.

A cold sunshine is whitening the dust on the window-panes. A pale sky, mottled with white. The gutters were frozen this morning. I am digesting dully near the stove; I know in advance that this is a wasted day. I shan't do anything good, except, perhaps, after nightfall. It's on account of the sun; it vaguely gilds dirty white wisps of mist hanging in the air above the yard, it flows into my room, all fair and pale, and it spreads four dull, false patches of light on my table.

My pipe is daubed with a golden varnish which at first catches the eye by means of its appearance of gaiety: you look at it, and the varnish melts, nothing is left but a big pale streak on a piece of wood. And everything is like that, everything, even my hands. When the sun begins shining like that the best thing to do would be to go to bed. Only I slept like a log last night, and I don't feel sleepy.

I liked yesterday's sky so much, a narrow sky, dark with rain, pressing against the window-panes like a ridiculous, touching face. This sun isn't ridiculous, quite the contrary. On everything I love, on the rust in the yards, on the rotten planks of the fence, a miserly, sensible light is falling, like the look you give, after a sleepless night, at the decisions you made enthusiastically the day before, at the pages you wrote straight off without a single correction. The four cafés on the boulevard Victor-Noir, which shine brightly at night, side by side, and which are much more than cafés — aquariums, ships, stars, or big wide eyes — have lost their ambiguous charm.

A perfect day to turn in upon oneself: these cold rays which the sun projects like a pitiless judgement on all creatures enter into me through my eyes; I am illuminated within by an impoverishing light. A quarter of an hour would be enough, I feel sure, for me to attain a feeling of supreme self-contempt. No, thank you very much, I can do without that. Nor shall I re-read what I wrote yesterday about Rollebon's stay in St Petersburg. I remain seated, my arms dangling, or else I write a few words, rather dispiritedly; I yawn, I wait for night to fall. When it is dark, the objects and I will come out of limbo.

Did Rollebon take part in the assassination of Paul I or didn't he? That is the question of the day: I have got as far as that and I can't go any further without deciding.

According to Tcherkov, he was paid by Count Pahlen. Most of the conspirators, says Tcherkov, would have been content with deposing and imprisoning the Tsar. (Alexander indeed seems to have been in favour of that solution.) But Pahlen allegedly wanted to get rid of Paul completely, and Monsieur de Rollebon is said to have been given the task of converting each conspirator individually to the plan for assassination.

'He visited each of them and, with incomparable power, mimed the scene which was to take place. Like that he introduced or developed in them the lust to kill.' But I distrust Tcherkov. He isn't a reasonable witness, but a half-mad, sadistic magus: he gives a demoniacal twist to everything. I simply cannot see Monsieur de Rollebon in this melodramatic role. Would he have mimed the assassination scene? Not on your life! He was a cold man, who didn't usually sweep other people off their feet: he didn't show things, he insinuated, and his pale, colourless method could succeed only with men of his kind, intriguers accessible to reason, politicians.

Adhémar de Rollebon [writes Madame de Charrières] did not paint pictures with his words, made no gestures, never changed the tone of his voice. He kept his eyes half-closed, and one could barely distinguish, between his lashes, the outer edges of his grey pupils. It has only been within the last few years that I have dared to admit to myself that he bored me more than I can say. He spoke rather in the way that the Abbé Mably used to write.

And this is the man who, by his gift for miming ... But then how did he manage to captivate women? And then there is this curious story which Ségur tells and which strikes me as plausible:

In 1787, at an inn near Moulins, an old man was dying – a friend of Diderot's, whose ideas had been moulded by the *philosophes*. The local priests were baffled: they had tried everything in vain; the good man refused the last sacraments, saying he was a pantheist. Monsieur de Rollebon, who was passing by and who believed in nothing, bet the Curé of Moulins that he would take less than two hours to bring the sick man back to Christian sentiments. The Curé took the bet and lost: taken in hand at three in the morning, the sick man confessed at five and died at seven. 'You must be very good at arguing,' said the Curé, 'to beat our own people!' 'I didn't argue,' replied Monsieur de Rollebon, 'I made him frightened of Hell.'

Now, did he take an effective part in the assassination? That evening, about eight o'clock, one of his officer friends accompanied him as far as his door. If he went out again, how did he manage to cross St Petersburg without being stopped? Paul, who was half-insane, had given orders that after nine o'clock at night all passers-by except midwives and doctors were to be arrested. Are we to believe the absurd legend that Rollebon disguised himself as a midwife in order to get to the palace? After all, he was quite capable of a thing like that. In any case, it seems proved that he was not at home on the night of the assassination. Alexander must have been deeply suspicious of him, since one of the first official acts of his reign was to send the Marquis away under the vague pretext of a mission to the Far East.

Monsieur de Rollebon bores me to tears. I get up. I move about in this pale light; I see it change on my hands and on the sleeves of my jacket: I cannot say how much it disgusts me. I yawn. I light the lamp on the table: perhaps its light will be able to fight the light of day. But no: the lamp does nothing more than spread a pitiful pool around its base. I turn it out; I get up. On the wall there is a white hole, the mirror. It is a trap. I know that I am going to let myself be caught in it. I have. The grey thing has just appeared in the mirror. I go over and look at it, I can no longer move away.

It is the reflection of my face. Often, during these wasted days, I stay here contemplating it. I can understand nothing about this face. Other people's faces have some significance. Not mine. I cannot even decide whether it is handsome or ugly. I think it is ugly, because I have been told so. But that doesn't strike me. At heart, I am indeed shocked that qualities of this sort can be applied to it, as if you called a piece of earth or a lump of rock beautiful or ugly.

All the same there is one thing which is a pleasure to see, above the flabby regions of the cheeks, above the forehead: it is that beautiful red flame which gilds my skull, it is my hair. That is something pleasant to see. At least it's a definite colour: I am glad I have red hair. It's there in the mirror, it catches the eye, it shines out. I'm still lucky: if my forehead was adorned with one of those dull heads of hair which can't make up their mind whether to be chestnut or fair, my face would be lost in a vague expanse, it would make me feel giddy.

My gaze travels slowly and wearily down over this forehead, these cheeks: it meets nothing firm, and sinks into the sand. Admittedly there is a nose there, two eyes and a mouth, but none of that has any significance, nor even a human expression. Yet Anny and Vélines thought I looked alive; it may be that I am too accustomed to my face. When I was small, my Aunt Bigeois used to tell me: 'If you look at yourself too long in the mirror, you'll see a monkey there.' I must have looked at myself even longer than that: what I can see is far below the monkey, on the edge of the vegetable world, at the polyp level. It's alive, I can't deny that; but this isn't the life that Anny was thinking of: I can see some slight tremors, I can see an insipid flesh blossoming and palpitating with abandon. The eyes in particular, seen at such close quarters, are horrible. They are glassy, soft, blind, and red-rimmed; anyone would think they were fish-scales. I lean my whole weight on the porcelain edge, I push my face forward until it touches the mirror. The eyes, the nose, the mouth disappear: nothing human is left. Brown wrinkles on each side of the feverish swelling of the lips, crevices, mole-hills. A silky white down runs along the wide slopes of the cheeks, two hairs protrude from the nostrils: it's a geological relief map. And, in spite of everything, this lunar world is familiar to me. I can't say that I *recognize* the details. But the whole thing gives me an impression of something seen before which numbs me: I slip gently into sleep.

I should like to pull myself together: a sharp, abrupt sensation would release me. I slap my left hand against my cheek, I pull the skin; I grimace at myself. An entire half of my face gives way, the left half of the mouth twists and swells, uncovering a tooth, the eye-socket opens on a white globe, on pink, bleeding flesh. That isn't what I was looking for: nothing strong, nothing new; soft, vague, familiar stuff! I'm going to sleep with my eyes open; already the face is growing larger, growing in the mirror; it is an immense, pale halo slipping in the light . . .

I lose my balance and that wakes me up with a start. I find myself sitting astride a chair, still quite dazed. Do other men experience as much difficulty in appraising their face? It seems to me that I see my own as I feel my body, through a dull, organic sensation. But the others? Rollebon, for example? Did it send him to sleep as well to look in a mirror at what Madame de Genlis calls

his little wrinkled face, clean and sharp-featured, all pitted with smallpox, in which there was a remarkable mischievousness which caught the eye at once, however much he tried to disguise it. He took [she adds] great care with his coiffure and I never saw him without a wig. But his cheeks were a blue verging on black, because he had a heavy growth and insisted on shaving himself, which he did extremely badly. It was his custom to daub his face with ceruse, as Grimm did. Monsieur de Dangeville used to say that with all that blue and white he looked like a Roquefort cheese.

It seems to me that he must have been very amusing. But that, after all, isn't the way he looked to Madame de Charrières. She, I believe, found him rather dull and quiet. Perhaps it is impossible to understand one's own face. Or perhaps it is because I am a solitary? People who live in society have learnt how to see themselves, in mirrors, as they appear to their friends. I have no friends: is that why my flesh is so naked? You might say – yes, you might say nature without mankind.

I no longer feel any inclination to work, I can do nothing more except wait for night to fall.

5.30

Things are bad! Things are very bad: I've got it, that filthy thing, the Nausea. And this time it's new: it caught me in a café. Until now cafés were my only refuge because

32

they are full of people and well lighted: from now on I shan't have even that; when I am run to earth in my room, I shall no longer know where to go.

I had come along for a fuck, but I had scarcely opened the door before Madeleine, the waitress, called out to me:

'The *patronne* isn't here, she's gone shopping in town.'

I felt a sharp disappointment in my prick, a long disagreeable tickling. At the same time I felt my shirt rubbing against my nipples and I was surrounded, seized by a slow, coloured whirlpool, a whirlpool of fog, of lights in the smoke, in the mirrors, with the benches shining at the back, and I couldn't see why it was there or why it was like that. I was on the doorstep, I was hesitating, and then there was a sudden eddy, a shadow passed across the ceiling, and I felt myself being pushed forward. I floated along, dazed by the luminous mists which were entering me from all directions at once. Madeleine came floating up to me to take off my overcoat and I noticed that she had drawn her hair back and put on earrings: I didn't recognize her. I looked at her big cheeks which stretched endlessly away towards her ears. In the hollow of the cheeks, under the cheek-bones, there were two isolated pink patches which looked as if they were feeling bored on that poor flesh. The cheeks stretched away, away towards the ears and Madeleine smiled:

'What will you have, Monsieur Antoine?'

Then the Nausea seized me, I dropped on to the bench, I no longer even knew where I was; I saw the colours slowly spinning around me, I wanted to vomit. And there it is: since then, the Nausea hasn't left me, it holds me in its grip.

I paid. Madeleine took away my saucer. My glass crushes a puddle of yellow beer, with a bubble floating in it, against the marble table top. The bench is broken just where I am sitting, and to avoid slipping I am forced to press the soles

33

of my shoes hard against the floor; it is cold. On the right, they are playing cards on a woollen cloth. I didn't see them when I came in; I simply sensed that there was a warm packet, half on the bench, half on the table at the back, with some pairs of arms waving about. Since then, Madeleine has brought them cards, the cloth, and the chips in a wooden bowl. There are three or five of them, I don't know how many, I haven't the courage to look at them. There's a spring inside me that's broken: I can move my eyes but not my head. The head is all soft and elastic, as if it had just been balanced on my neck; if I turn it, it will fall off. All the same, I can hear a short breath and now and then, out of the corner of my eye, I can see a reddish flash covered with white hairs. It is a hand.

When the *patronne* goes shopping it's her cousin who takes her place at the bar. His name is Adolphe. I began looking at him while I was sitting down and I went on because I couldn't turn my head. He is in shirt-sleeves with mauve braces; he has rolled the sleeves of his shirt above his elbows. The braces can scarcely be seen against the blue shirt; they are completely obliterated, buried in the blue, but this is false modesty; in point of fact they won't allow themselves to be forgotten, they annoy me with their sheep-like stubbornness, as if, setting out to become purple, they had stopped somewhere on the way without giving up their pretentions. You feel like telling them: 'Go on, *become* purple and let's hear no more about it.' But no, they remain in suspense, fixed in their unfinished effort. Sometimes the blue which surrounds them slips over them and covers them completely: for a moment I can't see them. But it is just a passing wave, and soon the blue goes pale in places and I see patches of hesitant mauve reappear, widen, join together, and reconstitute the braces. Cousin Adolphe has no eyes: his swollen, turned-up eyelids reveal just a little white. He smiles sleepily; now and then he snorts, yelps, and writhes feebly, like a dog having a dream.

His blue cotton shirt stands out cheerfully against a chocolate-coloured wall. That too brings on the Nausea. Or rather it *is* the Nausea. The Nausea isn't inside me: I can feel it *over there* on the wall, on the braces, everywhere around me. It is one with the café, it is I who am inside *it*.

On my right, the warm packet starts rustling, it waves its pairs of arms. 'Look, there's your trump.' 'What are trumps?' Long black spine bent over the game: 'Hahaha!' 'What? There's the trump, he's just played it.' 'I don't know, I didn't see . . .' 'Yes, I've just played trumps.' 'Ah, so hearts are trumps.' He sings softly: 'Hearts are trumps, hearts are trumps, hea-arts are trumps.' Spoken: 'What is it, Monsieur? What is it, Monsieur? I'll take it!'

Silence once more – the sugary taste of the air at the back of my throat. The smells, the braces.

The cousin has got up, taken a few steps, put his hands behind his back. He smiles, raises his head and leans back on his heels. In this position he goes to sleep. He is there, swaying, still smiling, with his cheeks trembling. He is going to fall. He bends backwards, bends, bends, his face turned completely up towards the ceiling, then, just as he is about to fall, he steadies himself adroitly on the edge of the bar and regains his balance. After which, he starts again. I have had enough, I call the waitress.

'Madeleine, please play me something on the gramophone. The one I like, you know: *Some of These Days*.'

'Yes, but it might bother these gentlemen; these gentlemen don't like music when they're playing. But I'll ask them.'

I make a great effort and turn my head. There are four of them. She bends over a red-faced old man with a pair of black-rimmed pince-nez on the end of his nose. He hides his cards against his chest and glances at me from under his glasses.

'Go ahead, Monsieur.'

Smiles. His teeth are rotten. The red hand doesn't belong to him, it belongs to his neighbour, a fellow with a black moustache. This fellow with the moustache has huge nostrils which could pump air for a whole family and which eat up half his face, but in spite of that he breathes through his mouth, panting slightly. With them there is also a young man with a face like a dog. I can't make out the fourth player.

The cards fall on to the woollen cloth, spinning through the air. Then hands with ringed fingers come and pick them up, scratching the cloth with their nails. The hands make white patches on the cloth, they look puffy and dusty. More cards fall all the time, the hands come and go. What a peculiar occupation: it doesn't look like a game, or a rite, or a habit. I think they do that to pass the time, nothing more. But time is too large, it refuses to let itself be filled up. Everything you plunge into it goes soft and slack. That gesture, for example, of the red hand falteringly picking up the cards: it's all flabby. It ought to be unstitched and cut down.

Madeleine turns the handle of the gramophone. I only hope she hasn't made a mistake and put on the principal theme from *Cavalleria Rusticana*, as she did the other day. But no, that's it, I recognize the tune from the very first bars. It's an old rag-time tune with a vocal refrain. I heard some American soldiers whistle it in 1917 in the streets of La Rochelle. It must date from before the War. But the recording is much more recent. All the same, it's the oldest record in the collection. A Pathé record for a sapphire needle.

The refrain will be coming soon: that's the part I like best and the abrupt way in which it flings itself forward, like a cliff against the sea. For the moment it's the jazz that's

36

playing; there's no melody, only notes, a host of little jolts. They know no rest, an unchanging order gives birth to them and destroys them, without ever giving them time to recover, to exist for themselves. They run, they hurry, they strike me with a sharp blow in passing and are obliterated. I should quite like to hold them back, but I know that if I managed to stop one, nothing would remain between my fingers but a vulgar, doleful sound. I must accept their death; I must even *will* it; I know few harsher or stronger impressions.

I am beginning to warm up again, to feel happy. This is nothing out of the ordinary as yet, just a little Nausea happiness; it spreads out at the bottom of the slimy puddle, at the bottom of *our* time – the time of mauve braces and broken benches – it's made of wide, soft moments, which grow outwards at the edges like an oil stain. It's no sooner born than it's already old, it seems as if I had known it for twenty years.

There's another happiness: outside, there's that band of steel, the narrow duration of the music, which crosses our time through and through, and rejects it and tears it with its dry little points; here's another time.

'Monsieur Randu plays hearts, you put down the ace.'

The voice slithers and disappears. Nothing bites on the ribbon of steel, neither the opening door, nor the gust of cold air flowing over my knees, nor the arrival of the vet with his little girl: the music pierces these vague shapes and passes beyond them. The little girl has scarcely sat down before she is seized: she holds herself rigid, her eyes wide open: she listens, rubbing the table with her fist.

Another few seconds and the Negress will sing. It seems inevitable, the necessity of this music is so strong: nothing can interrupt it, nothing which comes from this time in which the world is slumped; it will stop of its own accord, on orders. If I love that beautiful voice, it is above all because of that: it is neither for its fullness nor its sadness, but because it is the event which so many notes have prepared so far in advance, dying so that it might be born. And yet I feel anxious; it would take so little to make the record stop: a broken spring, a whim on the part of Cousin Adolphe. How strange it is, how moving, that this hardness should be so fragile. Nothing can interrupt it but anything can break it.

The last chord has died away. In the brief silence which follows, I feel strongly that this is it, that *something has happened*.

Silence.

> Some of these days
> You'll miss me honey!

What has just happened is that the Nausea has disappeared. When the voice sounded in the silence, I felt my body harden and the Nausea vanished. All of a sudden: it was almost painful to become so hard, so bright. At the same time the duration of the music dilated, swelled like a water spout. It filled the room with its metallic transparency, crushing our wretched time against the walls. I am *in* the music. Globes of fire revolve in the mirrors; rings of smoke encircle them and spin around, veiling and unveiling the hard smile of the light. My glass of beer has shrunk, it huddles up on the table: it looks dense and indispensable. I want to pick it up and weigh it, I stretch out my hand ... Good Lord! It's that which has changed most of all, it's my gestures. That movement of my arm unfolded like a majestic theme, it glided along the song of the Negress; it seemed to me that I was dancing.

Adolphe's face is there, set against the chocolate-coloured wall; he seems quite close. Just as my hand was closing, I saw his face; it had the obvious, necessary look of a conclusion.

I press my fingers against the glass, I look at Adolphe: I am happy.

'There!'

A voice rises above the general noise. It's my neighbour who is speaking, the drunken old man. His cheeks make a purple patch against the brown leather of the bench. He slaps a card down on the table. The queen of diamonds.

But the young man who looks like a dog smiles. The red-faced player, bent over the table, looks up at him, ready to spring.

'And there!'

The young man's hand emerges from the shadows, hovers for a moment, white, indolent, then suddenly drops like a kite and presses a card against the cloth. The fat red-faced man jumps into the air:

'Hell! He's trumped.'

The outline of the king of hearts appears between clenched fingers, then it is turned on its face and the game goes on. Handsome king, come from so far away, prepared for by so many combinations, by so many vanished gestures. Now he disappears in his turn, so that other combinations may be born, other gestures, attacks, counter-attacks, changes of fortune, a host of little adventures.

I am moved, I feel my body like a precision tool at rest. I for my part have had some real adventures. I can't remember a single detail, but I can see the rigorous succession of circumstances. I have crossed the seas, I have left cities behind me, and I have followed the course of rivers towards their source or else plunged into forests, always making for other cities. I have had women, I have fought with men; and I could never turn back, any more than a record can spin in reverse. And all that was leading me *where*? To this very moment, to this bench, in this bubble of light humming with music.

And when you leave me.

Yes, I who was so fond of sitting on the banks of the Tiber in Rome, or in the evening, in Barcelona, of walking a hundred times up and down the Ramblas, I who near Angkor, on the island of the Baray of Prah-Kan, saw a banyan tree knotting its roots around the chapel of the Nagas, I am here, I am living in the same second as these card players, I am listening to a Negress singing while the feeble night prowls outside.

The record has stopped.

Night has entered, smooth, hesitant. No one sees her, but she is there, veiling the lamps; you can breathe something thick in the air: it is she. It is cold. One of the players pushes the cards in an untidy heap towards another who picks them up. One card has been left behind. Can't they see it? It's the nine of hearts. Someone picks it up at last, and gives it to the dog-faced young man.

'Ah! It's the nine of hearts!'

Good, I'm off. The purple-faced old man bends over a sheet of paper, sucking the point of a pencil. Madeleine watches him with bright, empty eyes. The young man turns the nine of hearts over and over between his fingers. Good God! . . .

I get laboriously to my feet; in the mirror, above the vet's head, I see an inhuman face gliding along.

In a little while I'll go to the cinema.

The air does me good: it hasn't got the taste of sugar nor the winey smell of vermouth. But God, how cold it is.

It's half past seven, I'm not hungry and the cinema doesn't start till nine o'clock; what am I going to do? I have to walk quickly to keep warm. I hesitate: behind me the boulevard leads to the heart of the town, to the big fiery jewels of the central streets, to the Palais Paramount, the Imperial, the

Grands Magasins Jahan. That doesn't tempt me at all; it's apéritif time: for the time being I've seen enough of living things, of dogs, of men, of all the flabby masses which move about spontaneously.

I turn left, I'm going to plunge into that hole over there, at the end of the row of gas lamps: I'm going to follow the boulevard Noir as far as the avenue Galvani. An icy wind is blowing from the hole: yonder there is nothing but stones and earth. Stones are hard and don't move.

There is a tedious stretch at first: on the right-hand pavement, a gaseous mass, grey with streaks of fire, is making a noise like rattling shells: this is the old station. Its presence has fertilized the first hundred yards of the boulevard Noir – from the boulevard de la Redoute to the rue Paradis – has spawned a dozen street lamps there and, side by side, four cafés, the Rendez-vous des Cheminots and three others, which languish all day long but light up in the evening and cast luminous rectangles on the roadway. I take another three baths of yellow light, and see an old woman come out of the Rabache general stores who pulls her shawl over her head and starts running. Now it's finished. I'm on the curb of the rue Paradis, next to the last lamp-post. The asphalt ribbon breaks off sharply. On the other side of the street there is darkness and mud. I cross the rue Paradis. I put my right foot in a puddle of water, my sock is soaked through; the walk begins.

Nobody *lives* in this part of the boulevard Noir. The climate is too harsh here, the soil too barren for life to settle here and grow. The three saw-works of the Soleil Brothers (the Soleil Brothers provided the panelled arch of the church of Sainte-Cécile-de-la-Mer, which cost a hundred thousand francs) open on the west, with all their doors and windows, on to the quiet rue Jeanne-Berthe-Coeuroy, which they fill with purring sounds. On the boulevard Victor-Noir they

41

turn their three backs, joined by walls. These buildings border the left-hand pavement for four hundred yards: there isn't the smallest window, not even a skylight.

This time I've put both feet in the gutter. I cross the street; on the opposite pavement a solitary gas lamp, like a lighthouse at the far end of the earth, lights up a broken-down fence, which has been dismantled here and there.

Scraps of old posters are still sticking to the planks. A handsome face full of hatred grimaces against a green background, torn into the shape of a star; under the nose somebody has pencilled a curled-up moustache. On another scrap you can still make out the word *purâtre* in white letters from which red drops are falling, possibly drops of blood. It may be that the face and the word formed part of the same poster. Now the poster is torn, the simple, deliberate links which joined them have disappeared, but another unity has established itself of its own accord between the twisted mouth, the drops of blood, the white letters, and the termination *âtre*: it is as if a restless criminal passion were trying to express itself through these mysterious signs. Between the planks you can see the lights from the railway shining. The fence is followed by a long wall: a wall without any openings, without any doors, without any windows, a wall which stops two hundred yards farther on, against a house. I have gone out of range of the street lamp; I enter the black hole. Seeing my shadow at my feet melt into the darkness, I have the impression of plunging into icy water. In front of me, far ahead, through layers of black, I can make out a pale patch of pink: it is the avenue Galvani. I turn round; behind the gas lamp, far away, there is a hint of light: that is the station with the four cafés. Behind me, in front of me, there are people drinking and playing cards in pubs. Here there is nothing but darkness. Intermittently the wind carries a lonely, distant ringing to my ears. Familiar noises, the roar of motor-cars, shouts, and the barking of dogs scarcely stir from the lighted streets, they stay where it is warm. But this ringing sound pierces the darkness and reaches as far as here: it is harder, less human than the other noises.

I stop to listen to it. I am cold, my ears hurt; they must be all red. But I can't feel myself any longer; I am won over by the purity of my surroundings; nothing is alive; the wind whistles, straight lines flee into the darkness. The boulevard Noir doesn't have the indecent look of bourgeois streets, which try to charm the passers-by: it is simply a reverse side. The reverse side of the rue Jeanne-Berthe-Coeuroy, of the avenue Galvani. In the vicinity of the station, the people of Bouville still look after it a little: they clean it now and then because of the travellers. But, immediately afterwards, they abandon it and it rushes straight on, in total darkness, finally bumping into the avenue Galvani. The town has forgotten it. Sometimes a big mud-coloured lorry thunders across it at top speed. Nobody even commits any murders on it, for want of murderers and victims. The boulevard Noir is inhuman. Like a mineral. Like a triangle. We are lucky to have a boulevard like that at Bouville. Usually you find them only in capitals – in Berlin near Neukölln or again towards Friedrichshain; in London behind Greenwich. Straight, dirty corridors, with a howling draught and wide, treeless pavements. They are nearly always on the outskirts in those strange districts where cities are manufactured, near goods stations, tram depots, slaughter-houses, and gasometers. Two days after a downpour, when the whole city is moist in the sunshine and radiates damp heat, they are still cold, they keep their mud and puddles. They even have puddles of water which never dry up, except one month in the year, August.

The Nausea has stayed over there, in the yellow light. I am happy: this cold is so pure, this darkness is so pure; am I myself not a wave of icy air? To have neither blood, nor lymph, nor flesh. To flow along this canal towards that pallor over there. To be nothing but coldness.

Here are some people. Two shadows. What did they have to come here for?

It's a little woman pulling a man by his sleeve. She is talking in a small quick voice. On account of the wind I can't understand what she is saying.

'Are you going to shut your trap, or aren't you?' says the man.

She goes on talking. Suddenly he pushes her away. They look at each other, hesitant, then the man thrust his hands into his pockets and goes off without looking round.

The man has disappeared. Barely three yards separate me now from the woman. All of a sudden, deep, hoarse sounds rend her, tear themselves away from her and fill the whole street with extraordinary violence:

'Charles, please, you know what I told you? Charles, come back, I've had enough, I'm too miserable!'

I pass so close to her that I could touch her. It's . . . but how can I believe that this burning flesh, this face radiant with sorrow? . . . yet I recognize the head-scarf, the coat, and the big wine-coloured birth-mark on her right hand; it's she, it's Lucie, the charwoman. I dare not offer her my support, but she must be able to demand it if need be: I pass slowly in front of her, looking at her. Her eyes stare at me, but she doesn't seem to see me; she looks quite helpless in her suffering. I take a few steps. I turn round. . . .

Yes, it's she, it's Lucie. But transfigured, beside herself, suffering with an insane generosity. I envy her. She stands there, absolutely erect, holding her arms out as if she were waiting for the stigmata; she opens her mouth, she is choking. I have the impression that the walls have grown higher on each side of the street, that they have come closer together, that she is at the bottom of a well. I wait a few moments: I am afraid she is going to collapse: she is too sickly to endure this unexpected sorrow. But she doesn't move, she looks petrified like everything around her. For a moment I wonder if I haven't been mistaken about her, if this isn't her real nature which has suddenly been revealed to me. . . .

Lucie gives a little groan. She puts her hand to her throat, opening wide, astonished eyes. No, it isn't from herself that she is drawing the strength to suffer so much. It is coming to her from outside . . . from this boulevard. She needs to be taken by the shoulders and led to the lights, among people, into the pink, gentle streets: over there you can't suffer so acutely; she would soften up, she would recover her positive look and return to the ordinary level of her sufferings.

I turn my back on her. After all, she is lucky. I for my part have been much too calm these last three years. I can receive nothing more from these tragic solitudes, except a little empty purity. I walk away.

Thursday, 11.30

I have spent two hours working in the reading room. I have come down into the cour des Hypothèques to smoke a pipe. A square paved with pink bricks. The people of Bouville are proud of it because it dates from the eighteenth century. At the entrance to the rue Chamade and the rue Suspédard, some old chains bar the way to vehicles. These ladies in black, taking their dogs for a walk, glide beneath the arcade, hugging the walls. They rarely come right out into the daylight but they cast furtive, satisfied, girlish glances at the statue of Gustave Impétraz. They can't know the name of that bronze giant, but they can see from his frock coat and top hat that he was somebody in high society. He holds his hat in his left hand and rests his right hand on a pile of folio volumes: it is rather as if their grandfather were there on that pedestal, cast in bronze. They don't need to look at him for long to understand that he thought as they do, exactly as they do, on all subjects. At the service of their narrow, firm little ideas he has placed his authority and the immense erudition drawn from the folio volumes crushed under his heavy hand. The ladies in black feel relieved, they can attend peacefully to their household tasks, take their dogs out: they no longer have the responsibility of defending the sacred ideas, the worthy concepts which they derive from their fathers; a man of bronze has made himself their guardian.

The encyclopedia devotes a few lines to this personage; I read them last year. I had placed the volume on the window-sill; through the pane I could see Impétraz's green skull. I discovered that he was in his prime about 1890. He was a school inspector. He painted charming trifles and wrote three books: *Popularity among the Ancient Greeks* (1887), *Rollin's Pedagogy* (1891), and a poetic testament in 1899. He died in 1902, deeply mourned by his dependants and people of good taste.

I lean against the front of the library. I draw on my pipe which is threatening to go out. I see an old lady timidly emerge from the arcade and look at Impétraz with a shrewd, stubborn expression. She suddenly plucks up her courage, crosses the courtyard as fast as her legs can carry her, and stops for a moment in front of the statue with her jaws working. Then she runs away again, black against the pink pavement, and disappears through a crack in the wall.

This square may have been a cheerful place about 1800, with its pink bricks and its houses. Now there is something dry and evil about it, a delicate touch of horror. This is due to that fellow up there on his pedestal. When they cast that scholar in bronze, they turned him into a sorcerer.

I look Impétraz full in the face. He has no eyes, scarcely any nose, a beard eaten away by that strange leprosy which sometimes descends, like an epidemic, on all the statues in a particular district. He bows; his waistcoat has a big bright-green stain over his heart. He looks sickly and evil. He isn't alive, true, but he isn't inanimate either. A vague power emanates from him, like a wind pushing me away. Impétraz would like to drive me out of the cour des Hypothèques. I shan't go before I have finished this pipe.

A tall, thin shadow suddenly springs up behind me. I give a start.

'Excuse me, Monsieur, I didn't mean to disturb you. I saw your lips moving. You were probably repeating phrases from your book.' He laughs. 'You were hunting Alexandrines.'

I look at the Autodidact in amazement. But he seems surprised at my surprise:

'Shouldn't we take great care, Monsieur, to avoid Alexandrines in prose?'

I have gone down slightly in his estimation. I ask him what he is doing here at this time of day. He explains that his boss has given him the day off and he has come straight to the library; that he is not going to have any lunch, that he is going to read until closing time. I have stopped listening to him, but he must have strayed from his original subject, for I suddenly hear:

'. . . to have, like you, the good fortune of writing a book.'

I have to say something.

'Good fortune . . .' I say with a dubious look.

He mistakes the meaning of my reply and rapidly corrects himself:

'Monsieur, I should have said: "merit".'

We go up the staircase. I don't feel like working. Some-body has left *Eugénie Grandet* on the table, the book is open at page 27. I pick it up automatically and start reading page 27, then page 28: I haven't the courage to begin at the begin-ning. The Autodidact has gone swiftly over to the shelves along the wall; he brings back two books which he places on the table, looking like a dog which has found a bone.

'What are you reading?'

He seems reluctant to tell me: he hesitates a little, rolls his big wild eyes, then stiffly holds the books out to me. They are *Peat and Peateries* by Larbalétrier, and *Hitopadesa or Useful Education* by Lastex. Well? I can't see what's bothering him: these books strike me as perfectly respect-able. As a matter of form I glance through *Hitopadesa* and see nothing in it that isn't very high-minded.

3 p.m.

I have given up *Eugénie Grandet*. I have started work, but without any enthusiasm. The Autodidact, seeing that I am writing, watches me with a respectful concupiscence. Now and then I raise my head a little and see the huge stiff collar with his chicken-like neck coming out of it. His clothes are threadbare, but his shirt is dazzling white. From the same shelf he has just taken down another book, whose title I can make out upside down: *The Spire of Caudebec*, Norman chronicle, by Mademoiselle Julie Lavergne. The Autodi-dact's reading-matter always disconcerts me.

All of a sudden the names of the last authors whose works he has consulted come back to my mind: Lambert, Langlois, Larbalétrier, Lastex, Lavergne. It is a revelation; I have understood the Autodidact's method: he is teaching himself in alphabetical order.

I contemplate him with a sort of admiration. What willpower he must have to carry out, slowly, stubbornly, a plan on such a vast scale! One day, seven years ago (he told me once that he has been studying for seven years) he came ceremoniously into this reading room. He looked round at the countless books lining the walls, and he must have said, rather like Rastignac: 'It is between the two of us, Human Knowledge.' Then he went and took the first book from the first shelf on the far right; he opened it at the first page, with a feeling of respect and fear combined with unshakeable determination. Today he has reached 'L'. 'K' after 'J', 'L' after 'K'. He has passed abruptly from the study of coleopterae to that of the quantum theory, from a work on Tamerlane to a Catholic pamphlet against Darwinism: not for a moment has he been put off his stride. He has read everything; he has stored away in his head half of what is known about parthenogenesis, half the arguments against vivisection. Behind him, before him, there is a universe. And the day approaches when, closing the last book on the last shelf on the far left, he will say to himself: 'And now what?'

It is time for his afternoon snack; with an innocent air he eats a piece of bread and a bar of Gala Peter. His eyelids are lowered and I can study at leisure his beautiful curved lashes – a woman's eyelashes. He gives off a smell of old tobacco, mingled, when he breathes out, with the sweet scent of chocolate.

Friday, 3 p.m.

A little more and I would have fallen into the mirror trap. I avoided it, but only to fall into the window trap: with nothing to do, my arms dangling, I go over to the window. The Yard, the Fence, the Old Station – the Old Station, the Fence, the Yard. I give such a big yawn that tears come into my eyes. I am holding my pipe in my right hand and my packet of tobacco in my left. I ought to fill this pipe. But I haven't the heart to do it. My arms dangle, I press my forehead against the window pane. That old woman annoys me. She trots stubbornly along, with unseeing eyes. Sometimes she stops with a frightened expression, as if an invisible danger had brushed against her. Here she is under my window, the wind blows her skirts against her knees. She stops, she straightens her shawl. Her hands are trembling. She goes off again: now I see her from behind. The old woodlouse! I suppose she's going to turn right, into the boulevard Noir. That gives her a hundred yards to cover: at the rate she's going it will take her a good ten minutes, ten minutes during which I shall stay like this, watching her, my forehead glued to the window-pane. She's going to stop twenty times, start again, stop again . . .

I can *see* the future. It is there, stationed in the street, hardly any paler than the present. Why does it have to be fulfilled? What advantage will that give it? The old woman hobbles away, she stops, she tugs at a lock of grey hair escaping from her shawl. She walks on, she was there, now she is here . . . I don't know where I am any more: am I *seeing* her movements, or am I *foreseeing* them? I can no longer distinguish the present from the future and yet it is lasting, it is gradually fulfilling itself; the old woman advances along the empty street; she moves her heavy mannish shoes. This is time, naked time, it comes slowly into existence, it keeps you waiting, and when it comes you are disgusted because you realize that it's been there already for a long time. The old woman nears the corner of the street, she's nothing more now than a little bundle of black clothes. All right then, that's new, she wasn't there a moment ago. But that's a tarnished, deflowered newness, which can never take you by surprise. She is going to turn the corner of the street, she turns it – during an eternity of time.

I tear myself away from the window and stumble across the room; I am ensnared by the mirror, I look at myself, I disgust myself: another eternity. Finally I escape from my image and I go and throw myself on my bed. I look at the ceiling, I should like to sleep.

Calm. Calm. I can no longer feel the gliding movement, the slight touch of time. I see pictures on the ceiling. Rings of light at first, then crosses. They flutter about. And now another picture is forming; this time in the depths of my eyes. It is a big animal on its knees. I can see its front legs and its pack-saddle. The rest is in a haze. All the same I can recognize it: it's a camel I saw at Marrakesh, tethered to a rock. It knelt down and stood up six times running; some street urchins were laughing and exciting it with their shouts.

Two years ago, it was wonderful: I only had to close my eyes and straight away my head would start buzzing like a beehive: I could conjure up faces, trees, houses, a Japanese girl in Kamaishi bathing naked in a barrel, a dead Russian emptied by a great gaping wound, with all his blood in a pool beside him. I could recapture the taste of couscous, the smell of olive oil which fills the streets of Burgos at midday, the smell of fennel which floats through those of Tetuan, the piping of Greek shepherds; I was moved. This joy was worn out a long time ago, is it going to be reborn today?

A torrid sun glides stiffly through my head like a magic lantern slide. It is followed by a patch of blue sky; after a few jolts it becomes motionless, I am all gilded by it inside. From what Moroccan (or Algerian or Syrian) day has this brilliance suddenly detached itself? I let myself flow into the past.

Meknès. What was that man from the hills like who frightened us in a narrow street between the Berdaine mosque and that charming square shaded by a mulberry tree? He bore down upon us, Anny was on my right. Or on my left? That sun and that blue sky were only an illusion. This is the hundredth time I've let myself be caught. My memories are like the coins in the devil's purse: when it was opened, nothing was found in it but dead leaves.

Of the man from the hills, I can now see only a big dead eye, a milky-white colour. Is even this eye really his? The doctor at Baku who explained the principle of the state abortion-houses was also blind in one eye, and, whenever I try to remember his face, it is that same whitish globe which appears. Like the Norns, these two men have only one eye between them which they use in turn.

As for that square at Meknès, although I used to go there every day, it's even simpler: I can't see it at all now. All that remains is the vague feeling that it was charming, and these five words indissolubly linked together: a charming square at Meknès. No doubt if I close my eyes or stare vaguely at the ceiling I can reconstruct the scene: a tree in the distance, a short dark figure running towards me. But I am inventing all that for the sake of the thing. That Moroccan was tall and lean, besides I only saw him when he touched me. So I still *know* that he was tall and lean: certain abbreviated details remain in my memory. But I can't *see* anything any more: however much I search the past I can only retrieve scraps of images and I am not sure what they represent, nor whether they are remembered or invented.

Moreover there are many cases where even these scraps have disappeared: nothing is left but words: I could still tell the stories, tell them only too well (where anecdotes are concerned I can stand up to anybody except ships' officers and professionals), but they are only skeletons. They tell about a fellow who does this or that, but it isn't I, I have nothing in common with him. He travels through countries I know no more about than if I had never been in them.

Sometimes, in my story, I happen to pronounce some of those beautiful names you read in atlases, Aranjuez or Canterbury. They engender brand-new pictures in me, like the pictures which people who have never travelled create on the basis of their reading: I dream about words, that's all.

All the same, for a hundred dead stories there remain one or two living ones. These I evoke cautiously, occasionally, not too often, for fear of wearing them out. I fish one out, I see once more the setting, the characters, the attitudes. All of a sudden I stop: I have felt a worn patch, I have seen a word poking through the web of sensations. I sense that before long that word is going to take the place of several pictures I love. Straight away I stop and quickly think of something else; I don't want to tire my memories. In vain; the next time I evoke them, a good part will have congealed.

I make a vague movement as if to get up, and go and look for my photos of Meknès in the box I have pushed under my table. What's the use? These aphrodisiacs have scarcely any effect on my memory nowadays. The other day I found a faded little photo under my blotter. A woman was smiling, near a fountain. I looked at this person for a moment without recognizing her. Then on the back I read: 'Anny. Portsmouth, 7 April 27'.

Never have I felt as strongly as today that I was devoid of secret dimensions, limited to my body, to the airy thoughts which float up from it like bubbles. I build my memories with my present. I am rejected, abandoned in the present. I try in vain to rejoin the past: I cannot escape from myself.

There's a knock on the door. It's the Autodidact. I had forgotten him. I had promised to show him the photos of my travels. Damn him.

He sits down on a chair; his buttocks spread out and touch the back of it while his stiff torso leans forward. I jump off my bed and turn on the light.

'Do we need that, Monsieur? We were all right as we were.'

'Not for looking at photographs. . . .'

I relieve him of his hat which he doesn't know where to put.

'Really, Monsieur? You are going to show them to me?'

'Of course.'

It is a calculated risk: I hope he will keep quiet while he looks at them. I dive under the table, I push the box against his patent leather shoes, I deposit an armful of postcards and photos in his lap: Spain and Spanish Morocco.

But I can see from his frank, laughing expression that I was singularly mistaken in hoping to reduce him to silence. He glances at a view of San Sebastian taken from Monte Igueldo, places it cautiously on the table and remains silent for a moment. Then he sighs:

'Ah, Monsieur. You are lucky. If what they say is true, travel is the best school. Is that your opinion, Monsieur?'

I make a vague gesture. Luckily he hasn't finished.

'It must be such an upheaval. If I were to go on a voyage, I think I should like to make written notes of every aspect of my character before leaving, so that on my return I could compare what I used to be and what I have become. I've read that there are travellers who have changed physically and mentally to such an extent that their closest relatives didn't recognize them when they came back.'

He handles a thick packet of photographs absent-mindedly. He takes one and puts it on the table without looking at it; then he stares intently at the next photo, which shows a carving of St Jerome on a pulpit in Burgos Cathedral.

'Have you seen that Christ made of animal skin at Burgos? There's a very curious book, Monsieur, about those statues made of animal skin and even human skin. And the Black

54

Virgin? She isn't at Burgos, but at Saragossa, isn't she? But perhaps there's one at Burgos? The pilgrims kiss her, don't they? The one at Saragossa I mean. And isn't there a print of her foot on a flagstone? A flagstone in a hole, where mothers push their children?'

He stiffly pushes an imaginary child with both hands. You would think he was refusing the gifts of Artaxerxes.

'Ah, customs, Monsieur, they are . . . they are curious.'

A little out of breath, he juts his great ass's jaw-bone towards me. He smells of tobacco and stagnant water. His beautiful wild eyes shine like globes of fire and his spare hair rings his skull with a halo of mist. Under this skull Samoyeds, Nyam-nyams, Madagascans, and Fuegians are celebrating the strangest solemnities, eating their aged fathers and their children, spinning to the sound of tom-toms until they faint, giving themselves up to the frenzy of the amuck, burning their dead, exposing them on the roof-tops, abandoning them to the river current in a boat lighted by a torch, copulating at random, mother with son, father with daughter, brother with sister, mutilating themselves, castrating themselves, distending their lips with plates and having monstrous animals carved on their backs.

'Can one say, with Pascal, that custom is second nature?'

He has fixed his dark eyes on mine, he is begging for an answer.

'That depends,' I say.

He draws a deep breath.

'That's just what I told myself, Monsieur. But I distrust myself so much; one ought to have read everything.'

But at the next photograph he goes quite mad. He utters a cry of joy.

'Segovia! Segovia! But I've read a book about Segovia!'

He adds with a certain dignity:

'Monsieur, I can't remember the author's name any more.

I sometimes have these lapses of memory. N ... No ...
Nod ...'

'Impossible,' I tell him quickly, 'you've only got up to
Lavergne....'

I immediately regret my words: after all, he has never
spoken to me about this reading method of his, it must be a
secret madness. Sure enough, his face falls and thick lips jut
out as if he were going to cry. Then he lowers his head and
looks at a dozen postcards without a word.

But after half a minute I can see that he is swelling with a
powerful enthusiasm and that he will burst if he doesn't
speak.

'When I've finished my education (I'm allowing myself
another six years for that), I shall, if I'm allowed, join the
students and professors who go on an annual cruise to the
Middle East. I should like to extend my knowledge on certain
points,' he says unctuously, 'and I should also like something
unexpected, something new to happen to me – adventures
in fact.'

He has lowered his voice and assumed a roguish expression.

'What sort of adventures?' I ask him in surprise.

'Why, all sorts, Monsieur. Getting on the wrong train.
Stopping in an unknown town. Losing your wallet, being
arrested by mistake, spending the night in prison. Monsieur, it seems to me that you could define adventure as an
event which is out of the ordinary without being necessarily
extraordinary. People talk of the magic of adventures. Does
that expression strike you as accurate? I should like to ask
you a question, Monsieur.'

'What is it?'

He blushes and smiles.

'Perhaps it's indiscreet....'

'Ask me anyway.'

He leans towards me, his eyes half-closed, and asks:

'Have you had many adventures, Monsieur?'

'A few,' I reply automatically, drawing back to avoid his foul breath. Yes. I said that automatically, without thinking. Usually, in fact, I am rather proud of having had so many adventures. But today, I have no sooner uttered those words than I am filled with indignation against myself: it seems to me that I am lying, that I have never had the slightest adventure in the whole of my life, or rather that I don't even know what the word means any more. At the same time my shoulders feel weighed down by the same discouragement which affected me in Hanoi nearly four years ago when Mercier was urging me to join him and I was staring at a Khmer statuette without answering. And the IDEA is there, that big white mass which so disgusted me then: I hadn't seen it again for four years.

'Might I ask you . . .' says the Autodidact.

Good God! To tell him the story of one of those famous adventures. But I refuse to say another word on the subject.

'There,' I say, bending over his narrow shoulders and putting my finger on a photo, 'there, that's Santillana, the prettiest village in Spain.'

'The Santillana of Gil Blas? I didn't think it existed. Ah, Monsieur, how instructive your conversation is. Anybody can see you have travelled.'

I got rid of the Autodidact after stuffing his pockets with postcards, prints, and photos. He went off enchanted and I switched off the light. Now I am alone. Not quite alone. There is still that idea, waiting in front of me. It has rolled itself into a ball, it remains there like a big cat; it explains nothing, it doesn't move, it simply says no. No, I haven't had any adventures.

I fill my pipe, I light it, I stretch out on my bed, putting a coat over my legs. What astonishes me is to feel so sad and weary. Even if it were true that I had never had any adventures, what difference would that make to me? To begin with, it seems to me that it is simply a matter of words. That business at Meknès, for example, that I was thinking about a little while ago: a Moroccan jumped on me and tried to stab me with a big knife. But I lashed out at him and hit him just below the temple.... Then he started shouting in Arabic and a swarm of verminous characters appeared and chased us all the way to the Attarin souk. Well, you can call that whatever you like, but in any case it was an event which *happened to* ME.

It is completely dark and I'm not sure if my pipe is lit. A tram goes past: a red flash on the ceiling. Then a heavy lorry which makes the house tremble. It must be six o'clock.

I haven't had any adventures. Things have happened to me, events, incidents, anything you like. But not adventures. It isn't a matter of words; I am beginning to understand. There is something I longed for more than all the rest – without realizing it properly. It wasn't love, heaven forbid, nor glory, nor wealth. It was ... anyway, I had imagined that at certain moments my life could take on a rare and precious quality. There was no need for extraordinary circumstances: all I asked for was a little order. There is nothing very splendid about my life at present: but now and then, for example when they played music in the cafés, I would look back and say to myself: in the old days, in London, Meknès, Tokyo, I have known wonderful moments, I have had adventures. It is that which has been taken away from me now. I have just learnt, all of a sudden, for no apparent reason, that I have been lying to myself for ten years. Adventures are in books. And naturally, everything they tell you about in books can happen in real life, but not in the same way.

It was to this way of happening that I attached so much importance.

First of all the beginnings would have had to be real beginnings. Alas! Now I can see so clearly what I wanted. Real beginnings, appearing like a fanfare of trumpets, like the first notes of a jazz tune, abruptly, cutting boredom short, strengthening duration; evenings among those evenings of which you later say: 'I was out walking, it was an evening in May.' You are walking along, the moon has just risen, you feel idle, vacant, a little empty. And then all of a sudden you think: 'Something has happened.' It might be anything: a slight crackling sound in the shadows, a fleeting silhouette crossing the street. But this slight event isn't like the others: straight away you see that it is the predecessor of a great form whose outlines are lost in the mist and you tell yourself too: 'Something is beginning.'

Something begins in order to end: an adventure doesn't let itself be extended; it achieves significance only through its death. Towards this death, which may also be my own, I am drawn irrevocably. Each moment appears only to bring on the moments after. To each moment I cling with all my heart: I know that it is unique, irreplaceable – and yet I would not lift a finger to prevent it from being annihilated. This last minute I am spending – in Berlin, in London – in the arms of this woman whom I met two days ago – a minute I love passionately, a woman I am close to loving – it is going to come to an end, I know that. In a little while I shall leave for another country. I shall never find this woman again or this night. I study each second, I try to suck it dry; nothing passes which I do not seize, which I do not fix forever within me, nothing, neither the ephemeral tenderness of these lovely eyes, nor the noises in the street, nor the false light of dawn: and yet the minute goes by and I do not hold it back, I am glad to see it pass.

of a sudden something breaks off sharply.
s over, time resumes its everyday slackness.
behind me, that beautiful melodious form
tely into the past. It grows smaller, shrinking
d now the end is simply one with the be-
owing that golden spot with my eyes, I think
that I would agree – even if I had nearly died, lost a fortune,
a friend – to live it all over again, in the same circumstances,
from beginning to end. But an adventure never begins again,
is never prolonged.

Yes, it's what I wanted – alas! What I still want. I am so
happy when a Negress sings: what summits would I not
reach if my *own life* were the subject of the melody.

The Idea is still there, the unnameable Idea. It is waiting,
peacefully. At the moment it seems to be saying:

'Yes? Is *that* what you wanted? Well, that's exactly what
you've never had (remember that you fooled yourself with
words, you called the tinsel of travel, love affairs with
whores, brawls, and trinkets adventure) and that is what you
will never have – nor anyone but yourself.'

But why? WHY?

Saturday, noon

The Autodidact didn't see me come into the reading room.
He was sitting right at the end of the table at the back; he
had put a book in front of him, but he wasn't reading. He
was looking with a smile at his neighbour on the right, a
filthy-looking schoolboy who often comes to the library. The
schoolboy allowed himself to be looked at for a while, then
suddenly put his tongue out at him and pulled a horrible
face. The Autodidact blushed, hurriedly plunged his nose
back into his book, and became engrossed by his reading.

I have reconsidered my thoughts of yesterday. I was com-

pletely dried up: I didn't care if there we.
was simply curious to know whether there co.

This is what I have been thinking: for the mos.
place event to become an adventure, you must – and
all that is necessary – start *recounting* it. This is what fo.
people: a man is always a teller of tales, he lives surrounded
by his stories and the stories of others, he sees everything
that happens to him through them; and he tries to live his
life as if he were recounting it.

But you have to choose: to live or to recount. For example, when I was in Hamburg, with that Erna girl whom
I didn't trust and who was afraid of me, I led a peculiar
sort of life. But I was inside it, I didn't think about it. And
then one evening, in a little café at St Pauli, she left me to go
to the lavatory. I was left on my own, there was a gramophone playing *Blue Skies*. I started telling myself what had
happened since I had landed. I said to myself: 'On the third
evening, as I was coming into a dance hall called the Blue
Grotto, I noticed a tall woman who was half-seas over. And
that woman is the one I am waiting for at this moment,
listening to *Blue Skies*, and who is going to come back and
sit down on my right and put her arms round my neck.'
Then I had a violent feeling that I was having an adventure.
But Erna came back, she sat down beside me, she put her
arms around my neck, and I hated her without knowing
why. I understand now: it was because I had to begin living
again that the impression of having an adventure had just
vanished.

When you are living, nothing happens. The settings
change, people come in and go out, that's all. There are
never any beginnings. Days are tacked on to days without
rhyme or reason, it is an endless, monotonous addition.
Now and then you do a partial sum: you say: I've been
travelling for three years, I've been at Bouville for three

61

years. There isn't any end either: you never leave a woman, a friend, a town in one go. And then everything is like everything else: Shanghai, Moscow, Algiers, are all the same after a couple of weeks. Occasionally — not very often — you take your bearings, you realize that you're living with a woman, mixed up in some dirty business. Just for an instant. After that, the procession starts again, you begin adding up the hours and days once more. Monday, Tuesday, Wednesday. April, May, June. 1924, 1925, 1926.

That's living. But when you tell about life, everything changes; only it's a change nobody notices: the proof of that is that people talk about true stories. As if there could possibly be such things as true stories; events take place one way and we recount them the opposite way. You appear to begin at the beginning: 'It was a fine autumn evening in 1922. I was a solicitor's clerk at Marommes.' And in fact you have begun at the end. It is there, invisible and present, and it is the end which gives these few words the pomp and value of a beginning. 'I was out walking, I had left the village without noticing, I was thinking about my money troubles.' This sentence, taken simply for what it is, means that the fellow was absorbed, morose, miles away from an adventure, in exactly the sort of mood in which you let events go by without seeing them. But the end is there, transforming everything. For us, the fellow is already the hero of the story. His morose mood, his money troubles are much more precious than ours, they are all gilded by the light of future passions. And the story goes on in reverse: the moments have stopped piling up on one another in a happy-go-lucky manner, they are caught by the end of the story which attracts them and each of them in turn attracts the preceding moment: 'It was dark, the street was empty.' The sentence is tossed off casually, it seems superfluous; but we refuse to be taken in and we put it aside: it is a piece of information whose value we shall understand later on. And we have the impression that the hero lived all the details of that night like annunciations, promises, or even that he lived only those that were promises, blind and deaf to everything that did not herald adventure. We forget that the future was not yet there; the fellow was walking in a darkness devoid of portents, a night which offered him its monotonous riches pell-mell, and he made no choice.

I wanted the moments of my life to follow one another in an orderly fashion like those of a life remembered. You might as well try to catch time by the tail.

Sunday

I had forgotten, this morning, that it was Sunday. I went out and walked along the streets as usual. I had taken *Eugénie Grandet* with me. And then, all of a sudden, as I was pushing open the gate of the municipal park, I had the impression that something was signalling me. The park was bare and empty. But ... how shall I put it? It didn't have its usual look, it was smiling at me. I stayed for a moment leaning against the gate, and then, suddenly, I realized it was Sunday. It was there in the trees, on the lawns, like a faint smile. It was impossible to describe, you would have had to say very quickly: 'This is a municipal park, this is winter, this is a Sunday morning.'

I let go of the gate, I turned round towards the houses and the staid streets and I murmured: 'It's Sunday.'

It's Sunday: behind the docks, along the coast, near the goods station, all around the town there are empty warehouses and machines standing motionless in the darkness. In all the houses, men are shaving behind their windows: their heads are thrown back, they stare alternately at their mirror and at the cold sky to see whether it's going to be a fine day. The brothels are opening their doors to their first customers, peasants and soldiers. In the churches, in the light of the candles, a man is drinking wine in front of kneeling women. In all the suburbs, between the interminable walls of the factories, long black processions have set off, they are slowly advancing on the centre of the town. To receive them, the streets have assumed the appearance they have when there is rioting: all the shops, except for those in the rue Tournebride, have lowered their iron shutters. Soon, in complete silence, the black columns are going to invade these streets which are shamming death: the first to arrive will be the railway workers from Tourville and their wives who work in the Saint-Symphorin soap factories, then the small shop-keepers from Jouxtebouville, then the workers from the Pinot spinning-mills, then all the odd-job men from the Saint-Maxence district: the men from Thiérache will arrive last on the eleven o'clock tram. Soon the Sunday crowd will be born, between bolted shops and closed doors.

A clock strikes half past ten and I set off: on Sunday, at this hour, you can see a wonderful show at Bouville, but you mustn't arrive too late after the end of High Mass.

The little rue Joséphin-Soulary is dead, it smells like a cellar. But, as on every Sunday, it is full of a rich noise, a noise like a tide. I turn into the rue du Président-Chamart, where the houses have four stories, with long white venetian blinds. This street of notaries is entirely filled with the voluminous din of Sunday. In the passage Gillet, the noise is even greater and I recognize it; it is a noise made by men. Then suddenly, on the left, there is a sort of explosion of light and sound. I have arrived: this is the rue Tournebride, all I have to do is take my place among my fellows and I shall see the gentlemen of substance raising their hats to one another.

Only sixty years ago nobody would have dared to foresee the miraculous destiny of the rue Tournebride, which the inhabitants of Bouville today call the Little Prado. I have seen a map dated 1847 on which the street didn't even figure. At that time it must have been a dark, stinking alley, with a gutter along which fishes' heads and entrails floated between the paving stones. But, at the end of 1873, the National Assembly declared the construction of a church on the Montmartre hill to be of public utility. A few months later, the wife of the Mayor of Bouville had a vision: St Cécile, her patron saint, came and remonstrated with her. Was it tolerable that the cream of Bouville society should muddy themselves every Sunday going to Saint-René or Saint-Claudien to hear Mass with shopkeepers? Hadn't the National Assembly set an example? Bouville, thanks to the patronage of Heaven, now had a first-class economic position; wouldn't it be fitting to build a church in which to give thanks to the Lord?

These visions were approved: the municipal council held an historic meeting and the Bishop agreed to organize a subscription. All that remained to be done was to choose the site. The old families of business men and ship-owners were of the opinion that the building should be erected on the summit of the Coteau Vert, where they lived, 'so that St Cécile could watch over Bouville like the Sacré-Coeur de Jésus over Paris'. The new gentlemen of the boulevard Maritime, who were few as yet but extremely rich, objected: they would give what was needed, but the church would have to be built on the place Marignan; if they were going to pay for a church, they intended to be able to use it; they were not reluctant to give a taste of their power to that haughty bourgeoisie which treated them like parvenus. The Bishop hit on a compromise: the church was built half way between the Coteau Vert and the boulevard Maritime, on the place de la Halle-aux-Morues, which was baptized place Sainte-Cécile-de-la-Mer. This monstrous edifice, which was completed in 1887, cost no less than fourteen million francs.

The rue Tournebride, which was wide but dirty and ill-famed, had to be entirely rebuilt and its inhabitants were firmly driven back behind the place Sainte-Cécile; the Little Prado became – especially on Sunday mornings – the meeting-place of fashionable and distinguished people. One by one, fine shops opened upon the passage of the élite. They stay open on Easter Monday, all Christmas Eve, and every Sunday until noon. Next to Julien, the pork-butcher, who is renowned for his hot pies, Foulon the pastry-cook exhibits his famous specialities, wonderful cone-shaped petits-fours made of mauve butter, topped with a sugar violet. In the window of Dupaty's bookshop you can see the latest books published by Plon, a few technical works such as a theory of navigation or a treatise on sails, a large illustrated history of Bouville, and elegantly produced de luxe editions: *Koenigsmark*, bound in blue leather, *The Book of my Sons* by Paul Doumer, bound in beige leather with crimson flowers. Ghislaine (Haute Couture, Paris Models) separates Piégeois the florist from Paquin the antique dealer. The hairdresser Gustave, who employs four manicurists, occupies the first floor of a brand-new yellow-painted building.

Two years ago, at the corner of the impasse des Moulins-Gémeaux and the rue Tournebride, an impudent little shop still displayed an advertisement for the Tu-pu-nez insecticide. It had flourished at the time when codfish was hawked on the place Sainte-Cécile, it was a hundred years old. The display windows were rarely washed: you had to make an effort in order to distinguish, through the dust and mist, a crowd of little wax figures dressed in flame-coloured doublets, representing rats and mice. These animals were disembarking from a rated ship, leaning on sticks; they had scarcely touched the ground before a peasant girl, smartly dressed but ghastly pale and black with dirt put them to flight by sprinkling them with Tu-pu-nez. I was very fond of this shop, it had a cynical, obstinate look, it insolently recalled the rights of vermin and dirt a stone's throw from the most costly church in France.

The herborist died last year and her nephew sold the house. It was enough to knock down a few walls: it is now a small lecture hall, 'La Bonbonnière'. Last year Henry Bordeaux gave a talk on mountaineering there.

In the rue Tournebride you mustn't be in a hurry: the families walk slowly. Sometimes you move up one place because a whole family has gone into Foulon's or Piégeois'. But at other times you have to stop and mark time because two families, one belonging to the column going up the street and the other to the column coming down, have met and clasped each other firmly by the hands. I advance slowly. I stand a whole head higher than both columns and I see hats, a sea of hats. Most of them are black and hard. Now and then you see one fly off at the end of an arm, revealing the soft gleam of a skull; then, after a few moments of clumsy flight, it settles again. At No. 16 rue Tournebride, the hatter Urbain, who specializes in army caps, has hung up as a symbol a huge red archbishop's hat whose gold tassels hang six feet from the ground.

Everybody comes to a halt: a group has just formed right under the tassels. My neighbour waits without any sign of impatience, his arms dangling: I do believe that this pale little old man, as fragile as porcelain, is Coffier, the president of the Chamber of Trade. It seems that he is so intimidating because he never says anything. He lives at the top of the Coteau Vert, in a big brick house whose windows are always wide open. It's over now: the group has broken up, we start moving again. Another group has just collected, but it takes up less space: it has no sooner been formed than it presses against Ghislaine's window. The column doesn't even stop: it barely moves a little to one side; we walk past six people who are holding hands: 'Good morning, Monsieur. Good morning, my dear sir, how are you keeping? Do put your hat on again, Monsieur, you'll catch cold. Thank you, Madame, it isn't very warm, is it? Darling, allow me to introduce Doctor Lefrançois. Doctor, I am delighted to make your acquaintance, my husband is always talking to me about Doctor Lefrançois who took such good care of him, but do put your hat on, Doctor, in this cold weather you'll catch a chill. But the Doctor would cure himself quickly. Alas, Madame, it's doctors who are looked after worst of all. The Doctor is a remarkable musician. Heavens, Doctor, I didn't know, do you play the violin? The Doctor is very gifted.'

The little old man next to me must be Coffier; there's one of the women in the group, the brunette, who is eating him up with her eyes, while smiling at the same time at the doctor. She seems to be thinking: 'There's Monsieur Coffier, the president of the Chamber of Trade; how intimidating he looks, they say he's so cold.' But Monsieur Coffier hasn't deigned to see anything: these people are from the boulevard Maritime, they don't belong to society. Since I started coming to this street to see the Sunday hat-raising, I have learnt to distinguish between the people from the boulevard and those from the Coteau. When a fellow is dressed in a new overcoat, a soft felt hat, and a dazzling shirt, when he displaces air in passing, there's no possibility of a mistake: he is somebody from the boulevard Maritime. The people from the Coteau Vert can be recognized by an indefinable shabby, sunken look. They have narrow shoulders and an insolent expression on worn faces. This fat gentleman holding a child by the hand – I'd swear he comes from the Coteau: his face is all grey and his tie is knotted like a piece of string.

The fat gentleman comes towards us: he is staring hard at Monsieur Coffier. But, just before passing him, he turns his head away and starts joking in a fatherly way with his little boy. He takes a few more steps, bending over his son, his eyes gazing into the boy's eyes, nothing but a father; then, all of a sudden, turning quickly towards us, he darts a sharp glance at the little old man and gives a dry, ample salute with a sweep of his arm. Startled, the little boy hasn't taken off his cap: this is an affair between grown-ups.

At the corner of the rue Basse-de-Vieille, our column runs into a column of the faithful coming out of Mass: a dozen people bump into one another and greet one another, whirling round and round, but the hat-raising happens too quickly for me to spot the details; above this fat, pale crowd the church of Sainte-Cécile raises its monstrous white mass, chalk-white against a dark sky; behind these dazzling walls it retains within its flanks a little of the darkness of night. We move off again, in a slightly modified order. Monsieur Coffier has been pushed back behind me. A lady in navy blue has glued herself to my left side. She has come from Mass. She blinks her eyes, a little dazzled at coming back into the morning light. That gentleman who is walking in front of her and who has such a thin neck is her husband.

On the opposite pavement, a gentleman who is holding his wife by the arm has just whispered a few words in her ear and has started smiling. She promptly and carefully wipes all expression from her cream-coloured face and takes a few steps blindly. These signs are unmistakable: they are going to greet somebody. Sure enough, a moment later, the gentleman shoots his hand into the air. When his fingers are close to his felt hat, they hesitate for a second before settling delicately on the crown. While he is gently raising his hat, bowing his head a little to help the operation, his wife gives a little start and fixes a young smile on her face. A shadow passes them, bowing as it does so: but their twin smiles do not disappear straight away: they remain for a few moments on their lips, by a sort of residual magnetism. By the time the lady and gentleman pass me, they have regained their impassivity, but a gay expression still lingers around their mouths.

It's over: the crowd is thinner, the hat-raising less frequent, the shop windows less exquisite in character: I am at the end of the rue Tournebride. Shall I cross the street and go back up the opposite pavement? I think I have had enough, I have seen enough of these pink skulls, of these thin, distinguished, insipid faces. I am going to cross the place Marignan. As I am cautiously extricating myself from the column, a real gentleman's head springs out of a black hat close to me. It's the husband of the lady in navy blue. Ah, what a fine, long dolichocephalic skull, planted with thick, short hairs! What a handsome American moustache, scattered with silver threads! And above all what a smile, what an admirable cultured smile! There is also a pince-nez, somewhere on a nose.

Turning to his wife, he says:

'He's a new draughtsman at the factory. I wonder what he can be doing here. He's a nice young fellow, he's shy and he amuses me.'

Standing beside the window of Julien's, the pork-butcher's shop, the young draughtsman, who has just put his hat on again, still all pink, his eyes lowered, a stubborn look on his face, retains an appearance of intense pleasure. This is undoubtedly the first Sunday he has ventured to cross the rue Tournebride. He looks like a boy who has just had his First Communion. He has clasped his hands behind his back and turned his face towards the window with an air of positively exciting modesty; he is gazing unseeingly at four sausages shining with jelly, spread out on a bed of parsley.

A woman comes out of the shop and takes his arm. This is his wife, who is quite young, despite her wrinkled skin. She can roam about the rue Tournebride as much as she likes, nobody will take her for a lady; she is betrayed by the cynical sparkle of her eyes, by her intelligent, knowing look. Real ladies don't know the price of things, they like mad, extravagant gestures; their eyes are beautiful innocent flowers, hot-house flowers.

I reach the Brasserie Vézelize on the stroke of one o'clock. The old men are there as usual. Two of them have already started to eat. There are four who are playing cards and drinking apéritifs. The others are standing watching them play while their tables are being laid. The tallest, who has a flowing beard, is a stockbroker. Another is a retired commissioner from the Naval Conscription Board. They eat and drink like men of twenty. On Sunday they eat sauerkraut. The late arrivals call out to the others, who are already eating:

'What, the usual Sunday sauerkraut?'

They sit down and sigh happily:

'Mariette, my dear, a beer without a head on it and a sauerkraut.'

This Mariette is a strapping wench. As I am sitting down at a table at the back, a red-faced old man starts coughing furiously while she is pouring him a vermouth.

'Come on, pour me more than that,' he says, coughing.

But she gets angry herself: she hasn't finished pouring.

'Let me pour, will you? Anyway, what's the matter with you? You're like somebody who screams before he's hurt.'

The others start laughing.

'She's got you there!'

71

The stockbroker, on his way to his table, takes Mariette by the shoulders:

'It's Sunday, Mariette. Are you going to the cinema this afternoon with your boy-friend?'

'Oh, sure! This is Antoinette's day off. As far as boy-friends are concerned, I haven't a hope.'

The stockbroker has sat down opposite a clean-shaven old man with an unhappy face. The clean-shaven old man promptly launches out on an animated story. The stockbroker doesn't listen to him: he pulls faces and tugs at his beard. They never listen to each other.

I recognize my neighbours: they are small local shop-keepers. Sunday is their maid's day off. So they come here, always sitting at the same table. The husband eats a fine rib of under-done beef. He examines it closely and sniffs it now and then. The wife picks at her food. She is a heavy blonde of forty with red, downy cheeks. She has a pair of fine, hard breasts under her satin blouse. Like a man, she empties a bottle of claret at every meal.

I am going to read *Eugénie Grandet*. It isn't that I am en-joying it tremendously, but I have to do something. I open the book at random; the mother and daughter are talking about Eugénie's growing love:

Eugénie kissed her hand, saying:
'How kind you are, dear Mama!'
At these words, the motherly old face, withered by protracted suffering, lit up.
'Do you like him?' asked Eugénie.
Madame Grandet's only reply was a smile; then, after a moment's silence, she murmured:
'Are you already in love with him? That would be wrong.'
'Wrong?' Eugénie went on. 'Why? You like him, Nanon likes him, why shouldn't I like him? Come along, Mama, let's set the table for his luncheon.'

She put her needlework down, and her mother did likewise saying:

'You are mad.'

But she took pleasure in justifying her daughter's madness by sharing it. Eugénie called Nanon.

'What do you want now, Mamselle?'

'Nanon, you will have some cream for midday, won't you?'

'Ah, for midday, yes,' replied the old servant.

'Well, serve him some very strong coffee. I have heard Monsieur des Grassins say that they made coffee very strong in Paris. Put in a lot.'

'And where do you expect me to get it?'

'Buy some.'

'And what if Monsieur sees me?'

'He's out in the fields.'

My neighbours had remained silent since my arrival, but all of a sudden the husband's voice distracted me from my reading.

The husband, with an amused, mysterious air:

'I say, did you see that?'

The woman gives a start and, coming out of a dream, looks at him. He eats and drinks, and then goes on, with the same mischievous air:

'Ha, ha!'

A moment's silence, the woman has returned to her dream.

Suddenly she shivers and asks:

'What's that you were saying?'

'Suzanne yesterday.'

'Ah, yes,' the woman says, 'she had been to see Victor.'

'What did I tell you?'

The woman pushes her plate away impatiently.

'It's no good.'

The edge of her plate is decorated with lumps of gristle

73

she has spat out. The husband continues his train of thought:

'That little woman ...'

He stops and smiles vaguely. Opposite us the old stock-broker is stroking Mariette's arm and panting slightly. After a moment:

'I told you so, the other day.'

'What did you tell me?'

'Victor – that she'd go and see him. What's the matter?' he asks abruptly with a startled expression, 'don't you like it?'

'It's no good.'

'It isn't the same,' he says pompously, 'it isn't like it was when Hécart was here. Do you know where he is now, Hécart?'

'He's at Domrémy, isn't he?'

'Yes, that's right, who told you?'

'You did. You told me on Sunday.'

She eats a crumb of bread lying on the paper tablecloth. Then, smoothing the paper on the edge of the table with her hand, she says hesitatingly:

'You know, you're wrong, Suzanne is more ...'

'That may be, my dear, that may well be,' he replies absent-mindedly. He looks around for Mariette and beckons her.

'It's hot.'

Mariette leans familiarly on the edge of the table.

'Oh, yes, it is hot,' says the woman with a groan, 'it's stifling here and what's more the beef's no good, I'm going to tell the *patron*, it isn't like it used to be, do open the window a bit, Mariette dear.'

The husband assumes his amused expression again:

'I say, didn't you see her eyes?'

'When, pet?'

He apes her impatiently:

'When, pet? That's you all over: in summer when it's snowing.'

'Oh, you mean yesterday? I see.'

He laughs, he looks into the distance, he recites very quickly, with a certain application:

'The eyes of a cat on hot bricks.'

He is so pleased with himself that he seems to have forgotten what he wanted to say. She laughs in her turn, without malice.

'Ha, ha, you old rogue.'

She slaps him on the back.

'You old rogue, you old rogue.'

He repeats with more assurance:

'A cat on hot bricks.'

But she stops laughing:

'No, seriously, you know, she isn't like that.'

He leans forward, he whispers a long story in her ear. She listens for a moment with her mouth open, her face a little drawn and hilarious, like someone who is going to burst out laughing, then suddenly she throws herself back and scratches his hand.

'That isn't true, that isn't true.'

He says in a slow, reasonable voice:

'Listen, dear, he said so himself: if it wasn't true why would he have said so?'

'No, no.'

'But he said so: listen, suppose ...'

She starts laughing:

'I'm laughing because I'm thinking about René.'

'Yes.'

He laughs too. She goes on in a low, earnest voice:

'So that means he noticed on Tuesday.'

'Thursday.'

'No, Tuesday, you know because of the ...'

75

She sketches a sort of curve in the air.

A long silence. The husband dips a piece of bread in his sauce. Mariette changes the plates and brings them a couple of tarts. Later on I shall have a tart too. Suddenly the woman, a little dreamy with a proud and slightly shocked smile on her lips, says in a drawling voice:

'Oh no, really!'

There is so much sensuality in her voice that it stirs him, and he strokes the back of her neck with his fat hand.

'Charles, stop it, you're exciting me, darling,' she murmurs with a smile, her mouth full.

I try to go back to my reading:

'And where do you expect me to get it?'
'Buy some.'
'And what if Monsieur sees me?'

But I can still hear the woman, who is saying:

'I say, I'm going to make Marthe laugh, I'm going to tell her . . .'

My neighbours have fallen silent. After the tarts, Mariette has served them with prunes and the woman is busy gracefully laying the stones in her spoon. The husband, staring at the ceiling, taps out a military march on the table. You get the impression that their normal condition is silence and that speech is a slight fever which attacks them now and then.

'And where do you expect me to get it?'
'Buy some.'

I close the book, I'm going out for a walk.

When I left the Brasserie Vézelize, it was nearly three o'clock; I could feel the afternoon all through my heavy body. Not my afternoon, but theirs, the one a hundred thousand citizens of Bouville were going to live in common.

At this same moment, after their long and copious Sunday dinner, they were getting up from table and for them something had died. Sunday had spent its light-hearted youth. Now it was a matter of digesting the chicken and the tart, and getting dressed to go out.

The bell of the Ciné-Eldorado rang out in the clear air. This is a familiar Sunday sound, this ringing in broad daylight. Over a hundred people were queuing up alongside the green wall. They were eagerly awaiting the hour of soft shadows, of relaxation, of abandon, the hour when the screen, shining like a white pebble under water, would speak and dream for them. A vain longing: something in them would remain tense; they were too frightened of their lovely Sunday being spoilt. Before long, as on every Sunday, they would be disappointed: the film would be stupid, their neighbour would smoke a pipe or spit between his knees, or else Lucien would be unpleasant, he wouldn't have anything nice to say, or else, as if on purpose, today of all days, when for once they went to the cinema, the pain in their side would start up again. Soon, as on every Sunday, small, hidden rages would grow in the dark hall.

I walked along the quiet rue Bressan. The sun had scattered the clouds and it was fine. A family had just come out of a villa called 'The Wave'. The daughter was buttoning her gloves out on the pavement. She could have been about thirty. The mother, planted on the first of the flight of steps, was looking straight ahead with an assured expression, and breathing hard. Of the father I could see only the huge back. Bent over the keyhole, he was locking the door. The house would remain dark and empty until they got back. In the neighbouring houses, which were already bolted and deserted, the floors and furniture were creaking gently. Before going out they had put out the fire in the dining-room fireplace. The father joined the two women, and the family

77

set off without a word. Where were they going? On Sunday you go to the cemetery, or else you visit relatives, or else, if you are completely free, you go for a walk along the Jetty. I was free; I walked along the rue Bressan which comes out on the Jetty Promenade.

The sky was pale blue with a few wisps of smoke; now and then a drifting cloud passed in front of the sun. In the distance I could see the white cement balustrade which runs along the Jetty Promenade; the sea was shining through the openings. The family turned right, up the rue de l'Aumônier-Hilaire, which climbs up to the Coteau Vert. I saw them walking slowly upwards, they made three black patches on the glittering asphalt. I turned left and joined the crowd filing along the sea-shore.

It was more of a mixture than in the morning. It seemed as if all these men no longer had the strength to uphold that magnificent social hierarchy they were so proud of before lunch. Businessmen and civil servants walked side by side; they let themselves be elbowed, jostled, and even pushed to one side by shabby-looking clerks. Aristocracies, élites, and professional groups had melted away in this warm crowd. There remained men who were almost alone and no longer representative.

There was a puddle of light in the distance, the sea at low tide. A few reefs awash with water pierced that bright surface with their heads. On the sand there lay some fishing-boats, not far from the sticky stone cubes which have been thrown pell-mell at the foot of the jetty, to protect it from the waves, with gaps between them through which the sea rumbles. At the entrance to the outer harbour, the silhouette of a dredger stood out against the sun-bleached sky. Every evening until midnight it howls and groans and kicks up an infernal row. But on Sunday the workers stroll about on land, there is only a watchman on board: the boat is silent.

The sun was bright and diaphanous: a thin white wine. Its light barely touched people's bodies, gave them no shadows, no relief: faces and hands formed patches of pale gold. All these men in overcoats seemed to float gently along a few inches above the ground. Now and then the wind pushed shadows over us which trembled like water; faces lost their colour for a moment, turned chalky-white.

It was Sunday; boxed in between the balustrade and the gates of the villas, the crowd flowed away in little waves, to disappear in a thousand rivulets behind the Grand Hôtel de la Compagnie Transatlantique. And how many children there were! Children in prams, in arms, held by the hand or walking stiffly in twos or threes in front of their parents. I had seen all these faces a few hours before, almost triumphant in the youth of a Sunday morning. Now, dripping with sunlight, they no longer expressed anything but calm, relaxation, and a sort of obstinacy.

Few movements: admittedly there was a little hat-raising here and there, but without the grandiloquence, the nervous gaiety of the morning. The people all allowed themselves to lean back a little, their heads high, their eyes gazing into the distance, abandoned to the wind which pushed them along and puffed out their coats. Now and then a dry laugh, quickly stifled; the call of a mother, Jeannot, Jeannot, will you come here. And then silence. A faint aroma of mild tobacco: it's the shop assistants who are smoking. Salammbô, Aïcha, Sunday cigarettes. On a few faces, which were more relaxed, I thought I could detect a little sadness: but no, these people were neither sad nor gay: they were resting. Their wide-open, staring eyes passively reflected the sea and the sky. Soon they would go back home and drink a cup of tea all together around the dining-room table. For the moment they wanted to live as cheaply as possible, to economize on gestures, words, thoughts, to float along: they had only one day in which to smooth away their wrinkles, their crow's-feet, the bitter lines made by their work during the week. Only one day. They could feel the minutes flowing between their fingers; would they have time to stock up enough youth to start afresh on Monday morning? They filled their lungs because sea air is invigorating: only their breathing, as regular and deep as that of sleepers, still testified that they were alive. I walked along stealthily, I didn't know what to do with my hard, fresh body, in the midst of this tragic crowd taking its rest.

The sea was now the colour of slate; it was rising slowly. It would be high tide at nightfall; tonight the Jetty Promenade would be more deserted than the boulevard Victor-Noir. In front and on the left a red light would shine in the channel.

The sun went down slowly over the sea. On its way it lit up the window of a Norman chalet. A woman, dazzled by the light, wearily put her hand over her eyes and shook her head.

'Gaston, it's blinding me,' she said with a faltering laugh.

'Get along with you,' said her husband, 'that sun's all right, it doesn't warm you but it's very pleasant all the same.'

Turning towards the sea, she said:

'I thought we would have seen it.'

'Not a hope,' said the man, 'it's in the sun.'

They must have been talking about the Île Caillebotte, whose southern tip ought to have been visible between the dredger and the quay of the outer harbour.

The light grew softer. At this uncertain hour, something indicated the approach of evening. Already this Sunday had a past. The villas and the grey balustrade seemed like recent memories. One by one the faces lost their leisured look, several became almost tender.

A pregnant woman was leaning on a fair, rough-looking young man.

'There, there, there, look,' she said.

'Look at what?'

'There, there, the seagulls.'

He shrugged his shoulders: there were no seagulls. The sky had become almost pure, a little pink on the horizon.

'I heard them. Listen, they're crying.'

He replied:

'It was something creaking.'

A gas lamp shone suddenly. I thought it was the lamplighter who had gone past. The children watch for him because he gives the signal for them to go home. But it was only a last ray of the setting sun. The sky was still bright, but the earth was bathed in shadow. The crowd was getting thinner, you could distinctly hear the death-rattle of the sea. A young woman, leaning with both hands on the balustrade, lifted up towards the sky her blue face, barred in black by her lipstick. I wondered for a moment if I were not going to love mankind. But, after all, it was their Sunday and not mine.

The first light to come on was that of the Caillebotte lighthouse; a little boy stopped near me and murmured ecstatically: 'Oh, the lighthouse!'

Then I felt my heart swell with a great feeling of adventure.

I turn left and, by way of the rue des Voiliers, I return to the Little Prado. The iron shutters have been lowered over the shop windows. The rue Tournebride is bright but empty, it has lost its brief morning glory; at this time nothing distinguishes it any more from the neighbouring streets. A fairly strong wind has come up. I can hear the archbishop's metal hat creaking.

I am alone, most people have gone home, they are reading the evening paper and listening to the wireless. This Sunday which is drawing to a close has left them with a taste of ashes and already their thoughts are turning towards Monday. But for me there is neither Monday nor Sunday: there are days which push one another along in disorder, and then, all of a sudden, revelations like this.

Nothing has changed and yet everything exists in a different way. I can't describe it; it's like the Nausea and yet it's just the opposite: at last an adventure is happening to me and when I question myself I see that *it happens that I am myself and that I am here*: it is *I* who am piercing the darkness, I am as happy as the hero of a novel.

Something is going to happen: in the shadows of the rue Basse-de-Vieille there is something waiting for me, it is over there, just at the corner of that quiet street that my life is going to begin. I see myself advancing with a sense of fate. At the corner of the street there is a sort of white stone. From a distance it seemed black, and at each step I take it turns a little whiter. That dark body getting gradually lighter makes an extraordinary impression on me: when it is completely white, I shall stop just beside it and then the adventure will begin. It is so close now, that white beacon emerging from the shadows, that I am almost afraid: for a moment I think of turning back. But it is impossible to break the spell. I go forward, I stretch out my hand, I touch the stone.

Here is the rue Basse-de-Vieille and the huge mass of Sainte-Cécile crouching in the shadows, its stained-glass windows glowing. The metal hat creaks. I don't know whether the world has suddenly shrunk or whether it is I who am establishing such a powerful unity between sounds and shapes: I cannot even imagine anything around me being other than it is.

I stop for a moment, I wait, I can feel my heart beating; my eyes search the empty square. I see nothing. A fairly strong wind has come up. I was mistaken, the rue Basse-de-Vieille was only a stage; the *thing* is waiting for me at the far side of the place Ducoton.

I am in no hurry to start walking again. It seems to me that I have reached the summit of my happiness. In Marseille, in Shanghai, at Meknès, what haven't I done to try to obtain a feeling of such satisfaction? Today I expect nothing more, I am going home at the end of an empty Sunday: it is there.

I set off again. The wind carries the wail of a siren to my ears. I am all alone, but I walk like a band of soldiers descending on a town. At this very moment there are ships echoing with music on the sea; lights are going on in all the cities of Europe; Communists and Nazis are shooting it out in the streets of Berlin, unemployed are pounding the pavements of New York, women at their dressing-tables, in warm rooms, are putting mascara on their eyelashes. And I am here, in this empty street, and every shot fired from a window in Neukölln, every bloody hiccough of the wounded men being carried away, every precise, tiny gesture of the women making up answers my every footstep, my every heartbeat.

Standing in front of the passage Gillet, I no longer know what to do. Isn't something waiting for me at the end of the passage? But in the place Ducoton, at the end of the rue Tournebride, there is also a certain thing which needs me in order to come to life. I am full of anguish: the slightest gesture engages me. I can't imagine what is required of me. Yet I must choose: I sacrifice the passage Gillet, I shall never know what it held for me.

The place Ducoton is empty. Was I mistaken? I don't think I could bear it if I was. Will nothing really happen? I go towards the lights of the Café Mably. I am bewildered, I don't know whether to go in; I glance through the big, misted-up windows.

The place is packed. The air is blue with cigarette smoke and the steam rising from damp clothes. The cashier is at her counter. I know her well: she is red-haired like myself; she has some sort of stomach disease. She is rotting quietly under her skirts with a melancholy smile, like the smell of violets which is sometimes given off by decomposing bodies. I shudder from head to foot. It is . . . it is she who is waiting for me. She was there, holding her bust erect above the counter: she was smiling. From the far end of this café something goes back over the scattered moments of this Sunday and solders them together, gives them a meaning: I have gone through the whole of this day to end up here, with my forehead pressed against this window, to gaze at this delicate face blossoming against a red curtain. Everything has come to a stop; my life has come to a stop: this big window, this heavy air, as blue as water, this thick-leaved white plant at the bottom of the water, and I myself, we form a complete and motionless whole: I am happy.

When I found myself on this boulevard de la Redoute again nothing remained but bitter regret. I said to myself: 'Perhaps there is nothing in the world I value more than this feeling of adventure. But it comes when it pleases; it goes away so quickly and how dry I feel when it has gone! Does it pay me these brief, ironical visits in order to show me that my life is a failure?'

Behind me, in the town, in the big straight streets lit by the cold light of the street lamps, a tremendous social event was dying: it was the end of Sunday.

How could I have written this absurd, pompous sentence yesterday:

'I was alone, but I walked like a band of soldiers descending on a town.'

I have no need to speak in flowery language. I am writing to understand certain circumstances. I must beware of literature. I must let my pen run on, without searching for words.

What really disgusts me is having been sublime yesterday evening. When I was twenty I used to get drunk and then explain that I was a fellow in the style of Descartes. I knew very well that I was puffing myself up with heroism, but I let myself go, I enjoyed it. After that, the next day I felt as disgusted as if I had awoken in a bed full of vomit. I don't vomit when I'm drunk, but it would be better if I did. Yesterday I didn't even have the excuse of drunkenness. I got worked up like a fool. I need to clean myself up with abstract thoughts, as transparent as water.

This feeling of adventure definitely doesn't come from events: I have proved that. It's rather the way in which moments are linked together. This, I think, is what happens: all of a sudden you feel that time is passing, that each moment leads to another moment, this one to yet another and so on; that each moment destroys itself and that it's no use trying to hold back, etc., etc., and then you attribute this property to the events which appear to you *in* the moments; you extend to the contents what appertains to the form. In point of fact, people talk a lot about this famous passing of time, but you scarcely see it. You see a woman, you think that one day she will be old, only you don't *see* her grow old. But there are moments when you think you *see* her growing old and you feel yourself growing old with her: that is the feeling of adventure.

If I remember rightly, they call that the irreversibility of time. The feeling of adventure would simply be that of the irreversibility of time. But why don't we always have it? Is it because time isn't always irreversible? There are moments when you get the impression that you can do what you want, go forward or back, that it has no importance; and then other moments when you feel that the mesh has tightened, and in these cases it's not a question of failing in your attempt because you could never start again.

Anny used to get the most out of time. When she was at Djibouti and I was at Aden, and I used to go and see her for twenty-four hours, she contrived to multiply the mis-understandings between us until there were only sixty minutes, exactly sixty minutes, before I had to leave; sixty minutes, just long enough to make you feel the seconds pass-ing one by one. I remember one of those terrible evenings. I had to leave at midnight. We had gone to an open-air cinema; we were desperately unhappy, she as much as I. Only she led the dance. At eleven o'clock, at the beginning of the main picture, she took my hand and pressed it between her hands without a word. I felt myself flooded with a bitter joy and I understood, without needing to look at my watch, that it was eleven o'clock. From that moment on we began to feel the minutes passing. That time we were leaving each other for three months. At one moment they projected a com-pletely white picture on the screen, the darkness lifted, and I saw that Anny was crying. Then, at midnight, she let go of my hand, after pressing it violently; I got up and left without saying a single word to her. That was a job well done.

Seven o'clock in the evening

A working day. It didn't go too badly; I wrote six pages, with a certain pleasure. The more so in that they were six pages of abstract considerations on the reign of Paul I. After yesterday's orgy, I stayed tightly buttoned up all day. It would have been absolutely useless to appeal to my heart! But I felt quite at ease taking the Russian autocracy to pieces.

But this Rollebon irritates me. He makes a great mystery of the smallest things. What could he have been doing in the Ukraine in August 1804? He speaks of his trip in veiled terms:

Posterity will judge whether my efforts, which success was unable to reward, did not deserve something better than a brutal rejection and humiliations which I have had to bear in silence, when I carried in my breast the wherewithal to silence the scoffers and fill them with fear.

I let myself be caught once, when he was very reticent in a pompous way about a little trip he made to Bouville in 1790. I wasted a month checking up on all his movements. Finally it turned out that he had made the daughter of one of his tenant farmers pregnant. Can it be that he is nothing more than a hoaxer?

I feel full of ill-will towards that lying little fop. Perhaps this is out of injured vanity: I was delighted to find him lying to others, but I would have liked him to make an exception of me; I thought that we were as thick as thieves and that he would be sure to end up by telling me the truth. He has told me nothing, nothing at all; nothing more than he told Alexander or Louis XVIII whom he fooled to the top of their bent. It matters a great deal to me that Rollebon should have been a decent fellow. A rogue of course; who isn't? But a big rogue or a little one? I don't have a high enough regard for historical research to waste my time over a dead man whose hand, if he were alive, I wouldn't deign to touch. What do I know about him? You couldn't dream of a finer life than his: but did he live it? If only his letters weren't so formal. . . . Ah, I wish I had known the look in his eyes, perhaps he had a charming way of cocking his head to one side, or of shrewdly placing his long index finger against his nose, or else, sometimes, between two polite lies, flying into a sudden temper which he could promptly stifle. But he is dead: all that remains of him is a *Treatise on Strategy* and some *Reflections on Virtue*.

If I let myself go, I should imagine him so well: beneath his brilliant irony which has made so many victims, he is a simple man, almost an innocent. He thinks little, but at all times, thanks to a profound intuition, he does exactly what should be done. His rascality is frank, spontaneous, generous, as sincere as his love of virtue. And when he has thoroughly betrayed his benefactor and friends, he looks gravely back over the events, to draw a moral from them. He has never imagined that he had the slightest right over other people, any more than other people over him: he regards the gifts life has given him as unjustified and gratuitous. He attaches himself passionately to everything but detaches himself easily. And he has never written his letters or his works himself: he has always had them composed by the public letter-writer.

But if this is where all my work has led me, I would have been better off writing a novel about the Marquis de Rollebon.

Eleven o'clock in the evening

I had dinner at the Rendez-vous des Cheminots. Since the *patronne* was there, I had to fuck her, but it was really out of politeness. She disgusts me slightly, she is too white and besides she smells like a new-born baby. She pressed my head against her breast in a burst of passion: she thinks this is the right thing to do. As for me, I toyed absent-mindedly with her sex under the bedclothes; then my arm went to sleep. I was thinking about Monsieur de Rollebon: after all, why shouldn't I write a novel on his life? I let my arm move along the woman's side and suddenly I saw a little garden with low, wide-spreading trees from which huge hairy leaves were hanging. Ants were running about everywhere, centipedes and moths. There were some even more horrible animals: their bodies were made of slices of toast such as you put under roast pigeon; they were walking sideways with crab-like legs. The broad leaves were black with animals. Behind the cacti and the Barbary fig trees, the Velleda of the municipal park was pointing to her sex. 'This park smells of vomit,' I shouted.

'I didn't want to wake you up,' said the *patronne*, 'but the sheet got rucked up under my backside and besides I have to go down to attend to the customers from the Paris train.'

Shrove Tuesday

I gave Maurice Barrès a spanking. We were three soldiers and one of us had a hole in the middle of his face. Maurice Barrès came up and said to us: 'That's fine!' And he gave each of us a bunch of violets. 'I don't know where to put it,' said the soldier with the hole in his head. Then Maurice Barrès said: 'You must put it in the middle of the hole you've got in your head.' The soldier replied: 'I'm going to stick it up your arse.' And we turned Maurice Barrés over and took off his trousers. Under his trousers he was wearing a cardinal's red robe. We pulled the robe up and Maurice Barrès started shouting: 'Mind out, I'm wearing trousers with shoe straps.' But we spanked him until he bled, and then we drew Déroulède's head on his backside with the petals of the violets.

For some time now I have been remembering my dreams much too often. Besides, I must toss about a great deal in my sleep, because every morning I find my bedclothes on the

89

floor. Today is Shrove Tuesday, but that doesn't mean much at Bouville; in the whole town there are scarcely a hundred people who dress up for it.

As I was coming downstairs, the *patronne* called me.

'There's a letter for you.'

A letter: the last one I got was from the curator of Rouen Library last May. The *patronne* takes me into her office; she holds out a long thick yellow envelope: Anny has written to me. I hadn't heard from her for five years. The letter had been sent to my old Paris address, it is postmarked the first of February.

I go out; I hold the envelope between my fingers, I don't dare to open it; Anny hasn't changed her writing paper, I wonder if she still buys it at the little stationer's in Piccadilly. I imagine she has also kept her hair style, her heavy blonde locks she didn't want to cut. She must struggle patiently in front of mirrors to save her face: this isn't vanity or fear of growing old; she wants to stay as she is, exactly as she is. Perhaps that is what I liked best in her, that austere, steadfast loyalty to the slightest feature of her appearance.

The firm letters of the address, written in purple ink (she hasn't changed her ink either) still shine a little.

'Monsieur Antoine Roquentin.'

How I love to read my name on these envelopes. In a sort of mist I have recaptured one of her smiles, I have evoked her eyes, her head to one side: when I was sitting in a chair, she used to come and plant herself in front of me, smiling. Standing a head and shoulders higher than me, she would take me by the shoulders and shake me with outstretched arms.

The envelope is heavy, it must contain at least six pages. My former concierge has scrawled over this lovely writing of hers:

'Hôtel Printania – Bouville.'

These small letters don't shine.

When I open the letter, my disappointment makes me six years younger.

'I don't know how Anny manages to fill up her envelopes like this: there's never anything inside.'

I must have said that sentence a hundred times during the spring of 1924, struggling, as today, to extract a sheet of squared paper from the lining. The lining is a marvel in dark green with gold stars; you would think it was a piece of heavy, starched cloth. By itself it makes three-quarters of the envelope's weight.

Anny has written in pencil:

I am passing through Paris in a few days. Come and see me at the Hôtel d'Espagne on 20 February. Please [she has added 'Please' above the line and joined it to 'see me' with a curious spiral]. I *must* see you. Anny.

At Meknès, in Tangier, when I came home in the evening, I sometimes found a note on my bed: 'I want to see you straight away'. I would hurry round, Anny would open the door to me, her eyebrows raised, a surprised expression on her face: she no longer had anything to say to me; she was rather cross with me for coming. I'll go; she may refuse to see me. Or else they may tell me at the reception desk: 'Nobody of that name is staying here.' I don't think she'd do that. Only she may write to me, a week from now, to say that she's changed her mind and to make it some other time.

People are at work. This promises to be a very flat Shrove Tuesday. The rue des Mutilés smells strongly of damp wood, as it does every time it's going to rain. I don't like these peculiar days: the cinemas put on matinées, the school-children have the day off; there is a vague holiday feeling in the streets which never stops appealing for your attention but disappears as soon as you take any notice of it.

91

I am probably going to see Anny again but I can't say that the idea exactly fills me with joy. I have felt at a loose end ever since I got her letter. Luckily it is noon; I'm not hungry, but I'm going to eat to pass the time. I go into Camille's, in the rue des Horlogers.

It's a very quiet place; they serve sauerkraut or cassoulet all night. People come here for supper after the theatre; the police send travellers here who arrive during the night and are hungry. Eight marble-topped tables. A bench upholstered in leather runs along the walls. Two mirrors speckled with reddish stains. The panes of the two windows and of the door are of frosted glass. The bar is in an alcove. There is also a room at one side. But I have never been in it; it is reserved for couples.

'Give me a ham omelette.'

The waitress, a huge girl with red cheeks, can never prevent herself from laughing when she talks to a man.

'I can't. Would you like a potato omelette? The ham's locked up: the *patron* is the only one who cuts it.'

I order a cassoulet. The *patron* is called Camille and he's a tough character.

The waitress goes off. I am alone in this dark old room. In my wallet there is a letter from Anny. A feeling of false shame prevents me from reading it again. I try to remember the sentences one by one.

'My dear Antoine'.

I smile: it is certain, absolutely certain, that Anny didn't write 'My dear Antoine'.

Six years ago – we had just separated by mutual agreement – I decided to leave for Tokyo. I wrote her a brief note. I could no longer call her 'My dear love'; in all innocence I began: 'My dear Anny'.

'I like your nerve,' she replied. 'I have never been and I am not your dear Anny. And I must ask you to believe that you are not my dear Antoine. If you don't know what to call me, the best thing would be not to call me anything.'

I take her letter out of my wallet. She didn't write 'My dear Antoine'. Nor was there any conventional formula at the end of the letter: 'I must see you. Anny'. Nothing which could give me any indication of her feelings. I can't complain: I recognize here her love of perfection. She always wanted to enjoy 'perfect moments'. If the time was not convenient, she took no more interest in anything, the life went out of her eyes, and she trailed around lazily like a gawky schoolgirl at the awkward age. Or else she would pick a quarrel with me.

'You blow your nose solemnly like a bourgeois, and you cough into your handkerchief as if you were terribly pleased with yourself.'

The best thing was not to reply but just to wait: suddenly, at some signal which I could never recognize, she started, her beautiful languid features hardened, and she began her ant-like task. She had a magical quality which was imperious and charming; she hummed between her teeth, looking all around her, then she straightened up with a smile, came and shook me by the shoulders, and for a few moments seemed to give orders to the objects surrounding her. She explained to me, in a low rapid voice, what she expected of me.

'Listen, you will make an effort, won't you? You were so stupid last time. You do see how beautiful this moment could be? Look at the sky, look at the colour of the sunshine on the carpet. And I've put my green dress on and my face isn't made up, I'm quite pale. Go back, go and sit in the shadow; you understand what you have to do? Oh, come now! How stupid you are! Speak to me.'

I could feel that the success of the enterprise was in my hands: the moment had an obscure significance which had to be trimmed and perfected; certain gestures had to be made, certain words spoken: I was bowed down under the weight of my responsibility, I opened my eyes wide and saw nothing, I struggled in the midst of rites which Anny invented on the spur of the moment and I tore them with my long arms as if they had been spiders' webs. At those times she hated me.

I shall certainly go and see her. I still respect and love her with all my heart. I hope that somebody else has had better luck and has shown greater skill in the game of perfect moments.

'Your damned hair spoils everything,' she used to say. 'What can you do with a man with red hair?'

She would smile. To begin with I lost the memory of her eyes, then the memory of her long body. I kept her smile as long as I could, and then, three years ago, I lost that too. Just now, all of a sudden, as I was taking the letter from the hands of the *patronne*, it came back to me; I thought I could see Anny smiling. I try to remember it again: I need to feel all the tenderness that Anny inspires in me; it is there, that tenderness, it is close to me, only asking to be born. But the smile does not return: it is finished. I remain empty and dry.

A man has come in, shivering.

'Evening everybody.'

He sits down without taking off his greenish overcoat. He rubs his long hands together, clasping and unclasping his fingers.

'What are you going to have?'

He gives a start, a worried look in his eyes:

'Eh? Give me a Byrrh and water.'

The waitress doesn't move. In the mirror her face looks as if it were sleeping. In fact her eyes are open, but they are merely slits. She's like that, she's never in a hurry to serve customers, she always takes a moment to ponder over their orders. She must be thinking about the bottle she's going to take from above the bar, the white label with the red letters, the thick black syrup she's going to pour out: it's rather as if she were drinking it herself.

I slip Anny's letter into my wallet: it has given me all it could; I can't go back to the woman who took it in her hands, folded it, and put it in its envelope. Is it even possible to think of somebody in the past? As long as we were in love with each other we didn't allow the tiniest of our moments, the smallest of our sorrows to be detached from us and left behind. Sounds, smells, degrees of light, even the thoughts we had not told each other – we took all this with us and it all remained alive: we never stopped enjoying it and suffering from it in the present. Not a single memory; an implacable, torrid love, without a shadow, without a withdrawal, without an evasion. Three years present at one and the same time. That is why we separated: we no longer had enough strength to bear the burden. And then, when Anny left me, all at once, all together, the three years collapsed into the past. I didn't even suffer, I felt empty. Then time started flowing again and the emptiness grew larger. Then, in Saigon, when I decided to come back to France, all that was still left – foreign faces, squares, quays beside long rivers – all that was wiped out. And now my past is nothing but a huge hole. My present: this waitress in the black blouse dreaming near the bar, this little fellow. It seems to me as if everything I know about life I have learnt from books. The palaces of Benares, the terrace of the Leper King, the temples of Java with their great broken staircases, have been reflected for a moment in my eyes, but they have remained yonder, on the spot. The tram which passes the Hôtel Printania in the evening doesn't take away the reflection of the neon sign in its window panes; it flares up for a moment and moves away with dark windows.

That man doesn't take his eyes off me: he annoys me. He gives himself airs for a fellow of his size. The waitress finally makes up her mind to serve him. She lazily raises her long black arm, takes hold of the bottle and brings it to him with a glass.

'Here you are, Monsieur.'

'Monsieur Achille,' he says urbanely.

She pours without answering; all of a sudden he swiftly removes his finger from his nose and places both hands flat on the table. He has thrown his head back and his eyes are shining. He says in a cold voice:

'Poor girl.'

The waitress gives a start and I start too: he has an indefinable expression on his face, of astonishment perhaps as if it had been somebody else who had just spoken. All three of us feel embarrassed.

The fat waitress is the first to recover: she has no imagination. She looks Monsieur Achille up and down in a dignified way: she knows perfectly well that she could jerk him out of his seat and throw him out with one hand.

'And what makes you think I'm a poor girl?'

He hesitates. He looks at her, rather taken aback, then he laughs. His face creases up into a thousand wrinkles, he makes vague gestures with his wrist:

'That's annoyed her: it's the sort of thing you say without thinking. You say: poor girl. It doesn't mean anything.'

But she turns her back on him and goes off behind the counter: she is really offended. He laughs again:

'Ha, ha! It just slipped out, you know. Are you cross? She's cross,' he says, speaking vaguely to me.

I turn my head away. He raises his glass a little, but he isn't thinking about drinking: he blinks his eyes, looking surprised and intimidated; you would think he was trying to remember something. The waitress has sat down at the

cash desk; she picks up some sewing
turned to silence, but it isn't the same
started: it's tapping lightly against the
if there are still any children in fancy dr
going to spoil their cardboard masks a
run.

The waitress turns on the lights: it is
but the sky is black, she no longer has e
by. A soft glow; people are in their houses, they have probably turned on their lights too. They read, they look out of
the window at the sky. For them ... it's different. They
have grown older in another way. They live in the midst
of legacies and presents, and each piece of furniture is a
souvenir. Clocks, medallions, portraits, shells, paper-weights,
screens, shawls. They have cupboards full of bottles, material,
old clothes, newspapers; they have kept everything. The past
is a property-owner's luxury.

Where should I keep mine? You can't put your past in
your pocket; you have to have a house in which to store it.
I possess nothing but my body; a man on his own, with
nothing but his body, can't stop memories; they pass through
him. I shouldn't complain: all I have ever wanted was to
be free.

The little man stirs and sighs. He has huddled up in his
overcoat, but now and then he straightens up and takes
on a human appearance. He has no past either. If you looked
hard, you would probably find, in the house of some cousins
of his who no longer have anything to do with him, a photograph showing him at a wedding, with a wing-collar, a stiff
shirt, and a young man's prickly moustache. I don't think
that even that much remains of me.

Here he is looking at me again. This time he's going to
speak to me, I feel all stiff. It isn't a feeling of instinctive
attraction which exists between us: we are alike, that's all.

...ne like me, but sunk deeper than I am in solitude. ...ust be waiting for his Nausea or something of that ...t. So now there are people who *recognize* me, who after looking hard at me think: 'He's one of us.' Well? What does he want? He must know that we can't do anything for one another. The families are in their houses, in the midst of their memories. And here we are, two pieces of flotsam, neither of us with a memory. If he suddenly stood up and spoke to me, I should jump into the air.

The door opens noisily: it is Doctor Rogé.

'Afternoon everybody.'

He comes in, grim-faced and suspicious, swaying slightly on his long legs which can barely carry his torso. I often see him on Sundays in the Brasserie Vézelize, but he doesn't know me. He is built like the old gym instructors at Join-ville: arms like thighs, a chest measuring forty-three inches, and all this unsteady on its pins.

'Jeanne, my little Jeanne.'

He trots over to the coat rack to hang his wide-brimmed felt hat on the peg. The waitress has put her sewing on one side and comes across unhurriedly, almost sleep-walking, to help the doctor out of his raincoat.

'What will you have, Doctor?'

He studies her gravely. That's what I call a handsome face. Worn and furrowed by life and passions. But the doctor has understood life, mastered his passions.

'I really don't know what I want,' he says in a deep voice.

He has dropped on to the bench opposite me; he mops his forehead. As soon as he has taken his weight off his feet he feels at ease. His big eyes, black and imperious, are intimidating.

'I'll have ... I'll have, I'll have, I'll have – an old calva, my dear.'

The waitress, without moving a muscle, studies that huge

furrowed face. She is pensive. The little fellow has raised his head with a smile of relief. And it is true: this colossus has freed us. There was something horrible here which was going to take hold of us. I heave a sigh: we are among men now.

'Well, is that calvados coming?'

The waitress gives a start and goes off. He has stretched out his stout arms and grasped the table at both ends. Monsieur Achille is in high spirits; he would like to attract the doctor's attention. But he swings his legs and jumps about on the bench in vain, he is so tiny that he makes no noise.

The waitress brings the calvados. With a nod of her head she points out the little man to the doctor. Doctor Rogé slowly pivots his head and shoulders: he can't move his neck.

'Well, so it's you, you old swine,' he exclaims. 'So you aren't dead yet?'

He addresses the waitress:

'You let a fellow like that in here?'

He looks at the little man with his fierce eyes. A direct gaze which puts everything in its place. He explains:

'He's an old crackpot, that's what he is.'

He doesn't even take the trouble to show that he's joking. He knows that the old crackpot won't take offence, that he's going to smile. And sure enough, the other man smiles humbly. An old crackpot: he relaxes, he feels protected against himself; nothing will happen to him today. The queer thing is that I feel reassured too. An old crackpot: so that was it, that was all.

The doctor laughs, he darts an engaging, conspiratorial glance at me: because of my size, I suppose – and besides, I'm wearing a clean shirt – he is willing to let me in on his joke.

I don't laugh, I don't respond to his advances: so, without stopping laughing, he tries the terrible fire of his eyes on me. We consider each other in silence for a few seconds; he looks me up and down with half-closed eyes, he classifies me. In the crackpot category? Or in the scoundrel category?

All the same, he is the one who turns his head away: a tiny defeat at the hands of a fellow on his own, with no social importance, isn't worth talking about – it's the sort of thing you can forget straight away. He rolls a cigarette and lights it, then he stays motionless with his eyes hard and staring like an old man's.

He has all the best wrinkles: horizontal bars across the forehead, crow's feet, bitter creases at both corners of the mouth, not to mention the yellow cords hanging under his chin. There's a lucky man for you: as soon as you see him, you say to yourself that he must have suffered, that he is a man who has lived. Moreover, he deserves his face, for never, not even for a moment, has he misjudged the way to keep and use his past: he has quite simply stuffed it, he has turned it into experience to be used on women and young men.

Monsieur Achille is probably happier than he has been for a long time. He is agape with admiration; he drinks his Byrrh in little sips, puffing out his cheeks. The doctor certainly knew how to tackle him! The doctor isn't the man to let himself be fascinated by an old crackpot on the verge of having an attack; a good tongue-lashing, a few brusque, cutting words, that's what they need. The doctor has experience. He is a professional in experience: doctors, priests, magistrates, and officers know men as thoroughly as if they had made them.

I feel ashamed for Monsieur Achille. We are of the same sort, we ought to make common cause against them. But he has left me, he has gone over to their side: he honestly believes in Experience. Not in his, nor in mine. In Doctor Rogé's. A little while ago Monsieur Achille felt peculiar, he had the impression of being all alone; now he knows that there have been others like him, a great many others: Doctor Rogé has met them, he could tell Monsieur Achille the story of each one of them and say how it ended. Monsieur Achille is simply a case, and a case which allows itself to be easily reduced to a few commonplace ideas.

How I should like to tell him that he's being duped, that he's playing into the hands of self-important people. Professionals in experience? They have dragged out their lives in stupor and somnolence, they have married in a hurry, out of impatience, and they have made children at random. They have met other men in cafés, at weddings, at funerals. Now and then, caught in a current, they have struggled without understanding what was happening to them. Everything that has happened around them has begun and ended out of their sight; long obscure shapes, events from afar, have brushed rapidly past them, and when they have tried to look at them, everything was already over. And then, about forty, they baptize their stubborn little ideas and a few proverbs with the name of Experience, they begin to imitate slot machines; put a coin in the slot on the left and out come anecdotes wrapped in silver paper; put a coin in the slot on the right and you get precious pieces of advice which stick to your teeth like soft caramels. At this rate, I could get myself invited to people's houses and they would tell one another that I was a great traveller in the sight of Eternity. Yes: the Moslems squat to pass water; instead of ergotine, Hindu midwives use ground glass in cow dung; in Borneo, when a girl has a period, she spends three days and nights on the roof of her house. I have seen burials in gondolas in Venice, the Holy Week festivities in Seville, the Passion play at Oberammergau. Naturally, that's just a tiny sample of my experience: I could lean back in a chair and begin with a smile:

'Do you know Jihlava, Madame? It's a curious little town in Moravia where I stayed in 1924 . . .'

And the magistrate who has seen so many cases would add at the end of my story:

'How true that is, Monsieur, how human. I had a similar case at the beginning of my career. It was in 1902. I was deputy magistrate at Limoges . . .'

The trouble is that I had too much of all that when I was young. I didn't belong to a family of professionals, but there are amateurs too. These are the secretaries, the office workers, the shopkeepers, the people who listen to others in cafés: about the age of forty they feel swollen with an experience which they can't get rid of. Luckily they've made children and they force them to swallow it on the spot. They would like to make us believe that their past isn't wasted, that their memories have been condensed and gently transformed into Wisdom. Convenient past! Pocket-size past, little gilt-edged book full of fine maxims. 'Believe me, I'm talking from experience, I've learnt everything I know from life.' Are we to understand that Life has undertaken to think for them? They explain the new by the old – and the old they have explained by the older still, like those historians who describe Lenin as a Russian Robespierre and Robespierre as a French Cromwell: when all is said and done, they have never understood anything at all . . . behind their self-importance you can distinguish a morose laziness: they see a procession of semblances pass by, they yawn, they think that there's nothing new under the sun. 'An old crackpot' – and Doctor Rogé thought vaguely of other old crackpots, without being able to remember any one of them clearly. Now nothing Monsieur Achille can do will surprise us: *because* he's an old crackpot!

He isn't an old crackpot: he is frightened. What is he frightened of? When you want to understand something, you stand in front of it, all by yourself, without any help; all the past history of the world is of no use to you. And then it disappears and what you have understood disappears with it.

General ideas are more flattering. Besides, the professionals and even the amateurs always end up by being right. Their wisdom recommends you to make as little noise as possible, to live as little as possible, to allow yourself to be forgotten. Their best stories are about headstrong characters and eccentrics who have been punished. Why yes, that's how it happens and nobody will say anything to the contrary. Perhaps Monsieur Achille's conscience is a trifle uneasy. Perhaps he is telling himself that he wouldn't be like he is if he had listened to his father's advice or his elder sister's. The doctor is entitled to speak: he hasn't made a failure of his life: he has known how to make himself useful. He rises calm and powerful above this piece of flotsam; he is a rock.

Doctor Rogé has finished his calvados. His great body relaxes and his eyelids droop heavily. For the first time I see his face without the eyes: you might take it for a cardboard mask, like those they're selling in the shops today. His cheeks are a horrible pink colour. . . . The truth suddenly dawns upon me: this man is going to die before long. He must know it; he has only to look in a mirror: every day he looks a little more like the corpse he is going to become. That's what their experience amounts to, that's why I have told myself so often that it smells of death: it is their last defence. The doctor would like to believe in it, he would like to shut his eyes to the unbearable reality: that he is alone, without any attainments, without any past, with a mind which is growing duller, a body which is disintegrating. So he has carefully constructed, carefully furnished, and carefully padded his little compensatory fantasy: he tells himself that he is making progress. He has gaps in his thinking, moments when his head seems quite empty? That's because his judgement is no longer as impulsive as it was in his youth. He no longer understands what he reads in books? That's because he has left books so far behind. He can't make love any more? But he has made love in the past. To have made love is much better than to go on making it: looking back, you can judge, compare, and reflect. And to be able to bear the sight of this terrible corpse's face in mirrors, he tries to convince himself that the lessons of experience are engraved in it.

The doctor turns his head a little. His eyelids open slightly and he looks at me with eyes pink with sleep. I smile at him. I should like this smile to reveal to him all that he is trying to conceal from himself. That would wake him up, if he could say to himself: 'There's somebody who *knows* I'm going to die!' But his eyelids droop again: he falls asleep. I go off, leaving Monsieur Achille to watch over his slumber.

The rain has stopped, the air is mild, the sky is slowly rolling along beautiful black pictures: this is more than enough to make a frame for a perfect moment; to reflect these pictures, Anny would cause dark little tides to be born in our hearts. But I don't know how to take advantage of the opportunity: I wander along at random, calm and empty, under this wasted sky.

Wednesday

I must not be frightened.

Thursday

I have written four pages. Then a long moment of happiness. Must not think too much about the value of History. You run the risk of getting disgusted with it. Must not make public the fact that Monsieur de Rollebon now represents the only justification for my existence.

A week from today I am going to see Anny.

Friday

The fog was so thick on the boulevard de la Redoute that I thought it wise to keep close to the walls of the Barracks; on my right, the head-lamps of the motor-cars were driving a misty light along in front of them and it was impossible to tell where the pavement came to an end. There were people around me; I could hear the sound of their footsteps or, occasionally, the slight hum of their words: but I couldn't see anybody. Once a woman's face took shape on a level with my shoulder, but the mist promptly swallowed it up; another time somebody brushed past me, breathing hard. I didn't know where I was going, I was too absorbed: you had to move forward cautiously, feel the ground with the toe of your shoe, and even stretch your hands out in front of you. I wasn't enjoying this exercise. All the same, I didn't think of going back, I was caught. Finally, after half an hour, I caught sight of a bluish mist in the distance. Using it as a guide, I soon reached the edge of a big glow; in the middle, piercing the fog with its lights, I recognized the Café Mably.

The Café Mably has twelve electric lamps; but only two of them were on, one above the cash-desk, the other on the ceiling. The only waiter there pushed me forcibly into a dark corner.

'Not here, Monsieur, I'm cleaning up.'

He was wearing a jacket, without a waistcoat or a collar, and a white shirt with purple stripes. He kept yawning and looked at me sullenly, running his fingers through his hair.

'A black coffee and some croissants.'

He rubbed his eyes without answering and walked away. I was up to my eyes in shadow, an icy, dirty shadow. It was obvious that the radiator was not working.

I was not alone. A woman with a waxy complexion was sitting opposite me and her hands were moving all the time, sometimes smoothing her blouse, sometimes straightening her black hat. She was with a tall fair-haired man who was eating a brioche without saying a word. The silence struck me as oppressive. I wanted to light my pipe, but I would have felt uncomfortable attracting their attention by striking a match.

The telephone rang. The hands stopped: they remained pressed against the blouse. The waiter took his time. He calmly finished sweeping before going to unhook the receiver. 'Hullo, is that Monsieur Georges? Good morning, Monsieur Georges.... Yes, Monsieur Georges.... The *patron* isn't here.... Yes, he ought to be down.... Ah, with a fog like this.... He usually comes down about eight.... Yes, Monsieur Georges, I'll tell him. Good-bye, Monsieur Georges.'

The fog was weighing on the windows like a heavy curtain of grey velvet. A face pressed against the pane for a moment and disappeared.

The woman said plaintively:

'Do my shoe up for me.'

'It isn't undone,' the man said without looking. She became agitated. Her hands ran up her blouse and over her neck like big spiders.

'Yes, yes, do my shoe up.'

He bent down, looking peeved, and lightly touched her foot under the table:

'It's done.'

She gave a satisfied smile. The man called the waiter.

'How much do I owe you?'

'How many brioches have you had?' asked the waiter.

I lowered my eyes so as not to seem to be staring at them. After a few moments I heard a creaking noise and I saw the hem of a skirt and two boots stained with dry mud appear. The man's shoes followed, polished and pointed. They came towards me, stopped and turned round: he was putting on his coat. At that moment a hand started moving down the skirt at the end of a stiff arm; it hesitated slightly, and then scratched the skirt.

'Are you ready?' asked the man.

The hand opened and touched a large splash of mud on the right boot, then disappeared.

'Whew!' said the man.

He had picked up a suitcase near the coat rack. They went out, I saw them plunge into the fog.

'They're on the stage,' the waiter told me when he brought me my coffee. 'They've been doing the act in the interval at the Ciné-Palace. The woman blindfolds her eyes and reads out the name and age of people in the audience. They're leaving today because it's Friday and the programme changes.'

He went to get a plate of croissants from the table the couple had just left.

'Don't bother.'

I didn't feel like eating those particular croissants.

'I'll have to turn out the light. The *patron* would give me hell if he found two lamps on for a single customer at nine o'clock in the morning.'

The café was plunged into semi-darkness. A feeble light streaked with grey and brown was falling now from the tall windows.

'I'd like to see Monsieur Fasquelle.'

I hadn't seen the old woman come in. A gust of icy air made me shiver.

'Monsieur Fasquelle hasn't come down yet.'

'Madame Florent sent me,' she went on. 'She isn't well. She won't be coming today.'

Madame Florent is the cashier, the red-head.

'This weather,' said the old woman, 'is bad for her stomach.'

The waiter put on an important air:

'It's the fog,' he answered, 'it's the same with Monsieur Fasquelle; I'm surprised he isn't down yet. Somebody wanted him on the telephone. Usually he comes down at eight.'

The old woman looked automatically at the ceiling.

'He's up there, is he?'

'Yes, that's his room.'

In a drawling voice, as if she were talking to herself, the old woman said:

'Suppose he's dead. . . .'

'Well I never!' The waiter's face showed the liveliest indignation. 'What an idea!'

Suppose he were dead . . . this thought had occurred to me. It was just the sort of idea you get in foggy weather.

The old woman went off. I should have followed her example: it was cold and dark. The fog was filtering in under the door, it was going to rise slowly and envelope everything. At the municipal library I should have found light and warmth.

Once again a face came and pressed against the window; it made grimaces.

'Just you wait,' the waiter said angrily, and he ran out.

The face disappeared, I remained alone. I reproached myself bitterly for having left my room. By this time the fog would have invaded it; I would have been afraid to go back into it.

Behind the cash-desk, in the shadows, something creaked.

The noise came from the private staircase: was the manager coming down at last? No: nobody appeared; the stairs were creaking by themselves. Monsieur Fasquelle was still asleep. Or else he was dead up there above my head. Found dead in his bed, one foggy morning. Sub-heading: In the café, customers were drinking unsuspectingly . . .

But was he still in his bed? Hadn't he fallen out, dragging the sheets with him and bumping his head on the floor?

I know Monsieur Fasquelle very well; now and then he has asked after my health. He's a fat jolly fellow, with a carefully trimmed beard: if he is dead it must be from a stroke. He will be an aubergine colour, with his tongue hanging out of his mouth. His beard in the air; his neck purple under the curling hairs.

The private staircase disappeared into the dark. I could scarcely make out the knob of the bannister post. I would have to cross those shadows. The staircase would creak. Upstairs, I would find the door of the room. . . .

The body is there, above my head. I would turn the switch: I would touch that warm skin to see. — I can't stand it any longer, I get up. If the waiter catches me on the stairs, I'll tell him that I heard a noise.

The waiter came in suddenly, out of breath.

'Yes, Monsieur!' he cried.

The fool! He came towards me.

'That's two francs.'

'I heard a noise up there,' I told him.

'About time too!'

'Yes, but I think there's something wrong: it sounded like a death-rattle and then there was a thud.'

In that dark café, with that fog behind the window panes, this sounded perfectly natural. I shall never forget the look in his eyes.

'You ought to go up and see,' I added maliciously.

'Oh, no!' he said; then: 'I'd be afraid of him catching me. What time is it?'

'Ten o'clock.'

'I'll go up at half past ten, if he isn't down by then.'

I took one step towards the door.

'You're going? You aren't staying?'

'No.'

'It sounded like a real death-rattle?'

'I don't know,' I told him as I went out. 'Perhaps it was just because I was thinking about things like that.'

The fog had lifted a little. I hurried towards the rue Tournebride: I longed for its lights. It was a disappointment: true, there was plenty of light, it was streaming down the shop windows. But it wasn't a gay light: it was all white because of the fog and it fell on your shoulders like a shower.

A lot of people, especially women: maids, charwomen, ladies too – the sort who say: 'I do the shopping myself, it's safer.' They would have a look at the window displays and finally go in.

I stopped in front of Julien's, the pork-butcher's shop. Through the glass I could see now and then a hand pointing to the truffled pigs' feet and the sausages. Then a fat blonde bent forward, showing her bosom, and picked up the piece of dead flesh between her fingers. In his room, five minutes' walk from there, Monsieur Fasquelle was dead.

I looked around me for a support, for a defence against my thoughts. There was none: little by little the fog had broken up, but something disquieting still lingered in the street. Perhaps not a real menace: it was pale, transparent. But it was precisely that which ended up by frightening me. I pressed my forehead against the window. On the mayonnaise of a stuffed egg, I noticed a dark red drop: it was blood. This red on that yellow made me feel sick.

Suddenly I had a vision: somebody had fallen face forward and was bleeding in the dishes. The egg had rolled in the blood; the slice of tomato which crowned it had come off and fallen flat, red on red. The mayonnaise had run a little: a pool of yellow cream which divided the trickle of blood into two streams.

'This is really too silly, I must pull myself together. I'll go and work in the library.'

Work? I knew perfectly well that I shouldn't write a single line. Another day wasted. Crossing the municipal park, I saw a big blue cape, motionless on the bench where I usually sit. There's somebody who isn't cold.

When I entered the reading-room, the Autodidact was just coming out. He rushed at me:

'I really must thank you, Monsieur. Your photographs have given me some unforgettable hours.'

Seeing him, I had a moment's hope: perhaps it would be easier to get through the day if there were two of us. But with the Autodidact, you are never two in anything but appearance.

He tapped a quarto volume. It was a history of religion.

'Monsieur, nobody was better qualified than Nouçapié to attempt this vast synthesis. Is that true?'

He looked weary and his hands were trembling.

'You look ill,' I told him.

'Ah, Monsieur, I can well believe it! Something abominable has happened to me.'

The attendant was coming towards us: he is a bad-tempered little Corsican with mustachios like a drum major's. He walks for hours at a time between the tables, clicking his heels. In winter he spits into handkerchiefs which he dries out afterwards on the stove.

The Autodidact came close enough to breathe into my face:

'I shan't say anything to you in front of this man,' he said with a confidential air. 'Monsieur, if you would ...'

'Would what?'

He blushed and his hips swayed gracefully:

'Monsieur, I'm going to take the plunge. Would you do me the honour of lunching with me on Wednesday?'

'With pleasure.'

I had as much desire to lunch with him as to hang myself.

'How happy you have made me,' said the Autodidact. He added rapidly: 'I'll come and pick you up at your hotel, if you like,' and disappeared, probably for fear that I would change my mind if he gave me time.

It was half past eleven. I worked until a quarter to two. Poor work: I had a book in front of me, but my thoughts were constantly returning to the Café Mably. Had Monsieur Fasquelle come down by now? At heart, I didn't really believe he was dead and it was precisely that which irritated me: it was a floating idea of which I could neither convince myself nor rid myself. The Corsican's shoes creaked on the floor. Several times he came and planted himself in front of me, as if he wanted to speak to me. But he changed his mind and walked away.

About one o'clock, the last readers went off. I wasn't hungry; above all I didn't want to leave. I worked a little longer, then I gave a start: I felt buried in silence.

I raised my head: I was alone. The Corsican must have gone down to his wife who is the concierge of the library; I wanted to hear the sound of his footsteps. The most I could hear was that of a little coal falling inside the stove. The fog had invaded the room: not a real fog, which had gone a long time before, but the other fog, the one the streets were still full of, which was coming out of the walls and pavements. A sort of unsubstantiality of things. The books were still there of course, arranged in alphabetical order on the shelves, with their black or brown backs and their labels PU fl. 7·996 (Public Use – French Literature) or PU ns (Public Use – Natural Sciences). But . . . how can I put it? Usually, strong and stocky, together with the stove, the green lamps, the big windows, the ladders, they dam up the future. As long as you stay between these walls, whatever comes along must come along to the right or the left of the stove. If St Denis himself were to come in carrying his head in his hands, he would have to enter on the right, and walk between the shelves devoted to French Literature and the table reserved for women readers. And if he doesn't touch the ground, if he floats a foot above the floor, his bleeding neck will be exactly at the level of the third shelf of books. Thus these objects serve at least to fix the limits of probability. Well, today they no longer fixed anything at all: it seemed that their very existence was being called in question, that they were having the greatest difficulty in passing from one moment to the next. I gripped the volume I was reading tightly in my hands, but the strongest sensations were blunted. Nothing looked real; I felt surrounded by cardboard scenery which could suddenly be removed. The world was waiting, holding its breath, making itself small – it was waiting for its attack, its Nausea, like Monsieur Achille the other day.

I got up. I could no longer stay where I was in the midst of these enfeebled objects. I went to the window and glanced out at the skull of Impétraz. I murmured: '*Anything* can occur, *anything* can happen.' Obviously not the sort of horrible thing that men have invented; Impétraz wasn't going to start dancing on his pedestal: it would be something else.

I looked in alarm at these unstable creatures which, in another hour, in another minute, were perhaps going to collapse: yes, I was there, I was living in the midst of these books crammed full of knowledge, some of them describing the immutable forms of animal species, and others explaining that the quantity of energy in the world remained unchanged; I was there, standing in front of a window whose panes had an established index of refraction. But what weak barriers! It is out of laziness, I suppose, that the world looks the same day after day. Today it seemed to want to change. And in that case *anything, anything* could happen.

I had no time to lose: at the root of this uneasiness there was the Café Mably affair. I had to go back there, I had to see Monsieur Fasquelle alive, I had to touch his beard or his hands if need be. Then, perhaps, I would be free.

I grabbed my overcoat and threw it round my shoulders; I fled. Crossing the municipal park, I saw the fellow in the blue cape sitting in the same place; he had a huge pale face between two ears which were scarlet with cold.

The Café Mably was sparkling in the distance: this time the twelve lamps must be on. I hurried along: I had to get it over. First of all I glanced in through the big bay window; the place was empty. The cashier wasn't there, nor the waiter – nor Monsieur Fasquelle.

I had to make a great effort to go in; I didn't sit down. I shouted: 'Waiter!' Nobody answered. An empty cup on a table. A lump of sugar in the saucer.

'Is there anybody here?'

An overcoat was hanging on a peg. Some magazines were piled in black cardboard boxes on a small table. I listened intently for the slightest sound, holding my breath. The private staircase creaked slightly. Outside, a boat's hooter. I walked out backwards, keeping my eyes fixed on the staircase.

I know: at two in the afternoon customers are few and far between. Monsieur Fasquelle had influenza; he must have sent the waiter out on an errand – possibly to fetch a doctor. Yes, but I *needed* to see Monsieur Fasquelle. At the entrance to the rue Tournebride I turned round, I gazed in disgust at the bright, empty café. The venetian blinds on the first floor were closed.

An absolute panic took hold of me. I no longer knew where I was going. I ran along the docks, I turned into the deserted streets of the Beauvoisis district: the houses watched my flight with their mournful eyes. I kept saying to myself in anguish: 'Where shall I go? Where shall I go? *Anything* can happen.' Every now and then, with my heart pounding wildly, I would suddenly swing round: what was happening behind my back? Perhaps it would start behind me, and when I suddenly turned round it would be too late. As long as I could fix objects nothing would happen: I looked at as many as I could, pavements, houses, gas lamps; my eyes went rapidly from one to the other to catch them out and stop them in the middle of their metamorphosis. They didn't look any too natural, but I told myself insistently: 'This is a gas-lamp, that is a drinking fountain,' and I tried to reduce them to their everyday appearance by the power of my gaze. Several times I came across bars on my way: the Café des Bretons, the Bar de la Marine. I stopped, I hesitated in front of their pink net curtains: perhaps these cosy places had been spared, perhaps they still contained a bit of yesterday's world, isolated, forgotten. But I would have had to push open the door and go in. I didn't dare; I went on. The doors of the houses frightened me most of all. I was afraid that they might open by themselves. I ended up by walking in the middle of the street.

I suddenly came out on the quai des Bassins du Nord. Fishing boats, small yachts. I put my foot on a ring set in the stone. Here, far from the houses, far from the doors, I was going to know a moment's respite. On the calm water, speckled with black spots, a cork was floating.

'And *under* the water? Haven't you thought about what there may be *under* the water?'

A monster? A huge carapace, half embedded in the mud? A dozen pairs of claws slowly furrow the slime. The monster raises itself a little, every now and then. At the bottom of the water. I went nearer, watching for an eddy, a tiny ripple. The cork remained motionless among the black spots.

At that moment I heard some voices. It was time. I turned round and started running again.

I caught up with the two men who were talking in the rue de Castiglione. At the sound of my footsteps they gave a violent start and turned round together. I saw their anxious eyes look at me, then behind me to see if something else was coming. So they were like me, they were frightened too? When I passed them we looked at one another: we very nearly spoke. But our glances suddenly expressed mistrust: on a day like this you don't speak to just anybody.

I found myself back in the rue Boulibet, out of breath. Well, the die was cast: I was going to return to the library, take a novel and try to read. Walking by the railing of the municipal park, I caught sight of the man in the cape. He was still there in the deserted park; his nose had become as red as his ears.

I was going to push open the gate, but the expression on his face stopped me: he was wrinkling up his eyes and half-grinning, in a stupid, simpering way. But at the same time he was staring straight ahead at something I couldn't see, with a look so concentrated and intense that I suddenly swung round.

Opposite him, with one foot in the air and her mouth half-open, a little girl of about ten was watching him in fascination, tugging nervously at her scarf and thrusting her pointed face forward.

The fellow was smiling to himself, like somebody who is

about to play a good joke. All of a sudden he stood up, with his hands in the pockets of his cape, which reached down as far as his feet. He took a couple of steps forward and his eyes started rolling. I thought he was going to fall. But he went on smiling, with a sleepy air.

Suddenly I understood: the cape! I should have liked to stop him. It would have been enough for me to cough or to push open the gate. But I in my turn was fascinated by the little girl's face. Her features were drawn with fear and her heart must have been beating madly: but on that rat-like face I could also distinguish something potent and evil. It was not curiosity but rather a sort of assured expectation. I felt helpless: I was outside, on the edge of the park, on the edge of their little drama; but they were riveted to each other by the obscure power of their desires, they formed a couple. I held my breath, I wanted to see what expression would appear on that wizened face when the man, behind my back, opened the skirts of his cape.

But suddenly, released, the little girl shook her head and started running. The fellow in the cape had seen me: that was what had stopped him. For a second he remained motionless in the middle of the path, then he went off. His cape flapped against his calves.

I pushed open the gate and caught up with him in one bound.

'Hey, I say!' I cried.

He started trembling.

'A great menace is hanging over the town,' I said politely as I walked past him.

I went into the reading room and I picked up *La Chartreuse de Parme* from a table. I tried to bury myself in what I was reading, to find a refuge in Stendhal's bright Italy. I succeeded at moments, by means of brief hallucinations, then I fell back again into this threatening day, opposite a little old man who kept clearing his throat, and a young man who was leaning back in his chair, dreaming.

The hours went by, the windows had turned black. There were four of us, not counting the Corsican who was at his desk, stamping the library's latest acquisitions. There was that little old man, the fair-haired young man, a young woman who is working for her degree – and I. Now and then one of us would look up and glance rapidly and suspiciously at the other three, as if he were afraid of them. At one moment the little old man started laughing: I saw the young woman shudder from head to foot. But I had read upside down the title of the book he was reading: it was a humorous novel.

Ten minutes to seven. I suddenly remembered that the library closed at seven o'clock. I was going to be thrown out once more into the town. Where would I go? What would I do? The old man had finished his novel. But he didn't go off. He started drumming on the table with one finger, with sharp, regular taps.

'Gentlemen,' said the Corsican, 'it will be closing time soon.'

The young man gave a start and darted a swift glance at me. The young woman had turned towards the Corsican, then she picked up her book again and seemed to bury herself in it.

'Closing time,' said the Corsican five minutes later.

The old man shook his head with an uncertain air. The young woman pushed her book away, but without getting up.

The Corsican was at a loss what to do. He took a few hesitant steps, then turned a switch. The lamps on the reading tables went out. Only the centre bulb remained alight.

'Do we have to leave?' the old man asked quietly.

The young man got up slowly and regretfully, it was a

question of who was going to take the longest time putting on his coat. When I went out, the woman was still sitting in her chair, with one hand lying flat on her book.

Down below, the door gaped open into the night. The young man, who was walking in front, looked back, walked slowly downstairs, crossed the hall; he stopped for a moment on the threshold, then plunged into the darkness and disappeared.

When I reached the bottom of the stairs I looked up. After a moment the old man left the reading room, buttoning his overcoat. When he had come down the first three steps, I took off and dived out, closing my eyes.

I felt a cool little caress on my face. In the distance somebody was whistling. I opened my eyes: it was raining. A calm, gentle rain. The square was peacefully lighted by its four lamp-posts. A provincial square in the rain. The young man was walking away with great strides; it was he who was whistling: I felt like calling to the two others, who didn't know yet that they could leave without fear, that the menace had passed.

The little old man appeared at the door. He scratched his cheek with an embarrassed air, then he smiled broadly and opened his umbrella.

Saturday morning

Delightful sunshine, with a light mist which promises a fine day. I had my breakfast at the Café Mably.

Madame Florent, the cashier, gave me a gracious smile. I called out from my table:

'Is Monsieur Fasquelle ill?'

'Yes, Monsieur; a bad attack of flu: he'll have to stay in bed for a few days. His daughter arrived from Dunkirk this morning. She's going to stay here to look after him.'

For the first time since I got her letter, I feel really happy at the idea of seeing Anny again. What has she been doing these last six years? Shall we be embarrassed when we see each other again? Anny doesn't know what it is to feel embarrassed. She will greet me as if I had left her yesterday. I only hope I won't behave like a fool, and put her off right at the beginning. I must remember not to hold my hand out to her when I arrive: she hates that.

How many days shall we stay together? Perhaps I shall bring her back to Bouville. It would be enough if she lived here for only a few hours; if she spent one night at the Hôtel Printania. Afterwards, it wouldn't be the same; I couldn't feel frightened any more.

Saturday afternoon

Last year, when I paid my first visit to the Bouville museum, I was struck by the portrait of Olivier Blévigne. Was there something wrong with the proportions? With the perspective? I couldn't have said what it was, but something bothered me: this deputy didn't seem right on his canvas.

Since then I have been back several times to see him. But my impression that something was wrong persisted. I refused to believe that Bordurin, who had received the Prix de Rome and six medals, could have been guilty of faulty draughtsmanship.

Well, this afternoon, looking through an old collection of the *Satirique Bouvillois*, a blackmailing rag whose owner was accused of high treason during the war, I caught a glimpse of the truth. I promptly left the library and went over to the museum.

I walked quickly across the shadowy hall. My footsteps made no noise on the black and white tiles. Around me, a whole race of plaster people were twisting their arms.

Through a couple of large openings, I caught a glimpse in passing of some crackled vases, some plates, a blue and yellow satyr on a pedestal. It was the Bernard-Palissy Room, devoted to ceramics and the minor arts. But ceramics don't make me laugh. A lady and gentleman in mourning were respectfully contemplating these baked objects.

Above the entrance to the main hall – the Bordurin-Renaudas Room – a large canvas had been hung, probably only a little while before, which I didn't know. It was signed Richard Séverand and was entitled *The Bachelor's Death*. It was a gift from the State.

Naked to the waist, his torso a little green as befits a dead man, the bachelor was lying on an unmade bed. The disorder of the sheets and blankets bore witness to a long death-agony. I smiled, thinking of Monsieur Fasquelle. He wasn't alone: his daughter was looking after him. Already, on the canvas, the maid, a servant-cum-mistress with features marked by vice, had opened a drawer and was counting money. An open door revealed a man in a cap, a cigarette stuck on his lower lip, who was waiting in the shadows. Near the wall a cat was unconcernedly lapping up some milk.

This man had lived only for himself. As a severe and well-merited punishment nobody had come to his bedside to close his eyes. This picture gave me a final warning: there was still time, I could retrace my steps. But, if I ignored it, I should remember this: in the great hall I was about to enter, over a hundred and fifty portraits were hanging on the walls; with the exception of a few young people of whom their families had been prematurely deprived and the Mother Superior of an orphanage, none of the people depicted had died unwed, none of them had died childless or intestate, none without the last sacraments. All square, that day as every other day, with God and the world, these men had

slipped gently into death, to go and claim their share of
eternal life to which they were entitled.

For they were entitled to everything: to life, to work, to
wealth, to authority, to respect, and finally to immortality.

I thought for a moment and I went in. An attendant was
sleeping near a window. A pale light falling from the
windows was making patches on the pictures. Nothing alive
in this huge rectangular hall, except for a cat which took
fright at my arrival and fled. But I felt the gaze of a hundred
and fifty pairs of eyes upon me.

All who belonged to the Bouville élite between 1875 and
1910 were there, men and women, meticulously depicted by
Renaudas and Bordurin.

The men built Sainte-Cécile-de-la-Mer. In 1882, they
founded the Federation of Bouville Ship-owners and Mer-
chants 'to unite in a powerful group all men of goodwill, to
cooperate in the task of national recovery, and to hold in
check the parties of disorder ...'. They made Bouville the
best-equipped port in France for the unloading of coal and
timber. The lengthening and widening of the quays were
their work. They carried out necessary extensions to the harbour station and, by means of constant dredging, increased
the depth of the anchorage at low tide to thirty-five feet.
Thanks to them, in twenty years, the tonnage of the fishing
fleet, which was 5,000 barrels in 1869, rose to 18,000 barrels.
Stopping at no sacrifice to help the rise of the best elements
in the working class, they created, on their own initiative,
various centres of technical and professional training which
prospered under their lofty patronage. They broke the
famous dock strike of 1898 and gave their sons to their
country in 1914.

The women, worthy help-mates of these fighters, founded
most of the town's church clubs, day nurseries, and charity
needlework schools. But above all they were wives and

mothers. They raised fine children, taught them their rights and duties, religion, and respect for the traditions which have gone to the making of France. The general hue of the portraits bordered on dark brown. Bright colours had been banished, out of a sense of decency. However, in the portraits by Renaudas, who showed a preference for painting old men, the snowy white of the hair and side-whiskers stood out against the black backgrounds; he excelled in painting hands. Bordurin, who was less meticulous, sacrificed the hands to some extent, but the collars shone like white marble.

It was very hot and the attendant was snoring gently. I glanced all round the walls: I saw hands and eyes; here and there a patch of light covered part of a face. As I was walking towards the portrait of Olivier Blévigne, something brought me to a stop: from his place on the line, Pacôme the merchant was looking down at me with his bright eyes.

He was standing with his head thrown slightly back; in one hand he was holding a top hat and gloves against his pearl-grey trousers. I could not help feeling a certain admiration: I could see nothing mediocre about him, nothing to lay him open to criticism: small feet, delicate hands, broad wrestler's shoulders, quiet elegance with a hint of whimsy. He courteously offered visitors the unwrinkled purity of his face; the shadow of a smile was actually playing about his lips. But his grey eyes were not smiling. He could have been about fifty: he was as young and fresh as a man of thirty. He was very handsome.

I gave up trying to find any fault with him. But he for his part didn't let me go. I read a calm, implacable judgement in his eyes.

Then I realized what separated us: what I might think about him could not touch him; it was just psychology, the sort you find in novels. But his judgement pierced me like a sword and called in question my very right to exist. And it was true, I had always realized that: I hadn't any right to exist. I had appeared by chance, I existed like a stone, a plant, a microbe. My life grew in a haphazard way and in all directions. Sometimes it sent me vague signals; at other times I could feel nothing but an inconsequential buzzing.

But for this handsome, impeccable man, now dead, for Jean Pacôme, the son of the Pacôme of the Government of National Defence, it had been an entirely different matter: the beating of his heart and the dull rumblings of his organs reached him in the form of pure and instantaneous little rights. For sixty years, without a moment's failing, he had made use of his right to live. These magnificent grey eyes had never been clouded by the slightest doubt. Nor had Pacôme ever made a mistake.

He had always done his duty, all his duty, his duty as a son, a husband, a father, a leader. He had also unhesitatingly demanded his rights: as a child, the right to be well brought up, in a united family, the right to inherit a spotless name, a prosperous business; as a husband, the right to be cared for, to be surrounded with tender affection; as a father, the right to be venerated; as a leader, the right to be obeyed without demur. For a right is never anything but the other aspect of a duty. His extraordinary success (the Pacômes are now the richest family in Bouville) could never have surprised him. He had never told himself that he was happy, and when he indulged in a pleasure, he must have done so in moderation, saying: 'I am relaxing.' Thus pleasure, likewise acquiring the status of a right, lost its aggressive futility. On the left, a little above his bluish grey hair, I noticed some books on a shelf. The bindings were handsome; they must undoubtedly have been classics. Every evening, before going to sleep, Pacôme probably re-read a few pages of 'his old Montaigne' or one of Horace's odes in the original Latin. Sometimes, too, he must have read a

contemporary work to keep up to date. That was how he
had known Barrès and Bourget. After a little while he
would put the book down. He would smile. His gaze, losing
its admirable vigilance, would become almost dreamy. He
would say: 'How much simpler and how much more difficult it is to do one's duty!'

He had never gone any further in examining himself: he
was a leader.

There were other leaders hanging on the walls: indeed
there was nothing else. He was a leader, this tall verdigris
old man in his armchair. His white waistcoat was a happy
echo of his silver hair. (From these portraits, which were
painted above all for moral edification, and in which
accuracy was pushed to an exaggerated degree, artistic considerations were not entirely excluded.) He had placed his
long, delicate hand on the head of a little boy. An open
book was resting on his knees, which were covered with a
rug. But his eyes were gazing into the distance. He was
seeing all those things which are invisible to young people.
His name was written on his lozenge of gilded wood underneath his portrait: he must have been called Pacôme or
Parrottin, or Chaigneau. It didn't occur to me to look: for
his family, for this child, for himself, he was simply the
Grandfather; before long, if he considered the time had
come to reveal to his grandson the extent of his future
duties, he would speak of himself in the third person.

'You're going to promise your grandfather to be good, my
boy, to work hard next year. Perhaps Grandfather won't be
here any more next year.'

In the evening of life, he spread his indulgent kindness
over all and sundry. I myself, if he saw me – but I was
transparent to his gaze – I myself would find grace in his
eyes: he would think that I had once had grandparents. He
demanded nothing: a man has no more desires at that age.

125

Nothing except that people should lower their voices slightly when he came in, nothing except that their smiles should reveal a touch of affection and respect when he passed, nothing except that his daughter-in-law should sometimes say: 'Father is amazing; he is younger than all of us'; nothing except that he should be the only one able to calm his grandson's temper by putting his hands on the child's head, and able to say afterwards: 'Grandfather knows how to soothe these troubles', nothing except that his son should come several times a year to ask for his advice on delicate questions, nothing finally except that he should feel serene, calm, and infinitely wise. The old gentleman's hand scarcely weighed upon his grandson's curls; it was almost a benediction. What could he be thinking about? About his honourable past which conferred upon him the right to speak about everything and to have the last word on everything. I had not gone far enough the other day: Experience was much more than a defence against death; it was a right – the right of old men.

General Aubry, hanging on the line with his great sword, was a leader. Another leader was President Hébert, a well-read man and a friend of Impétraz. His face was long and symmetrical with an interminable chin, punctuated, just below the lip, by a tuft of hair: he thrust his jaw out slightly, with an amused expression as if he were putting on airs, pondering an objection on principle like a gentle belch. He was dreaming, holding a quill pen: he too was relaxing, dammit, this time by writing poetry. But he had the eagle eye of a leader.

And what about the soldiers? I was in the middle of the room, the cynosure of all these grave eyes. I was neither a grandfather, nor a father, nor even a husband. I didn't vote, I scarcely paid any taxes; I couldn't lay claim to the rights of a tax-payer, nor to those of an elector, nor even to the humble right to honour which twenty years of obedience confer on an employee. My existence was beginning to cause me serious concern. Was I a mere figment of the imagination?

'Hey,' I suddenly said to myself, 'I'm the one who is the soldier!' This made me laugh, without any suggestion of rancour.

A plump quinquagenarian politely returned a magnificent smile to me. Renaudas had painted him with loving attention, unable to find any touch too gentle for the fleshy, finely chiselled little ears, and above all for the hands, long sensitive hands with tapering fingers: real scientist's or artist's hands. His face was unknown to me: I must have passed the canvas often without noticing it. I went up to it and read: 'Rémy Parrottin, born at Bouville in 1849. Professor at the École de Médecine in Paris, by Renaudas.'

Parrottin: Doctor Wakefield had spoken to me about him: 'Once in my life I met a great man. It was Rémy Parrottin. I attended his lectures during the winter of 1904 (you know that I spent two years in Paris studying obstetrics). He made me understand what a leader is. He had a sort of life force in him, I swear he did. He electrified us, we would have followed him to the ends of the earth. And with all that he was a gentleman: he had a huge fortune and he used a good part of it to help poor students.'

That was how this prince of science, the first time I heard about him, had inspired a few strong feelings in me. Now I was standing before him and he was smiling at me. What intelligence and affability there was in his smile! His plump body rested comfortably in the hollow of a big leather armchair. This unpretentious savant put people at their ease straight away. If it hadn't been for the spirituality of his gaze you would even have taken him for a very ordinary man.

It wasn't hard to guess the reason for his prestige: he was loved because he understood everything; you could tell him anything. All in all he looked a little like Renan, with more distinction. He was one of those people who say:

'The Socialists? Why I go further than they do!' When you followed him along this perilous road, you soon had to abandon, with a shiver, family, country, the right to property, the most sacred values. You even doubted for a moment the right of the bourgeois élite to govern. Another step and suddenly everything was restored, miraculously founded on solid reasons, in the good old way. You turned round and you saw behind you the Socialists, already far away and tiny, waving their handkerchiefs and shouting: 'Wait for us!'

I knew too, through Wakefield, that the Master liked, as he used to say himself with a smile, 'to deliver souls'. Having remained young, he surrounded himself with young people: he often received young men of good family who were studying medicine. Wakefield had been to his house for luncheon several times. After the meal everyone moved into the smoking-room. The Master treated these students who had smoked their first cigarettes not long before like men: he offered them cigars. He stretched out on a divan and spoke at length, his eyes half-closed, surrounded by the eager crowd of his disciples. He evoked memories and told anecdotes, drawing an amusing and profound moral from each. And if, among these well-bred young men, there was one who showed a liking for advanced ideas, Parrottin would take a special interest in him. He encouraged him to speak, listened to him attentively, provided him with ideas and subjects for meditation. Inevitably the young man, full of generous ideas, excited by his family's hostility, and weary of thinking by himself and in opposition to everybody else, would ask the Master one day if he might see him alone, and, stammering with shyness, would confide to him his most intimate thoughts, his indignations, his hopes. Parrottin would clasp him in his arms. He would say: 'I understand you, I have understood you from the very first day.' They would talk together, and Parrottin would go far, further still, so far that the young man would have difficulty in following him. After a few conversations of this sort, a distinct improvement could be detected in the young rebel. He saw clearly in himself, he learned to know the close ties which linked him to his family, to his environment; finally he understood the admirable role of the élite. And in the end, as if by magic, the lost sheep, which had been following Parrottin step by step, found itself back in the fold, enlightened and repentant. 'He cured more souls,' Wakefield concluded, 'than I've cured bodies.'

Rémy Parrottin smiled affably at me. He hesitated, trying to understand my position, in order to outflank it and lead me back to the fold. But I wasn't afraid of him: I wasn't a sheep. I looked at his fine forehead, calm and unwrinkled, his little paunch, his hand resting flat on his knee. I returned his smile and left him.

Jean Parrottin, his brother, the President of the S.A.B., was leaning with both hands on the edge of a table loaded with papers; everything in his attitude indicated to the visitor that the audience was over. His gaze was extraordinary; it was almost abstract and shone with pure privilege. His dazzling eyes dominated the whole of his face. Below this glow I noticed two thin, tight lips, the lips of a mystic. 'That's funny,' I thought, 'he looks like Rémy Parrottin.' I turned towards the Master: examining him in the light of this resemblance, I suddenly saw something arid and desolate appear in his gentle face: the family resemblance. I came back to Jean Parrottin.

This man possessed the simplicity of an idea. Nothing

was left in him but bones, dead flesh, and Pure Privilege. A real case of possession, I thought. Once Privilege has taken hold of a man, there is no exorcistic spell which can drive it out; Jean Parrottin had devoted the whole of his life to thinking of his Privileges: nothing else. Instead of the slight headache which I could feel coming on, as it does every time I visit a museum, he would have felt in his temples the painful right to be looked after. It was important not to make him think too much, or to draw his attention to unpleasant realities, to the possibility of his dying, to other people's sufferings. Probably, on his death-bed, at that moment when, ever since Socrates, it has been the done thing to say a few uplifting words, he said to his wife, as an uncle of mine told his, after she had watched over him for twelve nights: 'You I don't thank, Thérèse; you have only done your duty.' When a man gets to that point, you have to take your hat off to him.

His eyes, which I gazed at in wonder, told me to go. I didn't leave, I was resolutely indiscreet. I knew, as a result of contemplating for a long time a certain portrait of Philip II in the library of the Escurial, that, when you look straight at a face ablaze with a sense of privilege, this fire dies out after a moment, and only an ashy residue remains: it was this residue which interested me.

Parrottin put up a good fight. But, all of a sudden, the light in his eyes went out, the picture grew dim.

What was left? Blind eyes, a mouth as thin as a dead snake, and cheeks. The pale, round cheeks of a child: they spread out over the canvas. The employees of the S.A.B. had never had any inkling of their existence: they never stayed for long enough in Parrottin's office. When they went in, they came up against that terrible gaze, as against a wall. The cheeks, white and flabby, were sheltered behind it. How long had it taken his wife to notice them? Two years? Five years? One day, I imagine, as her husband was sleeping beside her, with a ray of moonlight caressing his nose, or else as he was laboriously digesting, in the heat of the day, stretched out in an armchair, with his eyes half-closed and a puddle of sunlight on his chin, she had ventured to look him in the face: all this flesh had appeared to her without any defence, bloated, slavering, vaguely obscene. From that day on, Madame Parrottin had probably taken command.

I took a few steps backwards and embraced all these great figures in a single glance: Pacôme, President Hébert, the two Parrottins, and General Aubry. They had worn top hats; every Sunday, in the rue Tournebride, they used to meet Madame Gratien, the Mayor's wife, who saw St Cécile in a dream. They used to greet her with great ceremonious bows, the secret of which is now lost.

They had been painted with minute care; and yet, under the brush, their features had been stripped of the mysterious weakness of men's faces. Their faces, even the feeblest, were as clear-cut as porcelain: I looked at them in vain for some link with trees and animals, with the thoughts of earth or water. The need for this had obviously not been felt during their lifetime. But, on the point of passing on to posterity, they had entrusted themselves to a celebrated painter so that he should discreetly carry out on their faces the dredging, drilling, and irrigation by which, all around Bouville, they had transformed the sea and the fields. Thus, with the help of Renaudas and Bordurin, they had enslaved the whole of Nature: outside themselves and in themselves. What these dark canvases offered to my gaze was man re-thought by man, with, as his sole adornment, man's finest conquest: the bouquet of the Rights of Man and

Citizen. Without any mental reservation, I admired the reign of man.

A lady and gentleman had come in. They were dressed in black and were trying to make themselves inconspicuous. They stopped, dumbfounded, on the threshold, and the gentleman automatically took off his hat.

'Ah! Well I never!' said the lady, deeply moved.

The gentleman regained his composure more quickly. He said in a respectful tone of voice:

'It's a whole era!'

'Yes,' said the lady, 'it's my grandmother's era.'

They took a few steps and met Jean Parrottin's gaze. The lady stood there gaping, but the gentleman wasn't proud: he had a humble appearance, he must have been very familiar with intimidating gazes and brief interviews. He tugged gently at his wife's arm:

'Look at this one,' he said.

Rémy Parrottin's smile had always put humble folk at their ease. The woman went forward and painstakingly read out:

'Portrait of Rémy Parrottin, born at Bouville in 1849. Professor at the École de Médecine in Paris, by Renaudas.'

'Parrottin of the Académie des Sciences,' said her husband, 'by Renaudas of the Institut. That's History!'

The lady nodded her head, then looked at the Master.

'How handsome he is,' she said, 'how intelligent he looks!'

The husband made a sweeping gesture.

'These are the people who made Bouville what it is,' he said simply.

'It was a good idea to put them here, all together,' the lady said gently.

We were three soldiers drilling in that huge hall. The husband, who was laughing respectfully and silently, darted a worried glance at me and suddenly stopped laughing. I turned away and went and planted myself opposite the portrait of Olivier Blévigne. A sweet joy swept over me: well, I was right! It really was too funny for words!

The woman had drawn near me.

'Gaston,' she said, suddenly emboldened, 'come here!'

The husband came towards us.

'Look,' she went on, 'this one has a street named after him: Olivier Blévigne. You know, the little street that goes up to the Coteau Vert just before you get to Jouxtebouville.'

After a little while she added:

'He doesn't look very easy-going.'

'No. Grumblers and grousers must have met their match in him.' This remark was addressed to me. The gentleman looked at me out of the corner of his eye and started laughing, audibly this time, with a conceited, meddlesome air, as if he were Olivier Blévigne himself.

Olivier Blévigne did not laugh. He thrust his set jaw towards us and his Adam's apple jutted out.

There was a moment of ecstatic silence.

'Anybody'd think he was going to move,' said the lady.

The husband obligingly explained:

'He was a cotton merchant on a big scale. Then he went into politics, he was a deputy.'

I knew that. Two years ago I looked him up in the *Petit Dictionnaire des Grands Hommes de Bouville* by the Abbé Morellet. I copied out the article.

Blévigne, Olivier-Martial, son of the above, born and died at Bouville (1849–1908), studied law in Paris and obtained his degree in 1872. Deeply impressed by the Commune insurrection, which had forced him, like so many other Parisians, to take refuge at Versailles under the protection of the National Assembly, he swore, at an age when young men usually think of nothing but pleasure, 'to devote his life to the re-establishment of Order'. He kept his word: immediately after his return to our town, he founded the famous Club de l'Ordre, which, every evening for many years, brought together the principal businessmen and ship-owners of Bouville. This aristocratic circle, which was jokingly described as being more exclusive than the Jockey Club, exerted until 1908 a salutary influence on the destinies of our great commercial port. In 1880 Olivier Blévigne married Marie-Louise Pacôme, the youngest daughter of the merchant Charles Pacôme (see under Pacôme) and on the latter's death founded the company of Pacôme–Blévigne and Son. Soon afterwards he turned to political life and presented himself as a candidate for the Chamber of Deputies.

'The Country', he said in a famous speech, 'is suffering from the most serious of maladies: the governing class no longer wants to govern. But who is going to govern, gentlemen, if those whose heredity, education, and experience have rendered them most fit for the exercise of power, turn from it out of resignation or weariness? As I have often observed, to govern is not a right of the élite; it is the élite's principal duty. Gentlemen, I beg of you: let us restore the principle of authority!

Elected on the first ballot on 4 October 1885, he was consistently re-elected thereafter. Endowed with an energetic and vigorous eloquence, he delivered a great many brilliant speeches. He was in Paris in 1898 when the terrible strike broke out. He returned immediately to Bouville, where he became the moving spirit of the resistance. He took the initiative of negotiating with the strikers. These negotiations, inspired by a generous conciliatory spirit, were interrupted by the riot at Jouxtebouville. As is well known, calm was restored by the discreet intervention of the military.

The premature death of his son Octave, who had entered the École Polytechnique at an early age, and of whom he wanted to 'make a leader' was a terrible blow to Olivier Blévigne. He was never to recover from it and died a few years later, in February 1908.

Collected speeches; *Moral Forces* (1894. Out of print); *The Duty to Punish* (1900. The speeches in this volume were all given in connexion with the Dreyfus Case. Out of print); *Will-power* (1902. Out of print). After his death, his last speeches and a few letters to close friends were collected under the title *Labor Improbus* (Plon, 1910). Iconography: there is an excellent portrait of him by Bordurin, in Bouville museum.

An excellent portrait, granted. Olivier Blévigne had a little black moustache and his olive-tinted face somewhat resembled that of Maurice Barrès. The two men had undoubtedly met: they sat on the same benches. But the deputy from Bouville possessed none of the nonchalance of the President of the League of Patriots. He was as stiff as a poker and jumped out of the canvas like a jack-in-the-box. His eyes sparkled: the pupils were black, the corneas reddish. He pursed his fleshy little lips and held his right hand pressed against his chest.

How this portrait had bothered me! Sometimes Blévigne had struck me as too big and other times as too small. But today everything was clear to me. I had learned the truth while looking through the *Satirique Bouvillois*. The issue of 6 November 1905 was entirely devoted to Blévigne. He was depicted on the cover as a tiny figure clinging to the name of old Combes, with this caption: *The Lion's Louse*. And on the very first page, everything was explained: Olivier Blévigne was five feet tall. The paper made fun of his tiny stature and his croaking voice, which on more than one occasion had sent the whole Chamber into hysterics. It accused him of putting rubber lifts in his boots. On the other hand, Madame Blévigne, *née* Pacôme, was a horse. 'It must be said', the paper added, 'that his better half is his double.'

Five feet tall! Why, yes: Bordurin, with jealous care, had surrounded him with objects which ran no risk of diminish-

ing him: a hassock, a low armchair, a shelf with a few
small books, a little Persian table. Only he had given him the
same stature as his neighbour Jean Parrottin and the two
canvases were the same size. The result was that the little
table in one picture was almost as large as the huge table in
the other, and that the hassock would have come up to Parrottin's shoulder. The eye instinctively compared the two
portaits: my uneasiness had come from that.

Now I wanted to laugh: five feet tall! If I had wanted to
speak to Blévigne, I would have had to lean over or bend
my knees. I was no longer surprised that he stuck his nose
into the air so impetuously: the destiny of men of his size is
always worked out a few inches above their heads.

The power of art is truly admirable. Of this shrill-voiced
little man, nothing would go down to posterity except a
threatening face, a superb gesture, and the bloodshot eyes of
a bull. The student terrorized by the Commune, the bad-
tempered midget of a deputy: that was what death had
taken. But, thanks to Bordurin, the President of the Club
de l'Ordre, the orator of *Moral Forces*, was immortal.

'Oh, the poor boy!'

The lady had given a stifled cry: under the portrait of
Octave Blévigne, 'son of the former', a pious hand had
traced these words:

'Died at the École Polytechnique in 1904.'

'He's dead! Just like the Arondel boy. He looks intelligent. How upset his mother must have been! They make
them work too hard in those big schools. The boys' brains
go on working even when they're asleep. I must say I like
those two-cornered hats, they look so smart. Is that what
they call a cassowary?'

'No. A cassowary is what they wear at Saint-Cyr.'

I in my turn contemplated the prematurely dead polytechnician. His waxy complexion and his respectable moustache would have been enough to give anybody the impression of an early death. For that matter he had foreseen his destiny: a certain resignation could be read in his bright, far-seeing eyes. But at the same time he carried his head high; in this uniform he represented the French Army.

Tu Marcellus eris! Manibus date lilia plenis . . .

A cut rose, a dead polytechnician: what could be sadder?

I walked along the long gallery, greeting in passing, without stopping, the distinguished faces which emerged from the shadows: Monsieur Bossoire, President of the Commercial Court, Monsieur Faby, President of the Board of Directors of the Independent Port of Bouville, Monsieur Boulange, merchant, with his family, Monsieur Rannequin, Mayor of Bouville, Monsieur de Lucien, born at Bouville, French Ambassador to the United States and a poet as well, an unknown dressed in a prefect's uniform, Mother Sainte-Marie-Louise, Mother Superior of the Great Orphanage, Monsieur and Madame Théréson, Monsieur Thiboust-Gouron, President of the Conciliation Board, Monsieur Bobot, Chief Administrator of the Conscription Board, Messieurs Brion, Minette, Grelot, Lefebvre, Doctor and Madame Pain, and Bordurin himself, painted by his son Pierre Bordurin. Clear, cold gazes, delicate features, thin lips. Monsieur Boulange was huge and patient, Mother Sainte-Marie-Louise industrious in her piety. Monsieur Thiboust-Gouron was as hard on himself as on others. Madame Théréson struggled without weakening against a deep-seated illness. Her infinitely weary mouth spoke eloquently of her suffering. But this pious woman had never said: 'I feel ill.' She concealed her pain; she composed menus and presided over charitable societies. Sometimes, in the middle of a sentence, she would slowly close her eyes and all the life would go out of her face.

This attack would scarcely ever last more than a second; soon Madame Théréson would open her eyes again and finish her sentence. And in the workshop they would whisper: 'Poor Madame Théréson! She never complains.'

I had walked the whole length of the Bordurin-Renaudas Room. I turned round. Farewell, you beautiful lilies, elegant in your little painted sanctuaries, farewell, you beautiful lilies, our pride and *raison d'être*, farewell, you Bastards.

Monday

I've stopped writing my book about Rollebon; it's finished, I can't go on writing it. What am I going to do with my life?

It was three o'clock. I was sitting at my table; I had put the bundle of letters I stole in Moscow beside me; I was writing:

Care had been taken to spread the most sinister rumours. Monsieur de Rollebon must have allowed himself to be taken in by this trick since he wrote to his nephew on 13 September that he had just made his will.

The Marquis was present: pending the moment when I should have finally installed him in historical existence, I was lending him my life. I could feel him like a slight glow in the pit of my stomach.

I suddenly became aware of an objection which somebody would be sure to raise: Rollebon was far from frank with his nephew, whom he wanted to use, if the plot failed and he appeared before Paul I, as a defence witness. It was perfectly possible that he had made up the story of the will to give the impression that he was a simpleton.

This was a very unimportant objection; it was nothing to get worried about. But it was enough to plunge me into a fit of depression. I suddenly recalled the fat waitress at Camille's, the haggard face of Monsieur Achille, the room in which I had felt so clearly that I was forgotten and forsaken in the present. I told myself wearily:

'How on earth can I, who haven't had the strength to retain my own past, hope to save the past of somebody else?'

I picked up my pen and tried to get back to work; I was sick to death of these reflections on the past, the present, the world. I asked for only one thing: to be allowed to finish my book in peace.

But as my eyes fell on the pad of white sheets, I was struck by its appearance, and I stayed there, my pen raised, gazing at that dazzling paper: how hard and brilliant it was, how present it was. There was nothing in it that wasn't present. The letters which I had just written on it were not dry yet and already they no longer belonged to me.

'Care had been taken to spread the most sinister rumours . . .'

I had thought out this sentence, to begin with it had been a little of myself. Now it had been engraved in the paper, it had taken sides against me. I no longer recognized it. I couldn't even think it out again. It was there, in front of me; it would have been useless for me to look at it for some sign of its origin. Anybody else could have written it. But I, *I* wasn't sure that I had written it. The letters didn't shine any more, they were dry. That too had disappeared; nothing remained of their ephemeral brilliance. I looked anxiously around me: the present, nothing but the present. Light and solid pieces of furniture, encrusted in their present, a table, a bed, a wardrobe with a mirror – and me. The true nature of the present revealed itself: it was that which exists, and all that was not present did not exist. The past did not exist. Not at all. Neither in things nor even in my thoughts. True, I had realized a long time before that my past had escaped me. But until then I had believed that it had simply gone out of my range. For me the past was only a pensioning off: it was another way of existing, a state of holiday and inactivity; each event, when it had played its part, dutifully packed itself away in a box and became an honorary event: we find it so difficult to imagine nothingness. Now I knew. Things are entirely what they appear to be and *behind them* ... there is nothing.

For a few more minutes this thought absorbed my attention. Then I gave a violent shrug of my shoulders to free myself and I pulled the pad of paper towards me.

'... that he had just made his will.'

A feeling of immense disgust suddenly flooded over me and the pen fell from my fingers, spitting ink. What had happened? Had I got the Nausea? No, it wasn't that, the room had its paternal, everyday look. At the very most the table seemed a little heavier and more solid, and my fountain pen more compact. Only Monsieur de Rollebon had just died for the second time.

A little earlier he was there, inside me, quiet and warm, and now and then I could feel him stirring. He was quite alive, more alive to me than the Autodidact or the manageress of the Rendez-vous des Cheminots. Admittedly he had his whims, he could stay for several days without giving any sign of life; but often, on mysteriously fine days, like the man in a weather-box, he would put his nose out and I would catch sight of his pale face and his blue cheeks. And even when he didn't show up himself, he weighed heavily on my heart and I felt full up.

Now nothing remained of him. No more than anything remained, in those traces of dry ink, of the memory of their brilliance. It was my fault: I had uttered the only words that had to be avoided: I said that the past did not exist. And straight away, noiselessly, Monsieur de Rollebon had returned to his nothingness.

I picked up his letters in my hands, I felt them with a sort of despair:

'Yet it was he,' I said to myself, 'it was he who traced these characters one by one. He pressed on this paper, he put his finger on the sheets to prevent them from shifting under his pen.'

Too late: these words no longer had any meaning. Nothing existed any more but a bundle of yellow papers which I was clasping in my hands. True, there was this complicated story: Rollebon's nephew murdered in 1810 by the Tsar's police, his papers confiscated and taken to the Secret Archives, then, a hundred and ten years later, deposited by the Soviets, after they had taken power, in the State Library, from which I stole them in 1923. But this didn't seem true, and I retained no real memory of this theft which I had committed myself. It wouldn't have been difficult to find a hundred more plausible stories to explain the presence of these papers in my room: all of them, in the face of these coarse sheets of paper, would seem as light and hollow as bubbles. Rather than count on these papers to put me in communication with Rollebon, I would do better to resort straight away to table-turning. Rollebon was no more. No more at all. If there were still a few bones left of him, they existed for themselves, in absolute independence, they were nothing more than a little phosphate and calcium carbonate with salt and water.

I made one last attempt; I repeated to myself these words of Madame de Genlis by which I usually evoked the Marquis: 'His little wrinkled face, clean and sharp-featured, all pitted with smallpox, in which there was a remarkable mischievousness which caught the eye at once, however much he tried to disguise it.'

His face obediently appeared to me, his pointed nose, his blue cheeks, his smile. I was able to shape his features at will, perhaps indeed with greater facility than before. Only it was no longer anything but an image in me, a fiction. I sighed, I let myself lean back in my chair, with the impression of an unbearable loss.

Four o'clock strikes. I've been sitting here in my chair for an hour, with my arms dangling. It's beginning to get dark. Apart from that, nothing in this room has changed: the white paper is still on the table, next to the fountain pen and the inkwell . . . but I shall never write any more on this page I have started. Never again, following the rue des Mutilés and the boulevard de la Redoute, shall I go to the library to consult the archives there.

I want to jump up and go out, to do anything – anything at all – to dull my wits. But if I lift one finger, if I don't stay absolutely still, I know very well what will happen. I *don't want* that to happen to me yet. It will happen too soon as it is. I don't move; I read automatically, on the pad of paper, the paragraph I have left unfinished:

Care had been taken to spread the most sinister rumours. Monsieur de Rollebon must have allowed himself to be taken in by this trick, since he wrote to his nephew on 13 September that he had just made his will.

The great Rollebon affair has come to an end, like a great passion. I shall have to find something else. A few years ago, in Saigon, in Mercier's office, I suddenly emerged from a dream, I woke up. After that I had another dream, I was living in the court of the Tsars, in old palaces so cold that icicles formed in the doorways in winter. Today I wake up in front of a pad of white paper. The torches, the festivities, the uniforms, the lovely shivering shoulders have disappeared. In their place *something* remains in the warm room, something I don't want to see.

Monsieur de Rollebon was my partner: he needed me in

And so you drown yourself in the existence of others often fictional, or desirous idyllic images of your future self.

order to be and I needed him in order not to feel my being. I furnished the raw material, that material of which I had far too much, which I didn't know what to do with: existence, *my* existence. His task was to perform. He stood in front of me and had taken possession of my life in order to perform his life for me. I no longer noticed that I existed, I no longer existed in myself, but in him; it was for him that I ate, for him that I breathed, each of my movements had its significance outside, there, just in front of me, in him; I no longer saw my hand writing letters on the paper, nor even the sentence I had written – but, behind, beyond the paper, I saw the Marquis, who had called for that gesture, and whose existence was prolonged and consolidated by that gesture. I was only a means of making him live, he was my *raison d'être*, he had freed me from myself. What am I going to do now?

Above all not move, *not move* ... Ah!

I couldn't prevent that shrug of the shoulders. ...

The thing which was waiting has sounded the alarm, it has pounced upon me, it is slipping into me, I am full of it. – It's nothing: I am the Thing. Existence, liberated, released, surges over me. I exist.

I exist. It's sweet, so sweet, so slow. And light: you'd swear that it floats in the air all by itself. It moves. Little brushing movements everywhere which melt and disappear. Gently, gently. There is some frothy water in my mouth. I swallow it, it slides down my throat, it caresses me – and now it is starting up again in my mouth, I have a permanent little pool of whitish water in my mouth – unassuming – touching my tongue. And this pool is me too. And the tongue. And the throat is me.

I see my hand spread out on the table. It is alive – it is me. It opens, the fingers unfold and point. It is lying on its back. It shows me its fat under-belly. It looks like an animal upside down. The fingers are the paws. I amuse myself by making them move about very quickly, like the claws of a crab which has fallen on its back. The crab is dead: the claws curl up and close over the belly of my hand. I see the nails – the only thing in me which isn't alive. And even that isn't sure. My hand turns over, spreads itself out on its belly, and now it is showing me its back. A silvery, somewhat shiny back – you might think it was a fish, if it weren't for the red hairs near the knuckles. I feel my hand. It is me, those two animals moving about at the end of my arms. My hand scratches one of its paws with the nail of another paw; I can feel its weight on the table which isn't me. It's long, long, this impression of weight, it doesn't go. There's no reason why it should go. In the long run, it's unbearable . . . I withdraw my hand, I put it in my pocket. But straight away, through the material, I feel the warmth of my thigh. I promptly make my hand jump out of my pocket; I let it hang against the back of the chair. Now I feel its weight at the end of my arm. It pulls a little, not very much, gently, softly, it exists. I don't press the point: wherever I put it, it will go on existing; I can't suppress it, nor can I suppress the rest of my body, the damp warmth which soils my shirt, nor all this warm fat which turns lazily, as if somebody were stirring it with a spoon, nor all the sensations wandering about inside, coming and going, rising from my side to my armpit or else quietly vegetating, from morning till night, in their usual corner.

I jump to my feet: if only I could stop thinking, that would be something of an improvement. Thoughts are the dullest things on earth. Even duller than flesh. They stretch out endlessly and they leave a funny taste in the mouth. Then there are the words, inside the thoughts, the unfinished words, the sketchy phrases which keep coming back: 'I must fini . . . I ex . . . Dead . . . Monsieur de Roll is dead . . . I am not . . . I ex . . .' It goes on and on . . . and there's no end to it. It's worse than the rest because I feel responsible, I feel that I am to blame. For example, it is I who keep up this sort of painful rumination: *I exist*. It is I. The body lives all by itself, once it has started. But when it comes to thought, it is I who continue it, I who unwind it. I exist. I think I exist. Oh, how long and serpentine this feeling of existing is – and I unwind it, slowly . . . If only I could prevent myself from thinking! I try, I succeed: it seems as if my head is filling with smoke . . . And now it starts again: 'Smoke. . . . Mustn't think . . . I don't want to think . . . I think that I don't want to think. I musn't think that I don't want to think. Because it is still a thought.' Will there never be an end to it?

My thought is *me*: that is why I can't stop. I exist by what I think . . . and I can't prevent myself from thinking. At this very moment – this is terrible – if I exist, *it is because* I hate existing. It is I, *it is I* who pull myself from the nothingness to which I aspire: hatred and disgust for existence are just so many ways of *making me* exist, of thrusting me into existence. Thoughts are born behind me like a feeling of giddiness, I can feel them being born behind my head. . . . If I give way, they'll come here in front, between my eyes – and I go on giving way, the thought grows and grows and here it is, huge, filling me completely and renewing my existence.

My saliva is sugary, my body is warm; I feel insipid. My penknife is on the table. I open it. Why not? In any case it would be a change. I put my left hand on the pad and I jab the knife into the palm. The movement was too sudden; the blade slipped, the wound is superficial. It is bleeding. And what of it? What has changed? All the same, I look with a feeling of satisfaction at the white paper, where, across the lines I wrote a little while ago, there is this little

pool of blood which has at last stopped being me. Four lines
on a white paper, a splash of blood, together that makes a
beautiful memory. I must write underneath it: 'That day
I gave up writing my book about the Marquis de Rollebon.'

Am I going to see to my hand? I hesitate. I watch the
small, monotonous trickle of blood. Now it is coagulating.
It's over. My skin looks rusty round the cut. Under the
skin, there is nothing left but a small sensation like the rest,
perhaps even more insipid.

That is half past five striking. I get up, my cold shirt is
sticking to my flesh. I go out. Why? Well, because I have
no reason for not going out either. Even if I stay, even if
I curl up quietly in a corner, I shan't forget myself. I shall
be there, I shall weigh on the floor. I am.

I buy a newspaper on the way. Sensational news. Little
Lucienne's body has been found! Smell of ink, the paper
crumples up between my fingers. The murderer has fled.
The child was raped. They have found her body, the fingers
clutching at the mud. I roll the paper into a ball, my fingers
clutching at the paper; smell of ink; God, how strongly
things exist today. Little Lucienne was raped. Strangled. Her
body still exists, her bruised flesh. *She* no longer exists. Her
hands. She no longer exists. The houses. I am walking
between the houses, I am between the houses, upright on
the pavement; the pavement beneath my feet exists, the
houses close in on me, as the water closes over me, over the
paper in the shape of a swan, I am. I am, I exist, I think
therefore I am; I am because I think, why do I think? I
don't want to think any more, I am because I think that I
don't want to be, I think that I ... because ... Ugh! I flee,
the criminal has fled, her raped body. She felt that other flesh
slipping into hers. I ... now I ... raped. A sweet, bloody
longing for rape takes hold of me from behind, gently,

behind the ears, the ears race along behind me, the red hair, it is red on my head, wet grass, red grass, is it me too? and is this paper me too? hold the paper existence against existence, things exist against one another, I let go of the paper. The house juts out, it exists; in front of me I walk alongside the wall, alongside the long wall I exist, in front of the wall, a step, the wall exists in front of me, one, two, behind me, a finger which scratches inside my pants, scratches, scratches and pulls the little girl's finger soiled with mud, the mud on my finger which came out of the muddy gutter and falls back gently, gently, relaxing, scratching less hard than the fingers of the little girl who was being strangled, criminal, scratching the mud, the earth less hard, the finger slides gently, falls head first and caresses curled up warm against my thigh; existence is soft and rolls and tosses, I toss between the houses, I am, I exist, I think therefore I toss, I am, existence is a fallen fall, won't fall, will fall, the finger scratches at the window, existence is an imperfection. The gentleman. The fine gentleman exists. The gentleman feels that he exists. No, the fine gentleman passing by, as proud and gentle as a convolvulus, doesn't feel that he exists. To expand; my cut hand hurts, exists, exists, exists. The fine gentleman exists Legion of Honour, exists moustache, that's all; how happy one must be to be nothing more than a Legion of Honour and a moustache and nobody sees the rest, he sees the two pointed ends of moustache on both sides of the nose; I do not think therefore I am a moustache. He sees neither his gaunt body, nor his big feet, if you fumbled about inside his trousers, you would be sure to find a pair of little grey india-rubbers. He has the Legion of Honour, the Bastards have the right to exist: 'I exist because that is my right.' I have the right to exist, therefore I have the right not to think: the finger is raised. Am I going to ... caress in the splendour of white sheets the splendid white flesh which falls back gently, touch the blossoming moisture of the armpits, the elixirs and the liqueurs and the florescences of the flesh, enter into the other person's existence, into the red mucous membranes with the heavy, sweet, sweet smell of existence, feel myself existing between the soft wet lips, the lips red with pale blood, the throbbing, yawning lips all wet with existence, all wet with a transparent pus, between the wet sugary lips which cry like eyes? My body of living flesh, the flesh which swarms and turns gently liqueurs, which turns cream, the flesh which turns, turns, turns, the sweet sugary water of my flesh, the blood of my hand, it hurts, gentle to my bruised flesh which turns, walks, I walk, I flee, I am a criminal with bruised flesh, bruised with existence against these walls. I am cold, I take a step, I am cold, a step, I turn left, he turns left, he thinks that he turns left, mad, am I mad? He says that he is afraid of being mad, existence, you see child in existence, he stops, the body stops, he thinks that he stops, where does he come from? What does he do? He sets off again, he is afraid, terribly afraid, criminal, desire like a fog, desire, disgust, he says that he is disgusted with existence, is he disgusted, tired of disgusted with existence? He runs. What does he hope for? Does he run to flee from himself, to throw himself into the lake? He runs, the heart, the heart beating is a holiday. The heart exists, the legs exist, the breath exists, they exist running, breathing, beating softly, gently gets out of breath, gets me out of breath, he says that he is getting out of breath; existence takes my thoughts from behind and gently expands them *from behind*; somebody takes me from behind, they force me from behind to think, therefore to be something, behind me, breathing in light bubbles of existence, he is a bubble of fog of desire, he is pale in the mirror like a dead man, Rollebon is dead, Antoine Roquentin isn't dead, I'm fainting, he says that he would like to faint, he

runs, he runs races (from behind) from behind *from behind*,
little Lucienne assaulted from behind, raped by existence
from behind, he begs for mercy, he is ashamed of begging
for mercy, pity, help, help therefore I exist, he goes into the
Bar de la Marine, the little mirrors in the little brothel, he is
pale in the little mirrors in the little brothel the big soft
red-head who drops on to the bench, the gramophone plays,
exists, everything turns, the gramophone exists, the heart
beats: turn, turn liqueurs of life, turn jellies, syrups of my
flesh, sweetnesses . . . the gramophone.

> When that yellow moon begins to beam
> Every night I dream my little dream.

The voice, deep and husky, suddenly appears and the
world vanishes, the world of existences. A woman of flesh
had that voice, she sang in front of a record, in her best
dress and they recorded her voice. A woman: bah, she
existed like me, like Rollebon, I don't want to know her.
But there it is. You can't say that that exists. The spinning
record exists, the air struck by the vibrating voice exists,
the voice which made an impression on the record existed.
I who am listening, I exist. Everything is full, existence
everywhere, dense and heavy and sweet. But, beyond all this
sweetness, inaccessible, quite close, so far away alas, young,
merciless, and serene, there is this . . . this rigour.

Tuesday

Nothing. Existed.

Wednesday

There is a patch of sunlight on the paper tablecloth. In the
patch of sunlight, a fly is dragging itself along, dazed,
warming itself and rubbing its front legs against one

another. I am going to do it the favour of squashing it. It doesn't see this gigantic index-finger looming up with the gold hairs shining in the sun.

'Don't kill it, Monsieur!' cried the Autodidact.

It bursts, its little white guts come out of its belly; I have relieved it of existence. I say dryly to the Autodidact:

'I've done it a favour.'

Why am I here? — And why shouldn't I be here? It is midday, I am waiting for it to be time to sleep. (Fortunately sleep doesn't avoid me.) In four days I shall see Anny again: for the moment, that is my only reason for living. And afterwards? When Anny has left me? I know very well what I am secretly hoping: I am hoping that she will never leave me again. Yet I ought to know that Anny will never agree to grow old in front of me. I am weak and lonely, I need her. I should have liked to see her again while I was strong: Anny has no pity for flotsam.

'Is anything the matter, Monsieur? Do you feel all right?'

The Autodidact looks sideways at me with laughing eyes. He is panting slightly, his mouth open, like a dog out of breath. I have to admit it: this morning I was almost glad to see him again, I needed to talk.

'How glad I am to have you at my table,' he says. 'If you're cold, we could go and sit next to the stove. Those gentlemen are going to go soon, they have asked for their bill.'

Somebody is worrying about me, wondering if I am cold; I am speaking to another man: that hasn't happened to me for years.

'They're leaving, would you like to change places?'

The two gentlemen have lighted cigarettes. They go out, there they are in the pure air, in the sunshine. They walk along past the big windows, holding their hats on with both hands. They laugh; the wind puffs out their overcoats. No,

I don't want to change places. What would be the use? And then, through the windows, between the white roofs of the bathing-huts, I see the sea, green and compact.

The Autodidact has taken two rectangles of purple cardboard from his wallet. He will hand them over at the cash-desk later on. On the back of one I decipher the words:

> *Maison Bottanet, cuisine bourgeoise.*
> *Le déjeuner à prix fixe: 8 francs*
> *Hors-d'œuvre au choix*
> *Viande garnie*
> *Fromage ou dessert*
> *140 francs les 20 cachets*

That fellow eating at the round table, near the door – I recognize him now: he often stays at the Hôtel Printania, he's a commercial traveller. Now and then he turns his attentive and smiling gaze upon me; but he doesn't see me; he is too busy examining what he is eating. On the other side of the cash-desk, two stocky, red-faced men are eating mussels and drinking white wine. The smaller of the two, who has a thin yellow moustache, is telling a story which he himself is finding amusing. He pauses and laughs, revealing dazzling teeth. The other man doesn't laugh; his eyes are hard. But he often nods his head affirmatively. Near the window, a dark, thin man, with distinguished features and fine white hair brushed back from his forehead, is thoughtfully reading his paper. On the bench beside him, he has put a leather brief-case. He is drinking Vichy water. In a moment all these people are going to leave; weighed down by food, caressed by the breeze, their overcoats wide open, their heads a little hot and muzzy, they will walk along by the balustrade, looking at the children on the beach and the boats on the sea; they will go to work. I for my part will go nowhere, I have no work.

The Autodidact laughs innocently and the sunshine plays in his sparse hair:

'Would you like to order?'

He hands me the menu: I am entitled to choose one hors-d'œuvre: either five slices of sausage or radishes or shrimps or a dish of celery in sauce. There is an extra charge for the Burgundy snails.

'I'll have sausage,' I tell the waitress. He snatches the menu out of my hands:

'Isn't there anything better? Look, there are Burgundy snails.'

'The thing is that I'm not very fond of snails.'

'Oh! Then what about oysters?'

'They're four francs extra,' says the waitress.

'All right, oysters, Mademoiselle — and radishes for me.'

Blushing, he explains to me:

'I'm very partial to radishes.'

So am I.

'And afterwards?' he asks.

I look through the list of meat dishes. The braised beef would tempt me. But I know in advance that I shall have chicken, the only meat dish with an extra charge.

'This gentleman,' he says, 'will have chicken. Braised beef for me, Mademoiselle.'

He turns the menu round: the wine list is on the back:

'We shall have some wine,' he says with a somewhat solemn expression.

'Well I never,' says the waitress, 'we *are* letting ourselves go! You've never had any before.'

'But I can easily stand a glass of wine now and then. Mademoiselle, will you bring us a carafe of Anjou rosé.'

The Autodidact puts down the menu, breaks his bread into small pieces and rubs his knife and fork with his napkin.

He glances at the white-haired ▮▮▮▮▮▮▮▮▮▮▮▮▮▮▮▮
he smiles at me:

'Usually I come here with a book, ev▮
once advised me not to: you eat too quickly
chew. But I've got a stomach like an ostrich, I c▮
anything. During the winter of 1917, when I was a p▮
of war, the food was so bad that everybody fell ill. Natura▮
I went sick like everybody else: but there was nothing wrong
with me.'

He has been a prisoner of war. . . . This is the first time
he has ever spoken to me about it; I can't get over it: I
can't imagine him as anything but an autodidact.

'Where were you a prisoner?'

He doesn't reply. He has put down his fork and is looking
at me terribly hard. He is going to tell me his troubles: now
I remember that there was something wrong at the library.
I am all ears: I ask for nothing better than to sympathize
with other people's troubles, that will make a change for me.
I haven't any troubles, I have some money like a gentleman
of leisure, no boss, no wife, no children; I exist, that's all.
And that particular trouble is so vague, so metaphysical,
that I am ashamed of it.

The Autodidact doesn't seem to want to talk. What a
curious look he is giving me: it isn't a look to see with, but
rather one for a communion of souls. The Autodidact's soul
has risen to the surface of his magnificent blind man's eyes.
If mine does the same, if it comes and presses its nose against
the window panes, the two of them can exchange greetings.

I don't want a communion of souls, I haven't fallen so
low. I draw back. But the Autodidact leans forward across
the table, without taking his eyes off me. Fortunately the
waitress brings him his radishes. He slumps back in his
chair, his soul disappears from his eyes, he docilely starts
eating.

...ve you sorted out your troubles?'

He gives a start:

'What troubles, Monsieur?' he asks with a frightened look.

'You know, the other day you spoke to me about them.'

He blushes scarlet.

'Ha!' he says in a dry voice. 'Ha! Yes, the other day. Well, it's that Corsican, Monsieur, that Corsican in the library.'

He hesitates a second time, with the stubborn look of a sheep.

'They're just trivialities, Monsieur, that I don't want to bother you about.'

I don't pursue the matter. Without seeming to, he eats at an extraordinary speed. He has already finished his radishes by the time the waitress brings me the oysters. Nothing is left on his plate but a heap of green stalks and a little damp salt.

Outside, a young couple has stopped in front of the menu which a cardboard chef is holding out to them in his left hand (in his right he has a frying-pan). They hesitate. The woman is cold, she tucks her chin into her fur collar. The young man makes up his mind first, he opens the door and stands to one side to let his companion pass.

She comes in. She looks around her amiably and gives a little shiver:

'It's hot,' she says in a deep voice.

The young man closes the door.

'*Messieurs dames*,' he says.

The Autodidact turns round and says pleasantly:

'*Messieurs dames*.'

The other customers don't answer, but the distinguished-looking gentleman lowers his paper slightly and submits the new arrivals to a searching scrutiny.

'Thank you, don't bother.'

Before the waitress, who had run up to help him, could

make a move, the young man had slipped out of his raincoat. In place of a jacket, he is wearing a leather windcheater with a zip fastener. The waitress, a little disappointed, turns to the young woman. But once again he is ahead of her and helps his companion out of her coat with gentle, precise movements. They sit down near us, side by side. They don't look as if they'd known each other for long. The young woman has a tired pure face, with a somewhat sullen expression. She suddenly takes off her hat, shakes her black hair and smiles.

The Autodidact gazes at them for a long time, with a kindly eye; then he turns to me and gives me a meaning wink as if to say: 'What a good-looking pair they are!'

They are not ugly. They are silent, they are happy to be together, happy to be seen together. Sometimes, when we went into a restaurant in Piccadilly, Anny and I, we felt ourselves the objects of admiring attention. It annoyed Anny, but I must admit that I was rather proud of it. Above all, astonished; I have never had the neat look which becomes that young man so well and nobody could even say that my ugliness was touching. Only we were young: now I am at the age to be touched by the youth of others. I am not touched. The woman has dark, gentle eyes; the young man a rather leathery, orange-tinted skin and a charming, stubborn little chin. Yes, I do find them touching, but they also make me feel a little sick. I feel them so far away from me: the warmth is making them languid, they are pursuing a single dream in their hearts, so sweet, so low. They are at ease, they look confidently at the yellow walls, at the people, they consider that the world is fine as it is, just as it is, and for the moment each of them discovers the significance of his life in the life of the other. Soon the two of them will form just a single life, a slow, tepid life which will have no significance left at all – but they won't notice that.

They look as if they were intimidated by each other. Finally, the young man, in an awkward and determined manner, takes the young woman's hand with the tips of his fingers. She breathes heavily and they bend over the menu together. Yes, they are happy. But what of it?

The Autodidact assumes an amused, somewhat mysterious expression:

'I saw you the day before yesterday.'

'Where?'

'Ha, ha!' he says teasingly but respectfully.

He keeps me waiting for a moment, then:

'You were coming out of the museum.'

'Oh, yes,' I say, 'but not the day before yesterday: Saturday.'

The day before yesterday I was certainly in no mood for traipsing round museums.

'Have you seen that remarkable wood-carving of Orsini's attempted assassination?'

'I don't remember it.'

'Really? It's in a little room, on the right as you go in. It's the work of an insurgent in the Commune who lived at Bouville until the amnesty, hiding in an attic. He had intended to get on a boat for America, but the port here is very well policed. An admirable man. He spent his enforced leisure carving a great oak panel. The only tools he had were his penknife and a nail file. He did the intricate parts with the file: the hands and eyes. The panel is five feet long by three feet wide; the whole work is in one piece; there are seventy figures, each the size of my hand, not counting the two horses pulling the Emperor's carriage. And the faces, Monsieur, those faces carved with a nail file, they all have features, they all look human. Monsieur, if I may venture to say so, it is a work well worth seeing.'

I don't want to commit myself:

'I simply wanted to see Bordurin's pictures again.'

The Autodidact suddenly grows sad:

'Those portraits in the main hall? Monsieur,' he says, with a tremulous smile, 'I don't know anything about painting. Naturally I realize that Bordurin is a great painter, I can see that he knows his stuff, as they say. But pleasure, Monsieur, aesthetic pleasure is something I have never known.'

I tell him sympathetically:

'It's the same for me with sculpture.'

'Ah, Monsieur, for me too, alas. And with music, and with dancing. Yet I do possess a certain amount of knowledge. Well, believe it or not, I have seen some young people who didn't know half as much as I do, and who, standing in front of a painting, seemed to be experiencing pleasure.'

'They must have been pretending,' I say encouragingly.

'Perhaps. . . .'

The Autodidact reflects for a moment:

'What upsets me is not so much being deprived of a certain type of pleasure, it's rather that a whole branch of human activity should be foreign to me . . . yet I am a man and it is *men* that have made those pictures . . .'

Suddenly he goes on in a changed voice:

'Monsieur, at one time I ventured to think that beauty was only a matter of taste. Aren't there different rules for each period? Will you excuse me, Monsieur?'

To my surprise I see him take a black leather notebook out of his pocket. He goes through it for a moment: a lot of blank pages and, now and then, a few lines written in red ink. He has turned quite pale. He has put the notebook flat on the table and he places his great hand on the open page. He coughs with embarrassment.

'Sometimes things occur to me – I daren't call them

157

thoughts. It's very strange: I am sitting there reading and all of a sudden, I don't know where it comes from, I get a sort of revelation. At first I didn't take any notice of it, but then I made up my mind to buy a notebook.'

He stops and looks at me: he is waiting.

'Ah,' I say.

'Monsieur, these maxims are naturally only provisional: my education isn't complete yet.'

He picks up the notebook in his trembling hands, he is deeply moved:

'As it happens there is something here about painting. I should be happy if you would allow me to read it to you.'

'With pleasure,' I say.

He reads:

'Nobody believes any longer what the eighteenth century considered to be true. Why should we be expected to go on taking pleasure in the works which it considered to be beautiful?'

He looks at me beseechingly.

'What am I to think of that, Monsieur? Perhaps it's rather paradoxical? That's because I thought I could express my ideas in the form of a witty remark.'

'Well, I . . . I think it's very interesting.'

'Have you read it anywhere before?'

'No, certainly not.'

'Really, you really haven't read it anywhere? Then, Monsieur,' he says, his face falling, 'that means it isn't true. If it were true, somebody would have thought of it already.'

'Wait a minute,' I tell him, 'now that I come to think of it, I believe that I have read something like it.'

His eyes light up; he takes out his pencil.

'In a book by which author?' he asks me in a matter-of-fact tone of voice.

'By . . . by Renan.'

He is overjoyed.

'Would you be kind enough to give me the exact passage?' he says, sucking the point of his pencil.

'You know, it's a very long time since I read it.'

'Oh, it doesn't matter, it doesn't matter.'

He writes Renan's name in his notebook, underneath his maxim.

'I have had the same idea as Renan! I've written his name in pencil,' he explains delightedly, 'but this evening I'll go over it in red ink.'

He looks ecstatically at his notebook for a moment, and I wait for him to read me some more maxims. But he closes it carefully and stuffs it into his pocket. He probably considers that this is enough happiness for one time.

'How pleasant it is,' he says with a confidential air, 'to be able to talk freely at times, like this.'

This remark, as might be imagined, kills off our languishing conversation. A long silence follows.

Since the arrival of the young couple, the atmosphere of the restaurant has completely changed. The two red-faced men have fallen silent; they are shamelessly examining the young woman's charms. The distinguished-looking gentleman has put down his paper and is looking at the couple with a kindliness almost bordering on complicity. He is thinking that old age is wise and youth is beautiful, he nods his head with a certain coquetry: he is well aware that he is still handsome and well-preserved, that with his dark complexion and slim figure he is still attractive. He is playing at feeling paternal. The waitress's feelings seem to be simpler: she has planted herself in front of the young people and is staring at them open-mouthed.

They are talking quietly. The waitress has brought them their hors-d'œuvre, but they don't touch them. Straining my ears, I can make out snatches of their conversation. It is easier for me to distinguish what the woman is saying, in her rich, veiled voice.

'No, Jean, no.'

'Why not?' the young man murmurs with passionate vivacity.

'I've told you why.'

'That isn't a reason.'

There are a few words which escape me, then the young woman makes a charming, weary gesture:

'I've tried too often. I'm past the age when you can start your life again. I'm an old woman, you know.'

The young man laughs sarcastically. She goes on:

'I couldn't stand a ... disappointment.'

'You must have more confidence,' says the young man; 'the way you are now, you aren't living.'

She sighs.

'I know!'

'Look at Jeannette.'

'Yes,' she says, pulling a face.

'Well, I think it was splendid what she said. She showed courage.'

'You know,' says the young woman, 'the fact is, she really grabbed the chance. I can tell you that if I'd wanted, I could have had hundreds of chances like that. I preferred to wait.'

'You were right,' he says tenderly, 'you were right to wait for me.'

She laughs in her turn.

'What conceit! I didn't say that.'

I stop listening to them: they annoy me. They are going to sleep together. They know it. Each of them knows that the other knows it. But as they are young, chaste, and decent, as each wants to keep his self-respect and that of the other, and as love is a great poetic thing which mustn't be shocked, they go several times a week to dances and restaurants, to present the spectacle of their ritualistic, mechanical dances. . . .

After all, you have to kill time. They are young and well built, they have another thirty years in front of them. So they don't hurry, they take their time, and they are quite right. Once they have been to bed together, they will have to find something else to conceal the enormous absurdity of their existence. All the same . . . is it absolutely necessary to lie to each other? I look round the room. What a farce! All these people sitting there looking serious, eating. No, they aren't eating: they are reviving their strength in order to complete their respective tasks. Each of them has his little personal obstinacy which prevents him from noticing that he exists; there isn't one of them who doesn't think he is indispensable to somebody or something. Wasn't it the Autodidact who said to me the other day: 'Nobody was better qualified than Nouçapié to undertake this vast synthesis?' Every one of them does one little thing and nobody is better qualified than he to do it. Nobody is better qualified than the commercial traveller over there to sell Swan toothpaste. Nobody is better qualified than that interesting young man to fumble about under his neighbour's skirts. And I am among them and if they look at me they must think that nobody is better qualified than I to do what I do. But *I know*. I don't look very important but I know that I exist and that they exist. And if I knew the art of convincing people, I should go and sit down next to that handsome white-haired gentleman and I should explain to him what existence is. The thought of the look which would come on to his face if I did makes me burst out laughing. The Autodidact looks at me in surprise. I should like to stop, but I can't: I laugh until I cry.

'You are in a gay mood, Monsieur,' the Autodidact says to me with a guarded air.

'I was just thinking,' I tell him, laughing, 'that here we are, all of us, eating and drinking to preserve our precious existence, and that there's nothing, nothing, absolutely no reason for existing.'

The Autodidact has become serious, he makes an effort to understand me. I laughed too loud: I saw several heads turn towards me. Then I regret having said so much. After all, that's nobody's business.

He repeats slowly:

'No reason for existing . . . I suppose, Monsieur, you mean that life has no object. Isn't that what people call pessimism?'

He goes on thinking for a moment, then he says gently:

'A few years ago I read a book by an American author, called *Is Life Worth Living?* Isn't that the question you are asking yourself?'

No, that obviously isn't the question I'm asking myself. But I don't want to explain anything.

'He concluded,' the Autodidact tells me in a consoling voice, 'in favour of deliberate optimism. Life has a meaning if you choose to give it one. First of all you must act, you must throw yourself into some enterprise. If you think about it later on, the die is already cast, you are already involved. I don't know what you think about that, Monsieur?'

'Nothing,' I say.

Or rather I think that that is precisely the sort of lie that the commercial traveller, the two young people, and the white-haired gentleman keep on telling themselves.

The Autodidact smiles with a certain malice and much solemnity:

'It isn't my opinion either. I don't think we need look so far to find the meaning of our life.'

'Oh?'

'There is a goal, Monsieur, there is a goal . . . there are people.'

That's right: I was forgetting that he was a humanist. He remains silent for a moment, long enough to put away, neatly and inexorably, half his braised beef and a whole slice of bread. 'There are people . . .' He has just painted a complete portrait of himself, this tender-hearted fellow. Yes, but he doesn't know how to say his piece properly. His eyes are as soulful as could be, that can't be denied, but being soulful isn't enough. I knocked around with some Parisian humanists in the old days, and scores of times I've heard them say: 'There are people'. That was quite another matter! Virgan was unbeatable in this respect. He would take off his spectacles, as if to show himself naked, in his human flesh, and stare at me with his eloquent eyes, with a solemn, weary gaze which seemed to undress me in order to seize my human essence, and then he would murmur melodiously: 'There are people, old fellow, there are people,' giving the 'There are' a sort of awkward emphasis, as if his love of people, perpetually new and astonished, were getting caught up in its giant wings.

The Autodidact's mimicry hasn't acquired this smoothness; his love of mankind is naïve and barbaric: he is very much the provincial humanist.

'People,' I say to him, 'people . . . in any case you don't seem to worry about them very much: you are always alone, always with your nose in a book.'

The Autodidact claps his hands, he starts laughing mischievously:

'You're wrong. Ah, Monsieur, allow me to say how very wrong you are!'

He reflects for a moment and discreetly finishes swallowing. His face is as radiant as dawn. Behind him the young woman gives a gay laugh. Her companion is bending over her and whispering in her ear.

'Your mistake is perfectly natural,' says the Autodidact,

'I should have told you long ago ... but I am so shy, Monsieur: I was looking for an opportunity.'

'Here it is,' I tell him politely.

'I think so too. I think so too! Monsieur, what I am about to tell you ...' He stops, blushing: 'But perhaps I am imposing on you?'

I reassure him. He heaves a sigh of happiness.

'It isn't every day that one meets a man like you, Monsieur, in whom breadth of vision is linked with clear-sighted intelligence. I have been wanting to talk to you for months, to explain what I have been, what I have become. ...'

His plate is as empty and clean as if it had just been brought to him. I suddenly discover, next to mine, a little tin dish in which a drum-stick of chicken is swimming in a brown sauce. I have to eat that.

'A little while ago I mentioned my captivity in Germany. It was there that it all began. Before the war I was alone and I didn't realize it; I lived with my parents, who were good people, but I didn't get on with them. When I think of those years ... but how could I have lived like that? I was dead, Monsieur, and I never realized it; I had a collection of postage stamps.'

He looks at me and breaks off to say:

'Monsieur, you are pale, you look tired, I hope I'm not boring you?'

'You interest me greatly.'

'The war came and I enlisted without knowing why. I spent two years without understanding, because life at the front left little time for thought and besides, the soldiers were too coarse. At the end of 1917 I was taken prisoner. Since then I have been told that a lot of soldiers recovered their childhood faith during their captivity. Monsieur,' the Autodidact says, lowering his eyelids over burning pupils, 'I don't believe in God; his existence is disproved by

Science. But, in the internment camp, I learnt to believe in people.'

'They endured their fate bravely?'

'Yes,' he says vaguely, 'there was that too. Besides, we were treated well. But I wanted to speak of something else; during the last few months of the war, they gave us scarcely any work to do. When it rained, they made us go into a big wooden shed which held about two hundred of us at a pinch. They closed the door and left us there, squeezed up against one another, in almost total darkness.'

He hesitates for a moment.

'I don't know how to explain this to you, Monsieur. All those men were there, you could scarcely see them but you could feel them against you, you could hear the sound of their breathing. . . . One of the first times they locked us in that shed the crush was so great that at first I thought I was going to suffocate, then suddenly a tremendous feeling of joy came over me, and I almost fainted: at that moment I felt I loved those men like brothers, I would have liked to kiss them all. After that, every time I went back there, I felt the same joy.'

I have to eat my chicken, which must be cold by now. The Autodidact has finished a long time ago and the waitress is waiting to change the plates.

'That shed had taken on a sacred character in my eyes. Sometimes I managed to escape the attention of our guards. I slipped into it all alone and there, in the darkness, at the memory of the joys I had known there, I fell into a sort of ecstasy. Hours went by, but I paid no attention. Sometimes I burst out sobbing.'

I must be ill: there is no other way of explaining that terrible rage which has just overwhelmed me. Yes, a sick man's rage: my hands were shaking, the blood rushed to my head, and finally my lips too started trembling. All that simply because the chicken was cold. I was cold too, for that matter, and that was the worst of it: I mean that the heart of me had remained as it had been for the last thirty-six hours, absolutely cold and icy. Anger went through me like a whirlwind, it was something like a shudder, an effort by my conscience to react, to fight against this lowering of my temperature. It was all in vain: on the slightest pretext I should probably have rained blows and curses on the Auto-didact or the waitress. But my heart wouldn't really have been in it. My rage blustered on the surface, and for a moment I had the painful impression of being a block of ice enveloped in fire, an *omelette-surprise*. This superficial agitation disappeared and I heard the Autodidact say:

'Every Sunday I used to go to Mass. Monsieur, I have never been a believer. But couldn't one say that the real mystery of the Mass is the communion of souls? A French chaplain, who had only one arm, used to celebrate the Mass. We had a harmonium. We listened, standing, bare-headed, and as the sounds of the harmonium carried me away, I felt myself at one with all the men surrounding me. Ah, Monsieur, how I loved those Masses! Even now, in memory of them, I sometimes go to church on Sunday morning. We have a re-markable organist at Sainte-Cécile.'

'You must have often missed that life?'

'Yes, Monsieur, in 1919. That was the year I was released. I spent some utterly miserable months. I didn't know what to do, I wasted away. Whenever I saw some men gathered together I would insinuate myself into their group. There were times,' he adds with a smile, 'when I joined the funeral procession of a complete stranger. One day, in despair, I threw my stamp collection into the fire . . . but I found my vocation.'

'Really?'

'Somebody advised me . . . Monsieur, I know that I can

count on your discretion. I am – perhaps these are not your ideas, but you are so broad-minded – I am a Socialist.'

He has lowered his eyes and his long lashes are trembling:

'Since September 1921 I have been a member of the S.F.I.O. Socialist Party. That is what I wanted to tell you.'

He is radiant with pride. He looks at me, his head thrown back, his eyes half-closed, his mouth slightly open, looking like a martyr.

'That's excellent,' I say, 'that's very fine.'

'Monsieur, I knew that you would approve. And how could you disapprove of somebody who comes and tells you: I have arranged my life in such and such a way, and now I am perfectly happy?'

He has spread his arms out with his palms towards me and his fingers pointing to the ground, as if he were about to receive the stigmata. His eyes are glazed, I can see a dark pink mass rolling about in his mouth.

'Ah,' I say, 'as long as you're happy. . . .'

'Happy?' His gaze is disconcerting, he has raised his eyelids and is staring at me. 'You are going to be able to judge, Monsieur. Before taking that decision, I felt such utter loneliness that I thought of committing suicide. What held me back was the idea that nobody, absolutely nobody would be moved by my death, that I would be even more alone in death than in life.'

He straightens up, his cheeks puff out.

'I am no longer alone, Monsieur. And I shall never be alone again.'

'Ah, so you know a lot of people?' I say.

He smiles and I promptly realize my mistake.

'I mean that I no longer *feel* alone. But naturally, Monsieur, I don't have to be with anybody.'

'All the same,' I say, 'at the local branch of the party . . .'

'Ah, I know everybody there. But most of them only by

name. Monsieur,' he says mischievously, 'is one obliged to choose one's companions in such a narrow way? All men are my friends. When I go to the office in the morning, there are other men in front of me, behind me, going to their work. I see them, if I dared I would smile at them, I think that I am a Socialist, that they all form the purpose of my life, the object of my efforts, and that they don't know it yet. That's a positive holiday for me, Monsieur.'

He looks inquiringly at me: I nod my approval, but I can feel that he is a little disappointed, that he would like rather more enthusiasm. What can I do? Is it my fault if, in everything he tells me, I recognize borrowings, quotations? Is it my fault if, while he speaks, I see all the humanists I have known reappear? Alas, I've known so many of them! The radical humanist is a special friend of civil servants. The so-called 'Left wing' humanist's chief concern is to preserve human values; he belongs to no party because he doesn't want to betray humanity as a whole, but his sympathies go towards the humble; it is to the humble that he devotes his fine classical culture. He is generally a widower with beautiful eyes always clouded with tears; he weeps at anniversaries. He also loves cats, dogs, all the higher animals. The Communist writer has been loving men ever since the second Five-Year Plan; he punishes because he loves. Modest as all strong men are, he knows how to hide his feelings, but he also knows how, with a look or an inflection of his voice, to reveal, behind his stern justicial words, a glimpse of his bitter-sweet passion for his brethren. The Catholic humanist, the late-comer, the Benjamin, speaks of men with a wonder-struck air. What a beautiful fairy tale, he says, is the humblest life, that of a London docker, of a girl in a shoe factory! He has chosen the humanism of the angels; he writes, for the edification of the angels, long, sad, beautiful novels, which frequently win the Prix Femina.

Those are the principal types. But there are others, a swarm of others: the humanist philosopher who bends over his brothers like an elder brother who is conscious of his responsibilities; the humanist who loves men as they are, the one who loves them as they ought to be, the one who wants to save them with their consent, and the one who will save them in spite of themselves, the one who wants to create myths, and the one who is satisfied with the old myths, the one who loves man for his death, the one who loves man for his life, the happy humanist who always knows what to say to make people laugh, the gloomy humanist whom you usually meet at wakes. They all hate one another: as individuals, of course, not as men. But the Autodidact doesn't know it: he has locked them up inside him like cats in a leather bag and they are tearing one another to pieces without his noticing it.

He is already looking at me with less confidence.

'Don't you feel as I do, Monsieur?'

'Good heavens . . .'

Faced with his anxious, rather spiteful look, I feel a moment's regret at having disappointed him. But he goes on amiably:

'I know: you have your research, your books, you serve the same cause in your own way.'

My books, *my* research: the idiot. He couldn't have made a worse blunder.

'That isn't why I write.'

The Autodidact's face is immediately transformed: it is as if he had scented the enemy. I had never seen that expression on his face before. Something has died between us.

Feigning surprise, he asks:

'But . . . if I am not being indiscreet, why do you write, then, Monsieur?'

'Well . . . I don't know: just to write.'

He gives a satisfied smile, he thinks that he has caught me out:

'Would you write on a desert island? Doesn't one always write in order to be read?'

It was out of habit that he put that sentence in an interrogative form. In fact, he is making a statement. His veneer of gentleness and shyness has peeled off; I don't recognize him any more. His features reveal a massive obstinacy; he is a wall of complacency. I still haven't got over my astonishment when I hear him say:

'If somebody tells me: I write for a certain social class, for a group of friends, that's all right. Perhaps you write for posterity ... but, Monsieur, in spite of yourself you write for somebody.'

He waits for an answer. As it doesn't come, he smiles feebly.

'Perhaps you are a misanthrope?'

I know what this fallacious effort at conciliation hides. He is asking very little from me in fact: simply to accept a label. But this is a trap: if I consent, the Autodidact triumphs, I am promptly out-flanked, recaptured, overtaken, for humanism takes all human attitudes and fuses them together. If you stand up to it, you play its game; it lives on its opponents. There is a race of stubborn, stupid villains who lose to it every time: it digests all their violences and worst excesses, it turns them into a white, frothy lymph. It has digested anti-intellectualism, manicheism, mysticism, pessimism, anarchy, and egotism: they are nothing more than stages, incomplete thoughts which find their justification only in humanism. Misanthropy also has its place in this concert: it is simply a discord necessary to the harmony of the whole. The misanthrope is a man: it is therefore inevitable that the humanist should be misanthropic to a certain degree. But he is a scientific misanthrope who has succeeded in determining the extent of his hatred, who hates men at first only to love them better later.

I don't want to be integrated, I don't want my good red blood to go and fatten that lymphatic animal: I am not going to be fool enough to say that I am an 'anti-humanist'. I *am not* a humanist, that's all.

'I believe,' I say to the Autodidact, 'that one cannot hate men any more than one can love them.'

The Autodidact looks at me with a distant, patronizing air. He murmurs, as if he were paying no particular attention to his words:

'We must love them, we must love them. . . .'

'Whom must we love? The people here?'

'Them too. One and all.'

He turns round to look at the radiant young couple: that's what we must love. For a moment he contemplates the white-haired gentleman. Then his gaze returns to me; on his face I read a mute question. I shake my head. He looks as if he felt sorry for me.

'You don't love them either,' I tell him in irritation.

'Really, Monsieur? Will you allow me to disagree with you?'

He has become respectful again, respectful to his finger-tips, but he has the ironic look in his eyes of somebody who is tremendously amused. He hates me. I would have been a fool to worry about this maniac. I question him in my turn:

'So, those two young people behind you – you love them, do you?'

He looks at them again, he ponders:

'You want to make me say,' he says suspiciously, 'that I love them without knowing them. Well, Monsieur, I admit that I don't know them . . . unless, of course, love is true knowledge,' he adds with a silly laugh.

'But what do you love?'

'I see that they are young and it is youth that I love in them. Among other things, Monsieur.'

He breaks off and listens:

'Can you understand what they're saying?'

Can I understand it? The young man, emboldened by the sympathetic atmosphere around him, is describing in a loud voice a football match which his team won last year against a club from Le Havre.

'He's telling her a story,' I say to the Autodidact.

'Ah! I can't hear them properly. But I can hear their voices, a soft voice, a deep voice, they alternate. It's ... it's so attractive.'

'Only I can also hear what they're saying, unfortunately.'

'Well?'

'Well, they're play-acting.'

'Really? Playing at being young, perhaps?' he asks sarcastically. 'Allow me, Monsieur, to say that I consider that a very profitable exercise. Is it enough to play at being young to return to their age?'

I remain deaf to his sarcasm; I continue:

'You've got your back to them, you can't hear what they're saying. . . . What colour is the young woman's hair?'

He gets flustered:

'Well, I . . .' He shoots a glance at the young couple and recovers his composure. 'Black!'

'You see!'

'See what?'

'You see that you don't love them. You probably wouldn't be able to recognize them in the street. They are only symbols in your eyes. You aren't the least bit touched by them: you're touched by the Youth of Man, by the Love of Man and Woman, by the Human Voice.'

'Well? Doesn't all that exist?'

'Of course it doesn't exist! Neither Youth nor Maturity nor Old Age nor Death....'

The Autodidact's face, as hard and yellow as a quince, has frozen in lockjawed disapproval. Nevertheless I go on:

'It's like that old gentleman drinking Vichy water behind you. It's the Mature Man, I suppose, that you love in him; the Mature Man bravely heading towards his decline, and taking care of his appearance because he doesn't want to let himself go?'

'Exactly,' he says defiantly.

'And you can't see that he's a bastard?'

He laughs, he thinks I'm joking, he darts a quick glance at the handsome face framed in white hair:

'But, Monsieur, even supposing that he looks what you say, how can you judge that man by his face? A face, Monsieur, tells nothing when it is in repose.'

Blind humanists! That face is so eloquent, so clear – but their tender, abstract souls have never allowed themselves to be affected by the meaning of a face.

'How can you,' says the Autodidact, 'limit a man like that, how can you say that he *is* this or that? Who can drain a man dry? Who can know a man's resources?'

Drain a man dry! I salute in passing the Catholic humanism from which the Autodidact has unknowingly borrowed this formula.

'I know,' I tell him, 'I know that all men are admirable. You are admirable. I am admirable. In so far as we are God's creatures of course.'

He looks at me uncomprehendingly, then says with a thin smile:

'I suppose you are joking, Monsieur, but it is true that all men are entitled to our admiration. It is difficult, Monsieur, very difficult to be a man.'

Without noticing, he has abandoned the love of men in

Christ; he nods his head, and by a curious phenomenon of mimicry, he resembles that poor Guéhenno.

'Excuse me,' I say, 'but in that case I'm not quite sure of being a man: I had never found that very difficult. It always seemed to me that you only had to let yourself go.'

The Autodidact laughs openly, but his eyes remain spiteful:

'You are too modest, Monsieur. In order to endure your condition, the human condition, you, like everybody else, need a great deal of courage. Monsieur, the next moment may be the moment of your death, you know it and yet you can smile: come now, isn't that admirable? In the most insignificant of your actions,' he adds sourly, 'there is an immensity of heroism.'

'And what will you gentlemen have for dessert?' asks the waitress.

The Autodidact is quite white, his eyelids are half-lowered over eyes of stone. He makes a feeble gesture with his hand, as if inviting me to choose.

'Cheese,' I say heroically.

'And you, Monsieur?'

He gives a start.

'Eh? Oh, yes: Well, I won't have anything, I've finished.'

'Louise!'

The two fat men pay and go off. One of them limps. The *patron* shows them to the door: they are important customers, they were served with a bottle of wine in an ice-bucket.

I look at the Autodidact with a little remorse: he has been looking forward all week to this luncheon, at which he would be able to tell another man about his love of man. He so rarely has the opportunity of talking. And now I have spoilt his pleasure. In point of fact he is as lonely as I am: nobody cares about him. Only he doesn't realize his solitude.

Well, yes: but it wasn't up to me to open his eyes. I feel very ill at ease: I'm furious, it's true, but not with him, with Virgan and the others, all those who have poisoned that poor brain of his. If I could have them here in front of me, I'd have something to say to them, and no mistake. I shall say nothing to the Autodidact, I have nothing but sympathy for him: he is somebody like Monsieur Achille, somebody of my sort, who has deserted out of ignorance and good-will.

A burst of laughter from the Autodidact rouses me from my morose reflections:

'Forgive me, but when I think of the depth of my love for people, of the strength of the impulses which carry me towards them, and when I see us here, arguing and discussing . . . it makes me want to laugh.'

I say nothing, I give a forced smile. The waitress puts a plate in front of me with a piece of chalky Camembert on it. I glance round the room and a feeling of violent disgust comes over me. What am I doing here? Why did I get mixed up in a discusion about humanism? What are these people here? Why are they eating? It's true that *they* don't know that they exist. I want to leave, to go somewhere where I should be really *in my place*, where I would fit in . . . but my place is nowhere; I am unwanted.

The Autodidact calms down. He had been afraid that I would put up rather more resistance. He is willing to forget about all that I have said. He leans towards me in a confidential manner:

'At heart, you love them, Monsieur, you love them as I do: we are separated by words.'

I can't speak any more, I bow my head. The Autodidact's face is right up against mine. He smiles foolishly, right up against my face, just as people do in nightmares. I laboriously chew a piece of bread which I can't make up my mind to swallow. People. You must love people. People are admir-

175

able. I feel like vomiting – and all of a sudden, there it is: the Nausea.

A really bad attack: it shakes me from top to bottom. I had seen it coming for the last hour, only I didn't want to admit it. This taste of cheese in my mouth. . . . The Auto-didact babbles on and his voice buzzes gently in my ears. But I don't know what he's talking about any more. I nod my head mechanically. My hand is clutching the handle of the dessert knife. I can feel this black wooden handle. It is my hand which is holding it. My hand. Personally, I would rather leave this knife alone: what is the use of always touching something? Objects are not made to be touched. It is much better to slip between them, avoiding them as much as possible. Sometimes you take one of them in your hand and you are obliged to drop it as quickly as you can. The knife falls on the plate. The white-haired gentleman jumps at the noise and looks at me. I pick up the knife again, I press the blade against the table and I bend it.

So this is the Nausea: this blinding revelation? To think how I have racked my brains over it! To think how much I've written about it! Now I know: I exist – the world exists – and I know that the world exists. That's all. But I don't care. It's strange that I should care so little about everything: it frightens me. It's since that day when I wanted to play ducks and drakes. I was going to throw that pebble, I looked at it and that was when it all began: I felt that it *existed*. And then, after that, there were other Nauseas; every now and then objects start existing in your hand. There was the Nausea of the Rendez-vous des Cheminots and then another one before that, one night when I was looking out of the window; and then another one in the municipal park, one Sunday, and then others. But it had never been as strong as today.

'. . . of ancient Rome, Monsieur?'

The Autodidact is asking me a question, I think. I turn towards him and smile at him. Well? What's the matter with him? Why is he shrinking back into his chair? Do I frighten people now? It was bound to end up like that. I don't care anyway. They aren't completely wrong to be frightened. I can feel that I could do anything. For example plunge this cheese-knife into the Autodidact's eye. After that, all these people would trample on me and kick my teeth in. But that isn't what stops me: the taste of blood in my mouth instead of the taste of cheese would make no difference. Only it would be necessary to make a gesture, to give birth to a superfluous event: the cry the Autodidact would give would be superfluous – and so would the blood flowing down his cheek and the jumping-up of all these people. There are quite enough things existing already.

Everybody is looking at me; the two representatives of youth have interrupted their sweet conversation. The woman has her mouth open in a pout. Yet they ought to see that I am quite harmless.

I get up, everything spins about me. The Autodidact stares at me with his big eyes which I shan't put out.

'You're leaving already?' he murmurs.

'I'm a little tired. It was very nice of you to invite me. Good-bye.'

As I am leaving, I notice that I have kept the dessert-knife in my left hand. I throw it on my plate which makes a clinking noise. I cross the room in the midst of total silence. They have stopped eating: they are looking at me, they have lost their appetite. If I were to walk towards the young woman and say 'Boo!' she would start screaming, that's certain. It isn't worth it.

All the same, before going out, I turn round and I show them my face, so that they can engrave it in their memory.

'*Messieurs dames.*'

They don't reply. I go off. Now the colour will come back into their cheeks, they will start chattering.

I don't know where to go, I remain planted beside the cardboard chef. I don't need to turn round to know that they are watching me through the windows; they are looking at my back with surprise and disgust: they thought that I was like them, that I was a man, and I deceived them. All of a sudden, I lost the appearance of a man and they saw a crab escaping backwards from that all too human room. Now the unmasked intruder has fled: the show goes on. It annoys me to feel that swarm of eyes and frightened thoughts behind my back. I cross the street. The other pavement runs alongside the beach and the bathing huts.

There are a lot of people walking along the shore, turning poetic, springtime faces towards the sea; they're in holiday mood because of the sun. There are women in light-coloured dresses, who have put on their outfits from last spring; they pass by, as long and white as kid-gloves; there are also big boys from the *lycée* and the commercial school, and old men wearing decorations. They don't know one another, but they look at one another with a conspiratorial air, because it's such a fine day and they are people. People embrace one another without knowing one another on days when war is declared; they smile at one another every springtime. A priest walks slowly along, reading his breviary. Now and then he raises his head and looks at the sea approvingly: the sea too is a breviary, it speaks of God. Delicate colours, delicate perfumes, springtime souls. 'What lovely weather, the sea is green, I like this dry cold better than the damp.' Poets! If I grabbed one of them by the lapels of his coat, if I said to him: 'Come to my help,' he would think: 'What the devil is this crab?' and would run off, leaving his coat in my hands.

I turn my back on them, I lean both hands on the balustrade. The *real* sea is cold and black, full of animals; it crawls underneath this thin green film which is designed to deceive people. The sylphs all around me have been taken in: they see nothing but the thin film, that is what proves the existence of God. I see underneath! The varnishes melt, the shining little velvety skins, God's little peach-skins, explode everywhere under my gaze, they split and yawn open. Here comes the Saint-Elémir tram, I turn round and the things turn with me, as pale and green as oysters. Useless, it was useless to jump in since I don't want to go anywhere.

Bluish objects move jerkily past the windows, all stiff and brittle. People, walls; through its open windows a house offers me its black heart; and the window-panes give a pale blue tinge to everything that is black, give a blue colour to this big yellow brick building which advances hesitatingly, tremblingly, and which stops all of a sudden, taking a nose-dive forward. A gentleman gets on and sits down opposite me. The yellow building sets off again, it leaps up against the windows, it is so close that you can see only part of it, it has turned dark. The windows rattle. It rises, overwhelming, much higher than you can see, with hundreds of windows open on black hearts; it glides alongside the box, brushing past it; darkness has fallen between the rattling windows. It glides along endlessly, as yellow as mud, and the windows are sky-blue. And all of a sudden it is no longer there, it has stayed behind, a bright grey light invades the box and spreads everywhere with inexorable justice: it is the sky; through the windows you can still see layer on layer of sky, because we are going up Eliphar Hill and we have a clear view on both sides, on the right as far as the sea, on the left as far as the airfield. No smoking, not even a Gitane.

I lean my hand on the seat, but I pull it away hurriedly: the thing exists. This thing on which I'm sitting, on which

179

I leaned my hand just now, is called a seat. They made it on purpose for people to sit on, they took some leather, some springs, some cloth, they set to work with the idea of making a seat, and when they had finished, *this* was what they had made. They carried it here, into this box, and the box is now rolling and jolting along, with its rattling windows, and it's carrying this red thing inside it. I murmur: 'It's a seat,' rather like an exorcism. But the word remains on my lips, it refuses to settle on the thing. It stays what it is, with its red plush, thousands of little red paws in the air, all stiff, little dead paws. This huge belly turns upwards, bleeding, puffed up – bloated with all its dead paws, this belly floating in this box, in this grey sky, is not a seat. It could just as well be a dead donkey, for example, swollen by the water and drifting along, belly up on a great grey river, a flood river; and I would be sitting on the donkey's belly and my feet would be dangling in the clear water. Things have broken free from their names. They are there, grotesque, stubborn, gigantic, and it seems ridiculous to call them seats or say anything at all about them: I am in the midst of Things, which cannot be given names. Alone, wordless, defenceless, they surround me, under me, behind me, above me. They demand nothing, they don't impose themselves, they are there. Under the cushion of the seat, next to the wood, there is a thin line of shadow, a thin black line which runs along the seat with a mysterious, mischievous air, almost a smile. I know perfectly well that it isn't a smile and yet it exists, it runs under the whitish windows, under the rattle of the windows, it persists, under the blue pictures which pass behind the windows and stop and set off again, it persists, like the vague memory of a smile, like a half-forgotten word of which you can remember only the first syllable and the best thing you can do is turn your eyes away and think about something else, about that man half-lying on the seat opposite me, there. His terracotta face with its blue eyes. The whole of the right side of his body has collapsed, the right arm is stuck to the body, the right side is scarcely alive, it lives laboriously, avariciously, as if it were paralysed. But on the whole of the left side, there is a little parasitic existence which proliferates, a chancre: the arm started trembling and then it rose and the hand at the end was stiff. And then the hand too started trembling and, when it reached the height of the skull, a finger stretched out and started scratching the scalp with the nail. A sort of voluptuous grimace came and inhabited the right side of the mouth and the left side remained dead. The windows rattle, the arm trembles, the nail scratches, scratches, the mouth smiles under the staring eyes and the man endures without noticing it this little existence which is swelling his right side, which has borrowed his right arm and his right cheek to fulfil itself. The conductor blocks my way.

'Wait until the tram stops.'

But I push him aside and I jump off the tram. I couldn't stand it any more. I couldn't stand things being so close any more. I push open a gate, I go through, airy existences leap about and perch on the treetops. Now I recognize myself, I know where I am: I am in the municipal park. I flop on to a bench between the great black trunks, between the black, knotty hands reaching out towards the sky. A tree is scratching the earth under my feet with a black nail. I should so like to let myself go, to forget, to sleep. But I can't, I'm suffocating: existence is penetrating me all over, through the eyes, through the nose, through the mouth. . . .

And suddenly, all at once, the veil is torn away, I have understood, I have *seen*.

I can't say that I feel relieved or happy: on the contrary, I feel crushed. Only I have achieved my aim: I know what I wanted to know; I have understood everything that has happened to me since January. The Nausea hasn't left me and I don't believe it will leave me for quite a while; but I am no longer putting up with it, it is no longer an illness or a passing fit: it is me.

I was in the municipal park just now. The root of the chestnut tree plunged into the ground just underneath my bench. I no longer remembered that it was a root. Words had disappeared, and with them the meaning of things, the methods of using them, the feeble landmarks which men have traced on their surface. I was sitting, slightly bent, my head bowed, alone in front of that black, knotty mass, which was utterly crude and frightened me. And then I had this revelation.

It took my breath away. Never, until these last few days, had I suspected what it meant to 'exist'. I was like the others, like those who walk along the sea-shore in their spring clothes. I used to say like them: 'The sea *is* green; that white speck up there *is* a seagull', but I didn't feel that it existed, that the seagull was an 'existing seagull'; usually existence hides itself. It is there, around us, in us, it is *us*, you can't say a couple of words without speaking of it, but finally you can't touch it. When I believed I was thinking about it, I suppose that I was thinking nothing, my head was empty, or there was just one word in my head, the word 'to be'. Or else I was thinking ... how can I put it? I was thinking *appurtenances*, I was saying to myself that the sea belonged to the class of green objects, or that green formed part of the sea's qualities. Even when I looked at things, I was miles from thinking that they existed: they looked like stage

182

scenery to me. I picked them up in my hands, they served me as tools, I foresaw their resistance. But all that happened on the surface. If anybody had asked me what existence was, I should have replied in good faith that it was nothing, just an empty form which added itself to external things, without changing anything in their nature. And then, all of a sudden, there it was, as clear as day: existence had suddenly unveiled itself. It had lost its harmless appearance as an abstract category: it was the very stuff of things, that root was steeped in existence. Or rather the root, the park gates, the bench, the sparse grass on the lawn, all that had vanished; the diversity of things, their individuality, was only an appearance, a veneer. This veneer had melted, leaving soft, monstrous masses, in disorder – naked, with a frightening, obscene nakedness.

I took care not to make the slightest movement, but I didn't need to move in order to see, behind the trees, the blue columns and the lamp-post of the bandstand, and the Velleda in the middle of a clump of laurel bushes. All those objects ... how can I explain? They embarrassed me; I would have liked them to exist less strongly, in a drier, more abstract way, with more reserve. The chestnut tree pressed itself against my eyes. Green rust covered it half way up; the bark, black and blistered, looked like boiled leather. The soft sound of the water in the Masqueret Fountain flowed into my ears and made a nest there, filling them with sighs; my nostrils overflowed with a green, putrid smell. All things, gently, tenderly, were letting themselves drift into existence like those weary women who abandon themselves to laughter and say: 'It does you good to laugh', in tearful voices; they were parading themselves in front of one another, they were abjectly admitting to one another the fact of their existence. I realized that there was no half-way house between non-existence and this rapturous abundance. If you existed, you had to *exist to that extent*, to the point of mildew, blisters, obscenity. In another world, circles and melodies kept their pure and rigid lines. But existence is a curve. Trees, midnight-blue pillars, the happy bubbling of a fountain, living smells, wisps of heat haze floating in the cold air, a red-haired man digesting on a bench: all these somnolences, all these digestions taken together had a vaguely comic side. Comic.... No: it didn't go as far as that, nothing that exists can be comic; it was like a vague, almost imperceptible analogy with certain vaudeville situations. We were a heap of existents inconvenienced, embarrassed by ourselves, we hadn't the slightest reason for being there, any of us, each existent, embarrassed, vaguely ill at ease, felt superfluous in relation to the others. *Superfluous*: that was the only connexion I could establish between those trees, those gates, those pebbles. It was in vain that I tried to *count* the chestnut trees, to *situate* them in relation to the Velleda, to compare their height with the height of the plane trees: each of them escaped from the relationship in which I tried to enclose it, isolated itself, overflowed. I was aware of the arbitrary nature of these relationships, which I insisted on maintaining in order to delay the collapse of the human world of measures, of quantities, of bearings; they no longer had any grip on things. *Superfluous*, the chestnut tree, over there, opposite me, a little to the left. *Superfluous*, the Velleda....

And *I* – weak, languid, obscene, digesting, tossing about dismal thoughts – *I too was superfluous*. Fortunately I didn't feel this, above all I didn't understand it, but I was uneasy because I was afraid of feeling it (even now I'm afraid of that – I'm afraid that it might take me by the back of my head and lift me up like a ground-swell). I dreamed vaguely of killing myself, to destroy at least one of these superfluous existences. But my death itself would have been superfluous. Superfluous, my corpse, my blood on these pebbles, between these plants, in the depths of this charming park. And the decomposed flesh would have been superfluous in the earth which would have received it, and my bones, finally, cleaned, stripped, neat and clean as teeth, would also have been superfluous; I was superfluous for all time.

The word Absurdity is now born beneath my pen; a little while ago, in the park, I didn't find it, but then I wasn't looking for it either, I didn't need it: I was thinking without words, *about* things, *with* things. Absurdity was not an idea in my head, or the sound of a voice, but that long dead snake at my feet, that wooden snake. Snake or claw or root or vulture's talon, it doesn't matter. And without formulating anything clearly, I understood that I had found the key to Existence, the key to my Nausea, to my own life. In fact, all that I was able to grasp afterwards comes down to this fundamental absurdity. Absurdity: another word; I am struggling against words; over there, I touched the thing. But here I should like to establish the absolute character of this absurdity. A gesture, an event in the little coloured world of men is never absurd except relatively speaking: in relation to the accompanying circumstances. A madman's ravings, for example, are absurd in relation to the situation in which he finds himself, but not in relation to his madness. But I, a little while ago, experienced the absolute: the absolute or the absurd. That root – there was nothing in relation to which it was not absurd. Oh, how can I put that in words? Absurd: irreducible; nothing – not even a profound, secret aberration of Nature – could explain that. Obviously I didn't know everything, I hadn't seen the seed sprout or the tree grow. But faced with that big rugged paw, neither ignorance nor knowledge had any importance; the world of explanations and reasons is not that of existence. A circle is not absurd, it is clearly explicable by the rotation of a segment of a straight line around one of its extremities. But a circle doesn't exist either. That root, on the other hand, existed in so far that I could not explain it. Knotty, inert, nameless, it fascinated me, filled my eyes, repeatedly brought me back to its own existence. It was no use my repeating: 'It is a root' – that didn't work any more. I saw clearly that you could not pass from its function as a root, as a suction-pump, *to that*, to that hard, compact sea-lion skin, to that oily, horny, stubborn look. The function explained nothing; it enabled you to understand in general what a root was, but not *that one* at all. That root, with its colour, its shape, its frozen movement, was ... beneath all explanation. Each of its qualities escaped from it a little, flowed out of it, half-solidified, almost became a thing; each one was *superfluous in* the root, and the whole stump now gave me the impression of rolling a little outside itself, denying itself, losing itself in a strange excess. I scraped my heel against that black claw: I should have liked to peel off a little of the bark. For no particular reason, out of defiance, to make the absurd pink of an abrasion appear on the tanned leather: to *play* with the absurdity of the world. But when I took my foot away, I saw that the bark was still black.

Black? I felt the word subside, empty itself of its meaning with an extraordinary speed. Black? The root *was not* black, it was not the black there was on that piece of wood – it was ... something else: black, like the circle, did not exist. I looked at the root: was it *more than black* or *almost* black? But soon I stopped questioning myself because I had the feeling that I was on familiar ground. Yes, I had already scrutinized, with that same anxiety, unnameable objects, I had already tried – in vain – to think something *about them*: and I had already felt their cold, inert qualities escape, slip between my fingers. Adolphe's braces, the other evening, at the Rendez-vous des Cheminots. They *were not* purple. I recalled the two indefinable patches on the shirt. And the pebble, that wretched pebble, the origin of this whole business: it was not ... I couldn't remember exactly what it refused to be. But I hadn't forgotten its passive resistance. And the Autodidact's hand; I had taken it and shaken it one day at the library, and then I had had the feeling that it wasn't quite a hand. I had thought of a fat maggot, but it wasn't that either. And the suspicious transparency of a glass of beer in the Café Mably. Suspicious: that's what they were, the sounds, the smells, the tastes. When they shot past under your eyes, like startled hares, and you didn't pay too much attention to them, you could believe them to be simple and reassuring, you could believe that there was real blue in the world, real red, a real smell of almonds or violets. But as soon as you held on to them for a moment, this feeling of comfort and security gave way to a deep uneasiness: colours, tastes, smells were never real, never simply themselves and nothing but themselves. The simplest, most irreducible quality had a superfluity in itself, in relation to itself, in its heart. That black, there, against my foot, didn't look like black, but rather the confused effort to imagine black by somebody who had never seen black and who wouldn't have known how to stop, who would have imagined an ambiguous creature beyond the colours. It *resembled* a colour but also ... a bruise or again a secretion, a yolk – and something else, a smell for example, it melted into a smell of wet earth, of warm, moist wood, into a black smell spread like varnish over that sinewy wood, into a taste of sweet, pulped fibre. I didn't *see* that black in a simple way: sight is an abstract invention, a cleaned-up, simplified idea, a human idea. That black, a weak, amorphous presence, far surpassed sight, smell, and taste. But that richness became confusion and finally ceased to be anything at all because it was too much.

That moment was extraordinary. I was there, motionless

and frozen, plunged into a horrible ecstasy. But, in the very heart of that ecstasy, something new had just appeared; I understood the Nausea, I possessed it. To tell the truth, I did not formulate my discoveries to myself. But I think that now it would be easy for me to put them into words. The essential thing is contingency. I mean that, by definition, existence is not necessity. To exist is simply *to be there*; what exists appears, lets itself be *encountered*, but you can never *deduce* it. There are people, I believe, who have understood that. Only they have tried to overcome this contingency by inventing a necessary, causal being. But no necessary being can explain existence: contingency is not an illusion, an appearance which can be dissipated; it is absolute, and consequently perfect gratuitousness. Everything is gratuitous, that park, this town, and myself. When you realize that, it turns your stomach over and everything starts floating about, as it did the other evening at the Rendez-vous des Cheminots; that is the Nausea; that is what the Bastards – those who live on the Coteau Vert and the others – try to hide from themselves with their idea of rights. But what a poor lie: nobody has any rights; they are entirely gratuitous, like other men, they cannot succeed in not feeling superfluous. And in themselves, secretly, they *are superfluous*, that is to say amorphous and vague, sad.

How long did that spell last? I *was* the root of the chestnut tree. Or rather I was all consciousness of its existence. Still detached from it – since I was conscious of it – and yet lost in it, nothing but it. An uneasy consciousness and yet one which let itself hang with all its weight over that piece of inert wood. Time had stopped: a small black pool at my feet; it was impossible for anything to come after that particular moment. I should have liked to tear myself away from that atrocious pleasure, but I didn't even imagine that that was possible; I was inside; the black stump *did not pass*, it stayed there, in my eyes, just as a lump of food sticks in a windpipe. I could neither accept nor reject it. At the cost of what effort did I raise my eyes? And indeed did I actually raise them? Didn't I rather obliterate myself for a moment, to come to life again the next moment with my head thrown back and my eyes turned upwards? In fact, I was not aware of a transition. But, all of a sudden, it became impossible for me to think of the existence of the root. It had been wiped out. It was no use my repeating to myself: 'It exists, it is still there, under the bench, against my right foot', it didn't mean anything any more. Existence is not something which allows itself to be thought of from a distance; it has to invade you suddenly, pounce upon you, weigh heavily on your heart like a huge motionless animal – or else there is nothing left at all.

There was nothing left at all, my eyes were empty, and I felt delighted with my deliverance. And then, all of a sudden, something started moving before my eyes, slight, uncertain movements: the wind was shaking the top of the tree.

I wasn't sorry to see something move, it was a change from all those motionless existences which watched me like staring eyes. I said to myself, as I followed the swaying of the branches: 'Movements never quite exist, they are transitions, intermediaries between two existences, unaccented beats.' I got ready to see them come out of nothingness, gradually ripen, blossom: at last I was going to surprise existences in the process of being born.

It took only three seconds to dash all my hopes to the ground. In those hesitant branches which were groping about like blind men, I failed to distinguish any 'transition' to existence. That idea of transition was another invention of man. An idea which was too clear. All those tiny agitations cut themselves off, set themselves up on their own. They overflowed the branches and boughs everywhere. They whirled about those dry hands, enveloping them in tiny cyclones. Admittedly a movement was something different from a tree. But it was still an absolute. A thing. My eyes never met anything but repletion. There were swarms of existences at the ends of the branches, existences which constantly renewed themselves and were never born. The existing wind came and settled on the tree like a big fly; and the tree shivered. But the shiver was not a nascent quality, a transition from the potential to the act; it was a thing; a thing-shiver flowed into the tree, took possession of it, shook it, and suddenly abandoned it, going further on to spin around by itself. Everything was full, everything was active, there was no unaccented beat, everything, even the most imperceptible movement, was made of existence. And all those existents which were bustling about the tree came from nowhere and were going nowhere. All of a sudden they existed and then, all of a sudden, they no longer existed: existence has no memory; it retains nothing of what has disappeared; not even a recollection. Existence everywhere, to infinity, superfluous, always and everywhere; existence – which is never limited by anything but existence. I slumped on the bench, dazed, stunned by that profusion of beings without origin: bloomings, blossomings everywhere, my ears were buzzing with existence, my very flesh was throbbing and opening, abandoning itself to the universal burgeoning, it was repulsive. 'But why,' I thought, 'why so many existences, since they all resemble one another?' What was the use of so many trees which were all identical? So many existences failed and stubbornly begun again and once more failed – like the clumsy efforts of an insect which had fallen on its back? (I was one of those efforts). That abundance did not give the impression of generosity, far from it. It was dismal, sickly, encumbered by itself. Those trees, those big clumsy bodies ... I started laughing because I suddenly thought of the wonderful springtimes described in books, full of crackings, burstings, gigantic blossomings. There were fools who talked to you about willpower and the struggle for life. Hadn't they ever looked at an animal or a tree? That plane tree with its scaling bark, that half-rotten oak – they would have wanted me to take them for vigorous youthful forces thrusting towards the sky. And that root? I would probably have had to see it as a greedy claw, tearing the earth, snatching its food from it.

Impossible to see things that way. Weaknesses, frailties, yes. The trees were floating. Thrusting towards the sky? Collapsing rather: at any moment I expected to see the trunks shrivel like weary pricks, curl up and fall to the ground in a soft, black, crumpled heap. They did not want to exist, only they could not help it; that was the point. So they performed all their little functions, quietly, unenthusiastically, the sap rose slowly and reluctantly in the canals, and the roots penetrated slowly into the earth. But at every moment they seemed on the verge of dropping everything and obliterating themselves. Tired and old, they went on existing, unwillingly and ungraciously, simply because they were too weak to die, because death could come to them only from the outside: melodies alone can proudly carry their own death within them like an internal necessity; only they don't exist. Every existent is born without reason, prolongs itself out of weakness and dies by chance. I leaned back and I closed my eyes. But pictures, promptly informed, sprang forward and filled my closed eyes with existences: existence is a repletion which man can never abandon.

Strange pictures. They represented a host of things. Not real things, other things which looked like them. Wooden objects which looked like chairs, like clogs, other objects which looked like plants. And then two faces: the couple who were lunching near me, the other Sunday, at the Brasserie Vézelize. Fat, hot, sensual, absurd, with their ears all red. I could see the woman's shoulders and bosom. Existence in the nude. Those two – the idea suddenly horrified me – those two were still existing somewhere in Bouville: somewhere – in the midst of what smells? – that soft bosom was still rubbing up against cool material, nestling in lace, and the woman was still feeling her bosom existing in her blouse, thinking: 'My tits, my lovely fruits', smiling mysteriously, attentive to the blossoming of her breasts which were tickling her and then I cried out and I found myself with my eyes wide open.

Did I dream it up, that huge presence? It was there, installed on the park, tumbled into the trees, all soft, gumming everything up, all thick, a jelly. And I was inside with the whole of the park? I was frightened, but above all I was furious, I thought it was so stupid, so out of place, I hated that ignoble jelly. And there was so much of it, so much! It went up as high as the sky, it flowed away everywhere, it filled everything with gelatinous subsidence and I could see it going deeper and deeper, far beyond the limits of the park and the houses and Bouville, I was no longer at Bouville or anywhere, I was floating. I was not surprised, I knew perfectly well that it was the World, the World in all its nakedness which was suddenly revealing itself, and I choked with fury at that huge absurd being. You couldn't even wonder where it all came from, or how it was that a world should exist rather than nothing. It didn't make sense, the world was present everywhere, in front, behind. There had been nothing *before* it. Nothing. There had been no moment at which it might not have existed. It was that which irritated me: naturally there was *no reason* for it to exist, that flowing larva. *But it was not possible* for it not to exist. That was unthinkable: in order to imagine nothingness, you had to be there already, right in the world, with your eyes wide open and alive; nothingness was just an idea in my head, an existing idea floating in that immensity: this nothingness hadn't come *before* existence, it was an existence like any other and one which had appeared after a great many others. I shouted: 'What filth! What filth!' and I shook myself to get rid of that sticky dirt, but it held fast and there was so much of it, tons and tons of existence, indefinitely: I was suffocating at the bottom of that huge boredom. Then, all of a sudden, the park emptied as if through a big hole, the world disappeared in the same way it had come, or else I woke up – in any case I could not see it any more; there remained some yellow earth around me, out of which dead branches stuck up into the air.

I got up, I went out. When I got to the gate, I turned round. Then the park smiled at me. I leaned against the gate and I looked at the park for a long time. The smile of the trees, of the clump of laurel bushes, *meant* something; that was the real secret of existence. I remembered that one Sunday, not more than three weeks ago, I had already noticed in things a sort of conspiratorial air. Was it to me that it was addressed? I regretfully felt that I had no means of understanding. No means. Yet it was there, expectant, it resembled a gaze. It was there, on the trunk of the chestnut tree ... it was *the* chestnut tree. You could have sworn that things were thoughts which stopped half way, which forgot themselves, which forgot what they had wanted to think and which stayed like that, swaying to and fro, with a funny little meaning which went beyond them. That little meaning annoyed me: I *could not* understand it, even if I stayed leaning against the gate for a hundred and seven years; I had learned everything I could know about existence. I left, I came back to the hotel, and there you are, I wrote.

In the night

I have made up my mind: I no longer have any reason for staying at Bouville since I have stopped writing my book; I am going to live in Paris. On Friday I shall take the five o'clock train, on Saturday I shall see Anny; I think we shall spend a few days together. Then I shall come back here to settle a few things and pack my bags. By 1 March, at the latest, I shall be permanently installed in Paris.

Friday

At the Rendez-vous des Cheminots. My train leaves in twenty minutes. The gramophone. Strong feeling of adventure.

Saturday

Anny opens the door to me, in a long black dress. Naturally she doesn't hold her hand out to me, she doesn't say hello. I have kept my right hand in the pocket of my overcoat. Sulkily and very quickly, to get the formalities over with, she says:

'Come in and sit down anywhere you like, except in the armchair near the window.'

It's her, it's her all right. She lets her arms dangle by her sides, she has the sullen face which used to make her look like a little girl at the awkward age. But now she doesn't look like a little girl any more. She is fat, she has a big bosom.

She shuts the door, she says thoughtfully to herself:

'I don't know if I'm going to sit on the bed. . . .'

Finally she flops on to a sort of chest covered with a rug. Her walk is no longer the same: she moves with a majestic heaviness which is not ungraceful: she looks embarrassed by her youthful paunch. Yet in spite of everything it's her all right, it's Anny.

Anny bursts out laughing.

'What are you laughing for?'

As usual she doesn't answer straight away, and assumes a captious expression.

'Tell me why.'

'It's because of that big smile you've been wearing ever since you came in. You look like a father who's just married off his daughter. Come on, don't just stand there. Put your coat somewhere and sit down. Yes, there if you like.'

A silence follows, which Anny makes no attempt to break. How bare this room is! In the old days, wherever Anny went, she used to take with her a huge suitcase full of shawls, turbans, mantillas, Japanese masks, and popular pictures. As soon as she arrived at a hotel — even if it was only for one night — the first thing she did was to open that suitcase and take out all its treasures, which she hung on the walls, hooked on to the lamps, and spread over the tables or on the floor, following a changeable and complicated order; in less than half an hour the most ordinary room took on a heavy, sensual, almost unbearable personality. Perhaps the suitcase has got lost, or has been left at the cloakroom . . . this cold room, with the door into the bathroom half open, has something sinister about it. Though sadder and more luxurious, it looks like my room at Bouville.

Anny laughs again. How well I recognize that shrill, rather nasal little laugh.

'Well, you haven't changed. What are you looking for with that frantic look on your face?'

She smiles, but her eyes examine my face with an almost hostile curiosity.

'I was just thinking that this room doesn't look as if you were living in it.'

'Really?' she answers vaguely.

Another silence. Now she is sitting on the bed, very pale in her black dress. She hasn't cut her hair. She is still looking at me, calmly, raising her eyebrows slightly. Hasn't she anything to say to me then? Why did she ask me to come? This silence is unbearable.

Suddenly I say in a pitiful voice:

'I'm glad to see you.'

The last word sticks in my throat: if that's all I can find to say, I would have done better to keep quiet. She is going to lose her temper for sure. I expected the first quarter of an hour to be difficult. In the old days, when I saw Anny again, whether it was after an absence of twenty-four hours or on waking up in the morning, I could never find the words she expected, the right words to go with her dress, with the weather, with the last words we had spoken the night before. What does she want? I can't guess.

I raise my eyes again. Anny is looking at me with a sort of tenderness.

'So you haven't changed at all? You're still as big a fool as ever?'

Her face expresses satisfaction. But how tired she looks!

'You're a milestone,' she says, 'a milestone by the side of the road. You explain imperturbably and you'll go on explaining for the rest of your life that it's twenty-seven kilometres to Melun and forty-two to Montargis. That's why I need you so much.'

'Need me? You mean you've needed me these four years that I haven't seen you? Well, you've kept very quiet about it, I must say.'

I smiled as I spoke: she might think I bore her a grudge. I can feel this false smile on my mouth, I am uncomfortable.

'What a fool you are! Naturally I don't need to see you, if that's what you mean. You know you're not exactly a sight for sore eyes. I need you to exist and not to change. You're like that metre of platinum they keep somewhere in Paris or near by. I don't think anybody's ever wanted to see it.'

'That's where you're mistaken.'

'Anyway, it doesn't matter, I haven't. Well, I'm glad to know that it exists, that it measures exactly one ten millionth of a quarter of the meridian. I think of it every time anybody takes the measurements of a flat or sells me some material by the metre.'

'Really?' I say coldly.

'But you know, I could easily think of you only as an abstract virtue, a sort of limit. You ought to be grateful to me for remembering your face every time.'

Here we are again with those Alexandrian discussions which I had to put up with in the old days, when in my heart I had very simple, ordinary desires, such as a longing to tell her that I loved her, to take her in my arms. Today I have no desire. Except perhaps a desire to say nothing and to look at her, to realize in silence all the importance of this extraordinary event: Anny's presence opposite me. And for her, is this day like any other day? Her hands are not trembling. She must have had something to tell me the day she wrote to me – or perhaps it was just a whim. Now there has been no question of it for a long time.

Anny suddenly smiles at me with a tenderness so visible that tears come into my eyes.

'I've thought about you much more often than about the platinum metre. There hasn't been a day when I haven't thought about you. And I remembered exactly what you looked like down to the smallest detail.'

She gets up and comes and places her hands on my shoulders.

'You complain about me, but dare you say that you remembered my face?'

'That's not fair,' I say, 'you know perfectly well I have a bad memory.'

'You admit it: you'd forgotten me completely. Would you have recognized me in the street?'

'Naturally. It's not a question of that.'

'Did you so much as remember the colour of my hair?'

'Of course! It's fair.'

She bursts out laughing.

'You say that very proudly. Since you can see it in front of you, you don't deserve much credit.'

She ruffles my hair with her hand.

'And your hair is red,' she says, imitating me; 'the first time I saw you, I'll never forget it, you were wearing a soft hat which was practically mauve and it clashed horribly with your red hair. It hurt just to look at it. Where's your hat? I want to see if your taste is as bad as ever.'

'I don't wear one any more.'

She gives a low whistle, opening her eyes wide.

'You didn't think of that all by yourself! You did? Well, congratulations. Of course you shouldn't wear a hat. Only you had to think about it. That hair of yours can't stand anything, it clashes with hats, with armchair cushions, even with the wallpaper in the background. Or else, if you did wear a hat, you'd have to pull it down over your eyes like that felt hat you bought in London. You tucked that lock of yours under the brim, and nobody could tell whether you had any hair left at all.'

She adds, in the determined tone with which you end old quarrels:

'It didn't suit you at all.'

I can't remember what hat she's talking about.

'Did I say it suited me?'

'I should think you did! You never talked about anything

else. And you kept sneaking a look at yourself in the mirror when you thought I couldn't see you.'

This knowledge of the past depresses me. Anny doesn't even give the impression of evoking memories, she hasn't the tender, distant tone of voice suitable to that sort of occupation. She seems to be talking about today, or at the very most about yesterday; she has kept all her old opinions, prejudices, and spites fully alive. For me, on the contrary, everything is steeped in a vague poetic atmosphere; I am prepared to make any sort of concessions. Suddenly she says to me in a flat voice:

'You see, I'm getting fat, I'm getting old, I have to take care of my appearance.'

Yes, and how tired she looks! Just as I am about to say something, she adds:

'I did some acting in London.'

'With Candler?'

'No, not with Candler. That's just like you. You'd get it into your head that I was going to act with Candler. How many times have I got to tell you that Candler is a conductor? No, in a little theatre in Soho Square. We put on *The Emperor Jones,* some plays by Sean O'Casey and Synge, and *Britannicus.*'

'*Britannicus?*' I say in astonishment.

'Why yes, *Britannicus.* It was because of that that I left. I was the one who had given them the idea of putting on *Britannicus*; and they wanted me to play Junie.'

'Really?'

'Well naturally I couldn't play anybody but Agrippine.'

'And now what are you doing?'

It was a mistake to ask that. All the life goes out of her face. Yet she answers straight away:

'I'm not acting any more. I travel. There's a fellow who's keeping me.'

She smiles:

'Oh, don't look at me in that worried way, it isn't a tragedy. I always told you that I wouldn't object to being kept. Besides, he's an old man, he isn't any trouble.'

'An Englishman?'

'What business is that of yours?' she says in annoyance. 'We're not going to talk about him. He's of no importance whatever for you or for me. Would you like some tea?'

She goes into the bathroom. I hear her moving about, rattling saucepans and talking to herself; a shrill unintelligible murmur. On the table by her bed, there is, as always, a volume of Michelet's *History of France*. I can now see that over the bed she has hung a photo, a solitary one, a reproduction of the portrait of Emily Brontë painted by her brother.

Anny returns and brusquely tells me:

'Now you must talk to me about yourself.'

Then she disappears again into the bathroom. I remember that, in spite of my bad memory: that was the way she used to ask me those direct questions which I found extremely embarrassing, because I could feel in them both a genuine interest and a desire to get it over with as quickly as possible. In any case, after that question, there can be no doubt about it: she wants something from me. These are just the preliminaries: you get rid of anything that might prove awkward; you settle secondary questions once for all: 'Now you must talk to me about yourself.' In a little while she will talk to me about herself. Straight away I no longer have the slightest desire to tell her anything. What good would it do? The Nausea, fear, existence ... it would be better to keep all that to myself.

'Come on, hurry up,' she shouts through the partition.

She comes back with the teapot.

'What are you doing? Are you living in Paris?'

'I'm living at Bouville.'

'Bouville? Why? You aren't married, I hope?'

'Married?' I say, giving a start.

I find it very pleasant that Anny should have thought that. I tell her so.

'That's absurd. It's just the sort of naturalistic fantasy that you used to blame me for in the old days. You know, when I used to imagine you as a widow and the mother of two boys. And all those stories I used to tell you about what was going to become of us. You hated that.'

'And you loved it,' she replies quite calmly. 'You said that to show off. Besides, you put on a show of indignation like that in conversation, but you're quite shifty enough to get married one day on the sly. You swore indignantly for a whole year that you'd never go to see *Imperial Violets*. Then one day when I was ill, you went to see it by yourself at a little local cinema.'

'I am at Bouville,' I say with dignity, 'because I am writing a book about Monsieur de Rollebon.'

Anny looks at me with studied interest.

'Monsieur de Rollebon? Didn't he live in the eighteenth century?'

'Yes.'

'As a matter of fact you did tell me about him once,' she says vaguely. 'So it's a history book, is it?'

'Yes.'

'Ha, ha!'

If she asks me one more question I will tell her everything. But she asks nothing more. She apparently considers that she knows enough about me. Anny knows how to be a good listener, but only when she wants to be. I look at her; she has lowered her eyelids, she is thinking about what she is going to tell me, how she is going to begin. Must I question her in my turn? I don't think she wants me to. She will speak when she thinks fit. My heart is beating very fast.

She says suddenly:

'I have changed.'

That's the beginning. But now she falls silent. She pours tea into some white porcelain cups. She is waiting for me to speak: I must say something. Not just anything, but simply what she is expecting. I am on tenterhooks. Has she really changed? She has grown fatter, she looks tired; but that certainly isn't what she means.

'I don't know, I don't think so. I've already recognized your laugh, your way of getting up and putting your hands on my shoulders, your mania for talking to yourself. You're still reading Michelet's *History*. And then lots of other things. . . .'

That deep interest she takes in my eternal essence and her total indifference to everything that may happen to me in life – and then that funny affectation of hers, at once pedantic and charming – and then that way of abolishing right from the start all the mechanical formulas of politeness and friendship, everything that makes relationships between people easier, forcing the people she meets to keep on inventing.

She shrugs her shoulders:

'Yes, I have changed,' she says dryly, 'I have changed completely. I'm not the same person any more. I thought you'd notice that as soon as you saw me. And instead you talk to me about Michelet's *History*.'

She comes and plants herself in front of me:

'We'll see whether this man is as clever as he thinks he is. Come on, now: how have I changed?'

I hesitate; she taps her foot, still smiling but genuinely annoyed.

'There was something in the old days which used to make

you squirm. At least you said so And now it's gone, disappeared. You ought to have noticed that. Don't you feel more at ease?'

I don't dare to tell her that I don't: just as before, I am sitting on the edge of my chair, trying hard to avoid ambushes, to ward off inexplicable rages.

She has sat down again.

'Well,' she says, nodding her head with conviction, 'if you don't understand, that's because you've forgotten a great deal. Even more than I thought. Come on, don't you remember your misdeeds in the old days? You came, you spoke, you went away again: all in the wrong way. Suppose that nothing had changed: you would have come in, there would have been masks and shawls on the wall, I'd have been sitting on the bed and I'd have said to you:' (she throws her head back, dilates her nostrils and speaks in a theatrical voice, as if to make fun of herself) "Well? What are you waiting for? Sit down." and naturally I'd have carefully avoided telling you: "Anywhere except in the armchair near the window." '

'You used to set traps for me.'

'They weren't traps. . . . So naturally, being you, you'd have gone straight over to that armchair and sat down in it.'

'And what would have happened to me?' I ask, turning round and looking inquisitively at the armchair.

It is ordinary in appearance, it looks paternal and comfortable.

'Just something bad,' Anny replies curtly.

I don't press the point: Anny has always surrounded herself with things that were taboo.

'I think,' I tell her all of a sudden, 'that I have guessed something. But it would be so extraordinary. Wait a moment, let me think: yes, this room is completely bare. You must do me the justice of admitting that I noticed that straight away. All right, I would have come in, I would indeed have seen those masks on the wall, and the shawls and all the rest. The hotel always stopped at your door. Your room was something different. . . . You wouldn't have come and opened the door to me. I'd have seen you curled up in a corner, possibly sitting on the floor on that red rug you always took around with you, looking at me mercilessly, waiting. . . . I would have scarcely said a word, made a gesture, drawn a breath before you'd have started frowning and I would have felt deeply guilty without knowing why. Then with every moment that passed, I'd have made more blunders, I'd have plunged deeper into my guilt. . . .'

'How many times did that happen?'

'A hundred times.'

'At least. Are you any smarter, any cleverer now?'

'No!'

'I'm glad to hear you say so. Well then?'

'Well then, it's because there are no more. . . .'

'Ha, ha!' she cries in a theatrical voice, 'he scarcely dares to believe it!'

She goes on gently:

'Well, you can take my word for it: there are no more.'

'No more perfect moments?'

'No.'

I am astounded. I press the point.

'You mean at last you . . . It's all over, those . . . tragedies, those impromptu tragedies in which the masks, the shawls, the furniture, and I myself each had a minor part to play – and you had the lead?'

She smiles.

'What an ungrateful fellow! Sometimes I gave him more important parts than mine: but he never suspected. Well, yes: it's finished. Are you really surprised?'

'Oh, yes, I'm surprised! I thought that all that was a part

204

of you, that if it had been taken away from you it would have been like tearing the heart out of you.'

'I thought so too,' she says, looking as if she didn't regret anything.

She adds, with a sort of irony which makes a most unpleasant impression on me:

'But you can see that I can live without that.'

She has laced her fingers together and is holding one knee in her hands. She is gazing into the distance, with a vague smile which makes her whole face look younger. She looks like a fat little girl, mysterious and satisfied.

'Yes, I'm glad you've stayed the same. If you'd been moved, repainted, planted beside a different road, I'd have nothing stable to take my bearings by any longer. You are indispensable to me: I change, but it's understood that you stay motionless and I measure my changes in relation to you.'

I feel a little annoyed all the same.

'Well, that's quite inaccurate,' I say sharply. 'On the contrary, I've changed a great deal lately and, at heart, I . . .'

'Oh,' she says with crushing contempt, 'intellectual changes! I've changed down to the whites of my eyes.'

Down to the whites of her eyes. . . . What is it then which, in her voice, has just stirred me? In any case, all of a sudden, I gave a start. I have stopped looking for a vanished Anny. It's this girl here, this fat girl with a ruined look who moves me and whom I love.

'I have a sort of . . . physical certainty. I can feel that there are no perfect moments. I can feel it even in my legs when I am walking. I can feel it all the time, even when I'm asleep. I can't forget it. I have never had anything like a revelation; I can't say that on such and such a day, at such and such a time, my life was transformed. But now I always feel a bit as if that had suddenly been revealed to me the day before. I am dazzled, ill at ease, I can't get used to it.'

She says these words in a calm voice which retains a touch of pride at having changed so much. She balances herself on the chest with extraordinary grace. Not once since I came in has she looked so like the Anny of the old days, the Anny of Marseille. She has taken possession of me again, I have plunged back into her strange world, beyond absurdity, affectation, subtlety. I have even rediscovered that little fever which always took hold of me when I was with her, and that bitter taste at the back of my mouth.

Anny unclasps her hands and lets go of her knee. She is silent. It is a deliberate silence; as when, at the Opera, the stage remains empty for exactly seven bars of music. She drinks her tea. Then she puts down her cup and holds herself stiffly, leaning her clenched hands on the edge of the chest.

Suddenly she puts on her superb Medusa face which I used to love so much, all swollen with hatred, twisted, venomous. Anny scarcely ever changes expressions, she changes faces; as the actors of antiquity used to change masks: all of a sudden. And each of these masks is designed to create an atmosphere, to give the key to what is going to follow. It appears and stays in position without changing while she speaks. Then it falls, it detaches itself from her.

She stares at me without appearing to see me. She is going to speak. I expect a tragic speech, raised to the dignity of her mask, a dirge.

She says only a single phrase:

'I am outliving myself.'

The tone doesn't correspond in any way to the face. It isn't tragic, it is ... horrible: it expresses a dry despair, without tears, without pity. Yes, there is something irremediably desiccated in her.

206

The mask falls, she smiles.

'I'm not at all sad. I've often been surprised at that, but I was wrong: why should I be sad? I used to be capable of rather wonderful passions. I hated my mother passionately. And as for you,' she says defiantly, 'I loved you passionately.'

She waits for a retort. I say nothing.

'All that is over, of course.'

'How can you tell?'

'I know. I know that I shall never again meet anything or anybody that will inspire me with passion. You know, it's quite an undertaking to start loving somebody. You have to have energy, generosity, blindness. . . . There is even a moment, right at the start, where you have to jump across an abyss: if you think about it you don't do it. I know that I shall never jump again.'

'Why not?'

She looks at me ironically and doesn't answer.

'Now,' she says, 'I live surrounded by my dead passions. I try to recapture that splendid rage which hurled me out of a third-floor window, when I was twelve years old, one day my mother had whipped me.'

She adds, for no apparent reason, with a faraway look:

'It isn't good for me either to stare at things too long. I look at them to find out what they are, then I have to turn my eyes quickly away.'

'But why?'

'They disgust me.'

I could almost swear. . . . In any case there are certainly similarities. It has already happened once in London, we had both thought the same things about the same subjects, practically at the same time. I should like so much to . . . But Anny's mind takes a great many turnings: you can never be sure you've completely understood her. I have to be absolutely sure.

'Listen, I'd like to say something to you: you know that I never really understood what perfect moments were; you never really explained them to me.'

'Yes, I know, you made absolutely no effort. You just existed beside me like a log.'

'Maybe. But I know how much it cost me.'

'You deserved everything you got, it was all your fault; you annoyed me with your down-to-earth look, you seemed to be saying: I'm normal; and you set out to breathe health through every pore, you positively oozed moral well-being.'

'Still, I asked you a hundred times at least to explain to me what a . . .'

'Yes, but in what a tone of voice,' she says angrily; 'you condescended to inquire, that's what you did. You asked your question in a kindly, absent-minded way, like the old ladies who used to ask me what I was playing when I was a little girl. Now I come to think of it,' she says pensively, 'I wonder if you aren't the person I've hated most in my life.'

She makes an effort to compose herself, calms down and smiles, her cheeks still aflame. She is very beautiful.

'I don't mind explaining to you what they are. I'm old enough now to talk calmly to old women like you about my childhood games. Come on now, talk, what do you want to know?'

'What they were.'

'I've told you about privileged situations, haven't I?'

'I don't think so.'

'Yes I have,' she says with assurance. 'It was at Aix, in that square whose name I've forgotten. We were on the terrace of a café, out in the sun, under some orange parasols. You don't remember: we were drinking lemonade and I found some dead flies in the sugar.'

'Ah yes, perhaps. . . .'

'Well, I talked to you about that in that café. It came up in connexion with the big edition of Michelet's *History*, the one I had when I was little. It was a lot bigger than this one and the pages were a pale colour, like the inside of a mushroom, and they smelt like mushrooms too. When my father died, my Uncle Joseph got his hands on it and took all the volumes away. That was the day I called him an old pig, and my mother whipped me, and I jumped out of the window.'

'Yes, yes ... you must have told me about that *History of France* ... didn't you used to read it in the attic? You see, I remember. You can see that you were unfair just now when you accused me of having forgotten everything.'

'Be quiet. Yes, as you remember so well, I used to take those huge books up to the attic. There were very few pictures in them, possibly two or three in each volume. But each one had a big page all to itself, and the other side of the page was blank. That made all the more of an impression on me in that on the other pages the text had been arranged in two columns to save space. I had an extraordinary love for those pictures; I knew them all by heart, and when I re-read one of Michelet's books, I would wait for them fifty pages in advance; it always seemed a miracle to me to find them again. And then there was an added refinement: the scene they showed never had any connexion with the text on the adjoining pages, you had to go looking for the relevant event some thirty pages further on.'

'I beg you, please tell me about the perfect moments.'

'I'm telling you about the privileged situations. They were the ones shown in the pictures. It was I who called them privileged, I told myself they must have been terribly important for people to agree to make them the subject of those rare pictures. They had been chosen in preference to all the rest, you see: and yet there were a lot of episodes which had greater pictorial value, and others which had greater historical interest. For example, there were only three pictures for the whole of the sixteenth century: one for the death of Henri II, one for the assassination of the Duc de Guise, and one for the entry of Henry IV into Paris. Then it occurred to me that these events were of a special character. Besides, the pictures confirmed that idea: they were very badly drawn, the arms and legs were never properly attached to the bodies. But they were full of grandeur. When the Duc de Guise was assassinated, for example, the onlookers showed their amazement and indignation by stretching their hands out and turning their heads away: it was very beautiful, like a chorus. And don't imagine they didn't have any amusing, anecdotic details. You could see pages falling to the ground, little dogs running away, jesters sitting on the steps of the throne. But all these details were treated with so much grandeur and so much clumsiness that they were in perfect harmony with the rest of the picture: I don't think I've ever come across any pictures that had such a strict unity. Well, it started there.'

'The privileged situations?'

'The idea I formed of them. They were situations which had a very rare and precious quality, a style if you like. To be a king, for example, struck me as a privileged situation when I was eight years old. Or else to die. You may laugh, but there were so many people drawn at the moment of their death, and there were so many who uttered sublime words at that moment, that I honestly thought ... well, I thought that when you started dying you were transported yourself. Besides, it was enough just to be in the room of a dying person: death being a privileged situation, something emanated from it and communicated itself to everybody who was present. A sort of grandeur. When my father died, they took me up to his room to see him for the last time. Going upstairs, I was very unhappy, but I was also as it were drunk with a sort of religious ecstasy; I was at last going to enter a privileged situation. I leaned against the wall, I tried to make the proper gestures. But my aunt and my mother were there, kneeling by the bed, and they spoiled everything with their sobs.'

She says these last words angrily, as if the memory still hurt her. She breaks off; her eyes staring, her eyebrows raised. She is taking the opportunity to live the scene once more.

'Later on, I developed all that; to begin with, I added a new situation, love (I mean the act of making love). Look, if you've never understood why I refused . . . certain of your demands, now's your chance to understand: for me, there was something to be saved. And then I told myself that there were bound to be far more privileged situations than I could possibly count, finally I accepted the existence of an infinite number of them.'

'Yes, but what were they?'

'But I've told you,' she says in amazement, 'I've been explaining to you for the last quarter of an hour.'

'Yes, but was the most important thing for people to be in a great passion, carried away with hatred or love, for example; or was it the external appearance of the event which had to be great, I mean: what you could see of it. . . .'

'Both . . . it all depended,' she answers sulkily.

'And the perfect moments? Where do they come in?'

'They come afterwards. First there are some annunciatory signs. Then the privileged situation, slowly, majestically, enters into people's lives. Then the question arises whether you want to make a perfect moment out of it.'

'Yes,' I say, 'I understand. In each privileged situation, there are certain acts which have to be performed, certain attitudes which have to be assumed, certain words which have to be said – and other attitudes, other words are strictly prohibited. Is that it?'

'If you like. . . .'

'In other words, the situation is the raw material: it has to be treated.'

'That's it,' she says. 'First you had to be plunged into something exceptional and feel that you were putting it in order. If all these conditions had been fulfilled, the moment would have been perfect.'

'In fact, it was a sort of work of art.'

'You've already said that,' she says in irritation. 'No: it was . . . a duty. You *had* to transform privileged situations into perfect moments. It was a moral question. Yes, you can laugh if you like: a moral question.'

I am not laughing at all.

'Listen,' I say to her spontaneously, 'I'm going to recognize my short-comings too. I never really understood you, I never sincerely tried to help you. If I had known . . .'

'Thank you, thank you very much,' she says sarcastically. 'I hope you don't expect any gratitude for these tardy regrets of yours. In any case, I don't hold any grudges against you; I never explained anything to you clearly, I was all tied up, I couldn't talk to anybody about it, not even to you – especially not to you. There was always something which rang false about those moments. So I was all at sea. Yet I had the impression that I was doing everything I could.'

'But what had to be done? What actions?'

'What a fool you are. I can't give you any more examples, it all depends.'

'But tell me what you tried to do.'

'No, I don't want to talk about it. But if you like, there's a story which made a great impression on me when I was at school. There was a king who had lost a battle and had been taken prisoner. He was there in a corner in the victor's camp. He saw his son and daughter go by in chains. He didn't weep, he didn't say anything. Next he saw one of his servants go by, likewise in chains. Then he started groaning and tearing his hair. You can make up your own examples. You see: there are times when you mustn't cry – or else you'll be unclean. But if you drop a log on your foot, you can do what you like, groan, sob, or jump about on the other foot. The idiotic thing would be to be stoical all the time: you'd wear yourself out for nothing.'

She smiles:

'At other times, you had to be *more* than stoical. Naturally you don't remember the first time I kissed you, do you?'

'Yes I do, very clearly,' I say triumphantly, 'it was in Kew Gardens, on the banks of the Thames.'

'But what you never knew was that I was sitting on some nettles: my dress was hitched up, my thighs were covered with stings, and every time I made the slightest movement I was stung again. Well, stoicism wouldn't have been enough there. You didn't excite me at all, I had no particular desire for your lips, the kiss I was going to give you was much more important, it was an engagement, a pact. So you see, that pain was irrelevant, I wasn't at liberty to think about my thighs at a moment like that. It wasn't enough not to show that I was suffering: it was necessary not to suffer.'

She looks at me proudly, still surprised at what she had done:

'For more than twenty minutes, all the time you were insisting on having that kiss which I was quite determined to give you, all the time I was keeping you waiting – because I had to give it to you with proper formality – I managed to anaesthetize myself completely. Yet heaven knows that I have a sensitive skin: I felt *nothing* until we got up.'

That's it, that's it exactly. There are no adventures – there are no perfect moments ... we have lost the same illusions, we have followed the same paths. I can guess the rest – I can even speak for her and say myself what she still has to tell:

'So you realized that there were always women in tears, or a red-headed man or something else to spoil your effects?'

'Yes, naturally,' she says unenthusiastically.

'Isn't that it?'

'Oh, you know, I might have managed to resign myself in the end to the clumsiness of a red-headed man. After all, it was good of me to take an interest in the way in which other people played their parts.... No, it's rather that ...'

'That there are no privileged situations?'

'That's it, I used to think that hate, love, or death descended on us like tongues of fire on Good Friday. I used to think that one could radiate hate or death. What a mistake! Yes, I really thought that "Hate" existed, that it settled on people and raised them above themselves. Naturally, I am the only one, I am the one who hates, I am the one who loves. And that "I" is always the same thing, a dough which goes on stretching and stretching ... indeed, it looks so much like itself that you wonder how people got the idea of inventing names and making distinctions.'

She thinks as I do. I feel as if I had never left her.

'Listen carefully,' I say, 'for the last few minutes I've been thinking of something which pleases me much more than the role of a milestone which you generously allotted to me: it's that we have changed together and in the same way. I like that better, you know, than seeing you going further and further away and being condemned to mark your starting-point for ever. Everything you've told me, I had come to tell you – though admittedly in other words. We meet at the finishing-post. I can't tell you how much pleasure that gives me.'

'Really?' she says, softly but with a stubborn look, 'well, I'd still have liked it better if you hadn't changed; it was more convenient like that. I'm not like you, it annoys me rather to know that somebody has thought the same things as I have. Besides, you must be mistaken.'

I tell her about my adventures. I talk to her about existence – perhaps at too great length. She listens intently, her eyes wide open, her eyebrows raised.

When I finish, she looks relieved.

'Well, you don't think the same things as I do at all. You complain because things don't arrange themselves around you like a bunch of flowers, without taking the trouble to do anything. But I have never asked as much as that: I wanted to do things. You know, when we used to play at being adventurers, you were the one who had adventures, I was the one who made them happen. I used to say: "I'm a man of action." You remember? Well, now I simply say: "One can't be a man of action." '

I suppose I can't look convinced, for she gets excited and goes on more insistently:

'And then there are lots of other things I haven't told you, because it would take too long to explain. For example, I would have had to be able to tell myself, at the very moment I did something, that what I was doing would have ... fatal consequences. I can't explain that to you very well. . . .'

'But there's no need to,' I say somewhat pedantically. 'I've thought that too.'

She looks at me suspiciously.

'You seem to imagine that you've thought about everything in exactly the same way as I have: you surprise me.'

I can't convince her, I would only irritate her if I went on. I keep quiet. I want to take her in my arms.

All of a sudden she looks at me anxiously:

'But if you really have thought about all that, what can we do?'

I bow my head.

'I . . . I am outliving myself,' she repeats dully.

What can I say to her? Do I know any reasons for living? I don't feel the same despair as she does, because I never expected very much. I am rather . . . astonished at this life which is given to me – given for *nothing*. I keep my head bowed, I don't want to see Anny's face at this moment.

'I travel,' she goes on in a gloomy voice; 'I've just come back from Sweden. I stopped in Berlin for a week. There's that fellow who's keeping me . . .'

Should I take her in my arms? What good would it do? I can do nothing for her. She is alone like me.

She says to me, in a gayer voice:

'What are you muttering about?'

I raise my eyes. She is looking at me tenderly.

'Nothing. I was just thinking about something.'

'Oh mysterious person! Well, talk or shut up, but do one thing or the other.'

I tell her about the Rendez-vous des Cheminots, about the old rag-time I get them to play for me on the gramophone, about the strange happiness it gives me.

'I was wondering if we couldn't find something in that direction, or at least look for it. . . .'

She doesn't answer, I don't think she was very interested in what I've been telling her.

Still, after a moment, she goes on – and I don't know whether she is following her own train of thought or whether it is an answer to what I have just been saying.

'Pictures, statues can't be used: they're beautiful *facing me*. Music . . .'

'But at the theatre . . .'

'Well, what about the theatre? Are you going through all the fine arts one by one?'

'You used to say that you wanted to act because on the stage it must be possible to obtain perfect moments!'

'Yes, I've obtained them: for other people. I was in the dust, in the draughts, under glaring lights, between cardboard sets. I usually played opposite Thorndyke. I think you've seen him at Covent Garden. I was always afraid of bursting out laughing in his face.'

'But weren't you ever carried away by your part?'

'A little, now and then: never very strongly. The main thing, for all of us, was the black hole just in front of us, at the bottom of which there were people we couldn't see; to them we were obviously presenting a perfect moment. But, they didn't live in it; it unfolded in front of them. And do you think that we, the actors, lived inside it? In the end it wasn't anywhere, either on one side of the footlights or the other, it didn't exist; and yet everybody was thinking about it. So you see, my dear,' she says in a drawling, almost vulgar tone of voice, 'I dropped the whole thing.'

'I tried to write this book ...'

She interrupts me.

'I live in the past. I recall everything that has happened to me and I arrange it. From a distance, like that, it doesn't do any harm, it might almost take you in. Our story is all quite beautiful. I add a few touches here and there and it makes a whole string of perfect moments. Then I close my eyes and I try to imagine that I'm still living in it. I've got some other characters too. You have to know how to concentrate. You know what I've read? Loyola's *Spiritual Exercises*. I've found that very useful. There's a way of setting the scene first of all, and then bringing on the characters. Sometimes you can really *see*,' she adds with a mad look.

'Well,' I say, 'that wouldn't satisfy me at all.'

'Do you think it satisfies me?'

We remain silent for a moment. Dusk is falling; I can scarcely make out the pale patch of her face. Her black dress merges into the shadows which have invaded the room. I

217

automatically pick up my cup, which still has a little tea in it, and I raise it to my lips. The tea is cold. I should like to smoke, but I don't dare. I have the painful impression that we have nothing left to say to each other. Only yesterday, I had so many questions to ask her: where had she been, what had she done, whom had she met? But that interested me only in so far as Anny had given herself whole-heartedly. Now I have no curiosity: all those countries, all those cities she had passed through, all those men who have courted her and whom perhaps she has loved – all of that left her cold, all of that was fundamentally unimportant to her: little flashes of sunlight on the surface of a cold, dark sea. Anny is sitting opposite me, we haven't seen each other for four years, and we have nothing left to say to each other.

'You'll have to go now,' Anny says all of a sudden. 'I'm expecting somebody.'

'You're expecting. . . ?'

'No, I'm expecting a German, a painter.'

She starts laughing. This laughter sounds strange in the dark room.

'Now *there's* somebody who isn't like us – not yet. He acts, he exerts himself.'

I get up reluctantly.

'When shall I see you again?'

'I don't know, I'm leaving for London tomorrow evening.'

'Via Dieppe?'

'Yes, and I think I'll go to Egypt after that. I may be back in Paris next winter, I'll write to you.'

'I shall be free all day tomorrow,' I tell her timidly.

'Yes, but I've got a lot to do,' she answers in a dry voice. 'No, I can't see you. I'll write to you from Egypt. Just give me your address.'

'All right.'

In the semi-darkness I scribble my address on the back

of an envelope. I shall have to tell the Hôtel Printania to forward my letters when I leave Bouville. In my heart of hearts, I know very well that she won't write. Perhaps I shall see her again in ten years' time. Perhaps this is the last time I shall see her. I am not just terribly depressed at leaving her; I am terribly frightened of going back to my solitude.

She gets up; at the door she kisses me lightly on the mouth.

'That's to remind me of your lips,' she says, smiling. 'I have to rejuvenate my memories, for my "Spiritual Exercises".'

I take her by the arm and I draw her towards me. She doesn't resist, but shakes her head.

'No, that doesn't interest me any more. You can't begin again ... and then, for what you can do with people, the first good-looking fellow who comes along is just as good as you.'

'But what are you going to do then?'

'I've told you, I'm going to England.'

'No, I mean ...'

'Nothing!'

I haven't let go of her arms, I tell her softly:

'Then I must leave you after finding you again.'

Now I can see her face clearly. All of a sudden it becomes pale and drawn. An old woman's face, absolutely horrible; I'm quite sure that she didn't put that face on deliberately: it is there, unknown to her, or perhaps in spite of her.

'No,' she says slowly, 'No. You haven't found me again.'

She pulls her arm away. She opens the door. The corridor is ablaze with light.

Anny starts laughing.

'Poor fellow! He never has any luck. The first time he plays his part well, he gets no thanks for it. Go on now, be off with you.'

I hear the door close behind me.

Sunday

This morning I consulted the Railway Guide: assuming that she hadn't lied to me, she would be leaving by the Dieppe train at 5.38. But perhaps that fellow of hers would drive her to the coast, I wandered through the streets of Ménilmontant all morning, and then along the quays in the afternoon. A few steps, a few walls separated me from her. At 5.38 our conversation of yesterday would become a memory, the plump woman whose lips had brushed against my mouth would join in the past the thin little girl of Meknès, of London. But nothing had gone yet, since she was still there, since it was still possible to see her again, to persuade her, to take her away with me for ever. I didn't feel alone yet.

I wanted to stop thinking about Anny, because, as a result of imagining her body and her face, I had worked myself up into a highly nervous condition: my hands were trembling and icy shudders kept running through me. I started looking through the books on display in the second-hand boxes, and especially the obscene ones, because, in spite of everything, that occupies your mind.

The Gare d'Orsay clock struck five, I was looking at the pictures in a book entitled *The Doctor with the Whip*. There wasn't much variety about them: in most of them a tall bearded man was brandishing a riding whip above huge naked rumps. As soon as I realized it was five o'clock I threw the book back on the rest and I jumped into a taxi, which took me to the Gare Saint-Lazare.

I walked up and down the platform for about twenty minutes, then I saw them. She was wearing a heavy fur coat which made her look like a lady. And a short veil. The man had a camel-hair coat. He was sun-tanned, still young, very tall, very handsome. Obviously a foreigner, but not an Englishman; possibly an Egyptian. They got on the train without seeing me. They didn't speak to each other. Then the man got off again and bought some papers. Anny lowered the window of her compartment; she saw me. She looked at me for a long time, without any anger, with expressionless eyes. Then the man got back into the carriage and the train left. At that moment I had a clear vision of the restaurant in Piccadilly where we used to lunch together in the old days, then everything went blank. I walked. When I felt tired, I came into this café and I fell asleep. The waiter has just woken me up and I am writing this while I am still half-asleep.

Tomorrow I shall go back to Bouville by the midday train. Two days there will be enough for me to pack my bags and settle my account at the bank. I imagine the Hôtel Printania will want me to pay a fortnight extra because I haven't given them notice. I shall also have to return all the books I have borrowed from the library. In any case, I shall be back in Paris before the end of the week. And what shall I gain by the change? I shall still be in a town: this one is cut in two by a river, the other one is bordered by the sea, apart from that they are very similar. You take a piece of bare, sterile land, and you roll some big hollow stones on to it. Inside those stones, smells are held captive, smells which are heavier than air. Now and then you throw them out of the window into the streets and they stay there until the winds tear them apart. In bright weather, noises come in at one end of the town and go out at the other, after going through all the walls; at other times, they go round and round between these stones which are baked by the sun and split by the frost.

I am afraid of towns. But you mustn't leave them. If you venture too far, you come to the Vegetation Belt. The Vegetation has crawled for mile after mile towards the towns. It is waiting. When the town dies, the Vegetation will invade it, it will clamber over the stones, it will grip them, search them, burst them open with its long black pincers; it will bind the holes and hang its green paws everywhere. You must stay in the towns as long as they are alive, you must never go out alone into that great mass of hair waiting at their gates: you must let it undulate and crack all by itself. In a town, if you know how to go about it, and choose the times when the animals are digesting or sleeping in their holes, behind the heaps of organic detritus, you rarely come across anything but minerals, the least frightening of all existents.

I am going to go back to Bouville. The Vegetation is besieging Bouville on only three sides. On the fourth side, there is a big hole full of black water which moves all by itself. The wind whistles between the houses. The smells stay for a shorter time than anywhere else: driven out to sea by the wind, they race over the surface of the black water like little frolicsome mists. It rains. Plants have been allowed to grow between four railings. Castrated, domesticated plants, which are so thick-leaved that they are harmless. They have huge whitish leaves which hang down like ears. When you touch them, it feels like gristle. Everything is fat and white at Bouville, because of all that water which falls from the sky, I am going to go back to Bouville. How horrible!

I wake up with a start. It is midnight. Anny left Paris six hours ago. The boat has put out to sea. She is sleeping in a cabin, and on the deck the handsome sun-tanned fellow is smoking cigarettes.

Tuesday at Bouville

Is this what freedom is? Below me, the gardens slope gently towards the town, and in each garden there stands a house. I see the sea, heavy, motionless, I see Bouville. It is a fine day.

I am free: I haven't a single reason for living left, all the ones I have tried have given way and I can't imagine any more. I am still quite young, I still have enough strength to start again. But what must I start again? Only now do I realize how much, in the midst of my greatest terror and nauseas, I had counted on Anny to save me. My past is dead, Monsieur de Rollebon is dead, Anny came back only to take all hope away from me. I am alone in this white street lined with gardens. Alone and free. But this freedom is rather like death.

Today my life comes to an end. Tomorrow I shall have left the town which stretches out at my feet, where I have lived so long. It will no longer be anything but a name, stolid, bourgeois, very French, a name in my memory which is not as rich as the names of Florence or Baghdad. A time will come when I shall wonder: 'Whatever did I find to do all day long when I was at Bouville?' And of this sunshine, of this afternoon, nothing will remain, not even a memory.

My whole life is behind me. I can see it all, I can see its shape and the slow movements which have brought me this far. There is very little to say about it: it's a lost game, that's all. Three years ago I came to Bouville with a certain solemnity. I had lost the first round. I decided to play the second round and I lost again: I lost the whole game. At the same time, I learnt that you always lose. Only the bastards think they win. Now I'm going to do like Anny, I'm going to outlive myself. Eat, sleep. Sleep, eat. Exist slowly, gently, like these trees, like a puddle of water, like the red seat in the tram.

The Nausea is giving me a brief respite. But I know that it will come back: it is my normal condition. Only today my body is too exhausted to stand it. Sick people too have happy weaknesses which relieve them for a few hours of the consciousness of their suffering. Now and then I give such a big yawn that tears roll down my cheeks. It is a deep, deep boredom, the deep heart of existence, the very matter I am made of. I don't let myself go, far from it: this morning I took a bath, I shaved. Only, when I think back over all those careful little actions, I can't understand how I could bring myself to perform them. They are so futile. It was my habits, probably, which performed them for me. They aren't dead, my habits, they go on bustling about, gently, insidiously weaving their webs, they wash me, dry me, dress me, like nursemaids. Was it they too who brought me up on this hill? I can't remember now how I came here. Up the escalier Dautry I suppose: did I really climb its one hundred and ten steps one by one? What is perhaps even more difficult to imagine, is that in a little while I'm going to go down them again. Yet I know that I am: before long I shall find myself at the bottom of the Coteau Vert, and if I raise my head I shall be able to see the windows of these houses which are so close to me now light up. In the distance. Above my head; and this moment now, from which I cannot emerge, which shuts me in and hems me in on every side, this moment of which I am made will be nothing more than a confused dream.

I look at the grey shimmering of Bouville at my feet. In the sun it looks like heaps of shells, of splinters of bone, of gravel. Lost in the midst of that debris, tiny fragments of glass or mica give little flashes from time to time. An hour from now, the trickles, the trenches, the thin furrows running between the shells will be streets, I shall be walking in those streets, between walls. Those little black dots which I can make out in the rue Boulibet — an hour from now I shall be one of them.

How far away from them I feel, up on this hill. It seems

to me that I belong to another species. They come out of their offices after the day's work, they look at the houses and the squares with a satisfied expression, they think that it is *their* town. A 'good solid town'. They aren't afraid, they feel at home. They have never seen anything but the tamed water which runs out of the taps, the light which pours from the bulbs when they turn the switch, the half-breed, bastard trees which are held up with crutches. They are given proof, a hundred times a day, that everything is done mechanically, that the world obeys fixed, unchangeable laws. Bodies released in a vacuum all fall at the same speed, the municipal park is closed every day at four p.m. in winter, at six p.m. in summer, lead melts at 335°c., the last tram leaves the Town Hall at 11.05 p.m. They are peaceable, a little morose, they think about Tomorrow, in other words simply about another today; towns have only one day at their disposal which comes back exactly the same every morning. They barely tidy it up a little on Sundays. The idiots. It horrifies me to think that I am going to see their thick, self-satisfied faces again. They make laws, they write Populist novels, they get married, they commit the supreme folly of having children. And meanwhile, vast, vague Nature has slipped into their town, it has infiltrated everywhere, into their houses, into their offices, into themselves. It doesn't move, it lies low, and they are right inside it, they breathe it, and they don't see it, they imagine that it is outside, fifty miles away. I *see* it, that Nature, I *see* it . . . I know that its submissiveness is laziness, I know that it has no laws, that what they consider its constancy doesn't exist. It has nothing but habits and it may change those tomorrow.

What if something were to happen? What if all of a sudden it started palpitating? Then they would notice that it was there and they would think that their hearts were going to burst. What use would their dykes and ramparts and

power-houses and furnaces and pile-drivers be to them then?
That may happen at any time, straight away perhaps: the
omens are there. For example, the father of a family may
go for a walk, and he will see a red rag coming towards him
across the street, as if the wind were blowing it. And when
the rag gets close to him, he will see that it is a quarter of
rotten meat, covered with dust, crawling and hopping along,
a piece of tortured flesh rolling in the gutters and spasmodi-
cally shooting out jets of blood. Or else a mother may look
at her child's cheek and ask him: 'What's that – a pimple?'
And she will see the flesh puff up slightly, crack and split
open, and at the bottom of the split a third eye, a laughing
eye, will appear. Or else they will feel something gently
brushing against their bodies, like the caresses reeds give
swimmers in a river. And they will realize that their clothes
have become living things. And somebody else will feel
something scratching inside his mouth. And he will go to a
mirror, open his mouth: and his tongue will have become a
huge living centipede, rubbing its legs together and scraping
his palate. He will try to spit it out, but the centipede will be
part of himself and he will have to tear it out with his hands.
And hosts of things will appear for which people will have
to find new names – a stone-eye, a big three-cornered arm, a
toe-crutch, a spider-jaw, and somebody who has gone to
sleep in his comfortable bed, in his quiet, warm bedroom,
will wake up naked on a bluish patch of earth, in a forest of
rustling pricks, rising all red and white towards the sky like
the chimneys of Jouxtebouville, with big testicles half way
out of the ground, hairy and bulbous, like onions. And birds
will flutter around these pricks and peck at them with their
beaks and make them bleed. Sperm will flow slowly, gently,
from these wounds, sperm mingled with blood, warm and
vitreous with little bubbles. Or else nothing like that will
happen, no appreciable change will take place, but one morn-

226

ing when people open their blinds they will be surprised by a sort of horrible feeling brooding heavily over things and giving the impression of waiting. Just that: but if it lasts a little while, there will be hundreds of suicides. Well, yes, let things change a little, just to see, I ask for nothing better. Then we shall see other people suddenly plunged into solitude. Men all alone, entirely alone, with horrible monstrosities, will run through the streets, will go clumsily past me, their eyes staring, fleeing from their ills and carrying them with them, open-mouthed, with their tongue-insect beating its wings. Then I shall burst out laughing, even if my own body is covered with filthy, suspicious-looking scabs blossoming into fleshy flowers, violets and buttercups. I shall lean against a wall and as they go by I shall shout to them: 'What have you done with your science? What have you done with your humanism? Where is your dignity as a thinking reed?' I shan't be afraid – or at least no more than I am now. Won't it still be existence, variations on existence? All those eyes which will slowly eat up a face – no doubt they will be superfluous, but no more superfluous than the first two. Existence is what I am afraid of.

Dusk is falling, the first lights are going on in the town. Good Lord, how *natural* the town looks in spite of all its geometric patterns, how crushed by the evening it seems. It's so . . . so obvious from here; is it possible that I should be the only one to see it? Is there nowhere another Cassandra on the top of a hill, looking down at a town engulfed in the depths of Nature? But what does it matter to me? What could I possibly tell her?

My body turns very gently towards the east, wobbles slightly and starts walking.

I have looked all over the town for the Autodidact. He can't possibly have gone home. He must be walking about at random, filled with shame and horror, that poor humanist whom men don't want any more. To tell the truth, I was scarcely surprised when the thing happened: for a long time I had felt that his gentle, timid face was positively asking scandal to strike it. He was guilty in so small a degree: his humble, contemplative love for little boys is scarcely sensuality – rather a form of humanism. But it was inevitable that one day he should find himself alone again. Like Monsieur Achille, like myself: he is one of my own breed, he is full of good-will. Now he has entered into solitude – forever. Everything has collapsed at once, his dreams of culture, his dreams of an understanding with mankind. First there will be fear, horror, and sleepless nights, and then, after that, the long succession of days of exile. In the evening he will come back to wander round the cour des Hypothèques; from a distance he will look at the glowing windows of the library and his heart will miss a beat when he remembers the long rows of books, their leather bindings, the smell of their pages. I am sorry I didn't go with him, but he didn't want me to; it was he who begged me to leave him alone: he was beginning his apprenticeship in solitude. I am writing this in the Café Mably. I came here ceremoniously, I wanted to contemplate the manager and the cashier, and feel intensely that I was seeing them for the last time. But I can't stop thinking about the Autodidact, I can still see his drawn, reproachful face and his bloodstained collar. So I asked for some paper and I am going to tell what has happened to him.

I went to the library about two o'clock in the afternoon. I was thinking: 'The library. I am coming here for the last time.'

The reading room was almost empty. I found it hard to recognize it because I knew that I would never come back. It was as light as mist, almost unreal, all reddish; the setting sun was casting a reddish colour over the table reserved for women readers, the door, the spines of the books. For a second I had the delightful feeling that I was entering a thicket full of golden leaves; I smiled. I thought: 'What a long time it is since I last smiled.' The Corsican was looking out of the window, his hands behind his back. What did he see? The skull of Impétraz? 'I shall never see the skull of Impétraz again, or his top hat or his frock coat. In six hours' time I shall have left Bouville.' I placed the two volumes I had borrowed last month on the assistant librarian's desk. He tore up a green slip and handed me the pieces:

'There you are, Monsieur Roquentin.'

'Thank you.'

I thought: 'Now I owe them nothing more. I owe nothing more to anybody here. In a little while I shall go and say good-bye to the *patronne* of the Rendez-vous des Cheminots. I am free.' I hesitated for a minute: should I use these last moments to take a long walk through Bouville, to see the boulevard Victor-Noir again, the avenue Galvani, the rue Tournebride? But this thicket was so calm, so pure: it seemed to me that it scarcely existed and that the Nausea had spared it. I went and sat down near the stove. The *Journal de Bouville* was lying on the table. I stretched out my hand, I picked it up.

Saved by His Dog.
Last night, Monsieur Dubosc of Remiredon was cycling home from the Naugis Fair . . .

A fat lady came and sat down on my right. She put her felt hat beside her. Her nose was planted in her face like a knife in an apple. Under the nose, an obscene little hole was wrinkled up in disdain. She took a bound book out of her bag and leaned her elbows on the table, resting her head on her fat hands. In front of me, an old gentleman was sleeping. I knew him: he had been in the library the evening I had been so frightened. I think he had been frightened too. I thought: 'How far away all that is.'

At half past four the Autodidact came in. I should have liked to shake hands with him and say good-bye. But our last meeting must have left him with unpleasant memories: he nodded distantly to me and went quite a long way away from me to put down a small white packet which presumably contained, as usual, a slice of bread and a bar of chocolate. After a moment, he came back with an illustrated book which he placed near his packet. I thought: 'I am seeing him for the last time.' Tomorrow evening, the evening of the day after tomorrow, and all the following evenings, he would come back to read at that table, eating his bread and chocolate, he would patiently continue his rat-like nibbling, he would read the works of Nabaud, Naudeau, Nodier, Nys, breaking off now and then to jot down a maxim in his little notebook. And I would be walking in Paris, in the streets of Paris, I would be seeing new faces. What would happen to me while he was here, while the lamp was lighting up his heavy, meditative face? I realized just in time that I was going to let myself be caught once more by the mirage of adventure. I shrugged my shoulders and went back to my reading.

Bouville and district.
Monistiers:
Operations of the Gendarmerie Brigade during 1932. Sergeant-Major Gaspard, commanding the Monistiers Brigade and his four gendarmes, Messieurs Lagoutte, Nizan, Pierpont, and

Ghil, have scarcely been idle during 1932. Our gendarmes have in fact had to record 7 crimes, 82 misdemeanours, 159 offences, 6 suicides, and 15 motor-car accidents, 3 of which were fatal.

Jouxtebouville:

Friendly Society of the Trumpet Players of Jouxtebouville. Final rehearsal today: issue of tickets for the annual concert.

Compostel:

Presentation of the Legion of Honour to the Mayor.

The Bouville Tourist (Bouville Scout Foundation, 1924):

Monthly meeting this evening at 8.45 p.m., 10 rue Ferdinand-Byron, Room A. Agenda: Minutes. Correspondence. Annual Dinner. Subscriptions for 1932. Programme of outings in March. Miscellaneous matters. New Members.

Bouville Society for the Prevention of Cruelty to Animals:

Public meeting next Thursday, from 3 p.m. to 5 p.m. Room C, 10 rue Ferdinand-Byron, Bouville. Correspondence to be sent to the President, at the above address or at 154 avenue Galvani.

Bouville Watchdog Club . . . Bouville Association of Disabled Veterans . . . Taxi-Owners' Union . . . Bouville Committee of the Friends of the Training Colleges . . .

Two boys with satchels came in. Schoolboys from the *lycée.* The Corsican likes the schoolboys from the *lycée,* because he can keep a fatherly eye on them. Often, for his own pleasure, he lets them play about on their chairs and chatter, and then creeps up behind them and scolds them: 'Is that the way for big boys to behave? If you don't mend your manners, the librarian is going to complain to the headmaster.' And if they protest, he glares at them with his terrible eyes: 'Give me your names.' He also controls their reading: in the library, certain volumes are marked with a red cross; these are the forbidden books – works by Gide, Diderot, and Baudelaire, and some medical treatises. When a schoolboy asks for one of these books, the Corsican beckons to him, takes him into a corner and questions him. After a moment he explodes and his voice fills the reading room: 'But there are more interesting books for a boy of your age. Educational books. First of all have you finished your homework? What form are you in? The fifth form? And you've got nothing to do after four o'clock? Your master often comes in here and I'm going to tell him about you.'

The two boys remained standing near the stove. The younger one had fine brown hair, an almost excessively delicate skin, and a tiny mouth, proud and wicked. His friend, a big strapping fellow with a hint of a moustache, touched his elbow and murmured a few words. The little brown-haired boy didn't reply, but he gave an almost imperceptible smile, full of arrogance and self-assurance. Then the two of them nonchalantly took a dictionary from one of the shelves and went over to the Autodidact, who was staring at them with tired eyes. They seemed to be unaware of his existence, but they sat right up against him, the little brown-haired boy on his left and the big strapping fellow on the left of his friend. They promptly started looking through their dictionary. The Autodidact let his gaze wander round the room, then he returned to his reading. Never had any library offered such a reassuring sight: I couldn't hear a sound, except for the short breathing of the fat lady, and I couldn't see anything but heads bent over octavo volumes. Yet, at that moment, I had the impression that something unpleasant was going to happen. All those people with their heads bent so studiously seemed to be play-acting: a few moments earlier, I had felt something like a breath of cruelty pass over us.

I had finished reading, but I couldn't make up my mind to leave: I waited, pretending to read my paper. What increased my curiosity and my uneasiness was that the others were waiting too. It seemed to me that my neighbour was turning the pages of her book more rapidly. A few minutes went by, then I heard some whispering. I cautiously raised my head. The two boys had closed their dictionary. The little brown-haired boy wasn't talking, his face, marked with deference and interest, was turned to the right. Half hidden behind his shoulder, the fair-haired boy was listening and laughing silently. 'Then who's talking?' I wondered.

It was the Autodidact. He was bending over his young neighbour, eye to eye, and smiling at him; I could see his lips moving and, now and then, his long eyelashes trembling. I had never seen him look so young before, he was almost charming. But, from time to time, he broke off and looked anxiously over his shoulder. The boy seemed to be drinking in his words. There was nothing extraordinary about this little scene and I was going to return to my reading when I saw the boy slowly slide his hand behind his back along the edge of the table. Thus hidden from the Autodidact's eyes, it moved along for a moment and started groping about, then, meeting the fair-haired boy's arm, it pinched hard. The other boy, too absorbed in silent enjoyment of the Autodidact's words, hadn't seen it coming. He gave a start and his mouth opened wide under the influence of surprise and admiration. The little dark-haired boy had kept his look of respectful interest. One might have doubted whether that mischievous hand belonged to him. 'What are they going to do to him?' I thought. I knew that something horrible was going to happen, and I saw too that there was still time to prevent it. But I couldn't manage to guess what it was that had to be prevented. For a second I thought of getting up, going and tapping the Autodidact on the shoulder, and starting a conversation with him. But at the same moment he caught sight of me looking at him. He stopped talking straight away and pursed his lips with an irritated expression. Discouraged, I quickly turned my eyes away and returned to my paper to keep myself in countenance. Meanwhile the fat lady had pushed her book away and raised her head. She seemed fascinated. I could distinctly feel that the drama was going to begin; they all *wanted* it to begin. What could I do? I glanced at the Corsican: he wasn't looking out of the window any more, he had half-turned towards us.

A quarter of an hour went by. The Autodidact had started whispering again. I didn't dare to look at him any more, but I could easily imagine his young and tender expression and those heavy gazes which were weighing on him without his knowing it. At one moment I heard his laugh, a childish, piping little laugh. It wrung my heart: I felt as if some nasty brats were going to drown a cat. Then, all of a sudden, the whispering stopped. The silence struck me as tragic: it was the end, the death-blow. I bent my head over my newspaper and I pretended to read: but I wasn't reading: I lifted my eyebrows and I raised my eyes as high as I could in an attempt to see what was happening in that silence in front of me. By turning my head slightly, I managed to catch sight of something out of the corner of my eye: it was a hand, the small white hand which had slid along the table a little earlier. Now it was lying on its back, relaxed, soft, and sensual, it had the indolent nudity of a woman sunning herself on the beach. A brown hairy object approached it hesitantly. It was a thick finger yellowed by tobacco; beside that hand, it had all the grossness of a male organ. It stopped for a moment, rigid, pointing at the fragile palm, then, all of a sudden, it timidly started stroking it. I wasn't surprised, more than anything I was furious at the Autodidact: couldn't he restrain himself, the fool, didn't he realize the risk he was running? He still had a chance, a small chance: if he put both his hands on the table, on either side of his book, if he stayed absolutely still, he might be able to escape his destiny this time. But I *knew* that he was going to miss his chance: the finger passed gently, humbly, over the inert flesh, scarcely touching it, without daring to exert any pressure: it was as if it were conscious of its ugliness. I raised my head abruptly, I couldn't stand that stubborn little back-and-forth movement any longer: I tried to catch the Autodidact's eye and I coughed loudly to warn him. But he had closed his eyes, he was smiling. His other hand had disappeared under the table. The boys had stopped laughing, they had turned very pale. The little brown-haired one was pursing his lips, he was frightened, he looked as if he felt that things had gone beyond his control. Yet he didn't draw his hand away, he left it on the table, motionless, scarcely clenched. His friend's mouth was open in a stupid, horrified expression.

It was then that the Corsican started shouting. He had come up without being heard and placed himself behind the Autodidact's chair. He was crimson and he looked as if he were laughing, but his eyes were flashing. I sat up with a start, but I felt almost relieved; the waiting period had been such a strain. I wanted it to be all over as soon as possible. They could throw him out if they wanted, provided they got it over with. The two boys, white as a sheet, grabbed their satchels in a flash and disappeared.

'I saw you,' cried the Corsican, drunk with rage, 'I saw you this time, don't try and tell me it isn't true. You're going to tell me it isn't true, are you? You think I didn't see your little game, do you? I've got eyes in my head, I'd have you know. Patience, I said to myself, patience, and when I catch him he'll pay for it. Oh, yes, you'll pay for it. I know your name, I know your address, I've checked up on you, you see. I know your boss too, Monsieur Chuillier. And won't he be surprised tomorrow morning, when he gets a letter from the librarian. Eh? Shut up!' he said, rolling his eyes. 'And don't imagine it's going to stop there. There are courts in France for people like you. So you were studying, were you? So you were completing your education, were you? So you kept on bothering me all the time, for information or for books. You never fooled me for a moment, you know.'

The Autodidact didn't look surprised. He must have been expecting this to happen for years. A hundred times he must have imagined what would happen, the day the Corsican would creep up behind him and a furious voice would suddenly bellow in his ears. And yet he came back every evening, he feverishly went on with his reading, and then, from time to time, like a thief, he stroked the white hand or perhaps the leg of a little boy. What I read on his face was resignation rather than anything else.

'I don't know what you mean,' he stammered. 'I've been coming here for years ...'

He was feigning indignation and surprise, but without conviction. He knew perfectly well that the event was there, and that nothing could hold it back any longer, that he had to live through the minutes of it one by one.

'Don't listen to him,' said my neighbour, 'I saw him.' She had struggled to her feet: 'And that isn't the first time I've seen him; no later than last Monday I saw him and I didn't say anything because I couldn't believe my eyes and I would never have thought that in a library, a serious place where people come to study, things would happen fit to make you blush. I haven't any children, but I pity the mothers who send theirs to work here, thinking they're quite safe, then there are monsters here with no respect for anything and who prevent them from doing their homework.'

The Corsican went up to the Autodidact.

'You hear what that lady says?' he shouted in his face. 'There's no need to put on an act. We saw you, you filthy swine!'

'Monsieur, I must ask you to be polite,' the Autodidact

said with dignity. He was playing his part. Perhaps he would have liked to confess, to run away, but he had to play his part to the end. He was not looking at the Corsican, his eyes were almost closed. His arms hung limply by his sides; he was horribly pale. And then, all of a sudden, a flush of blood rose to his face.

The Corsican was choking with rage.

'Polite? You swine! Perhaps you think I didn't see you. I was watching you, I tell you. I've been watching you for months.'

The Autodidact shrugged his shoulders and pretended to return to his reading. Scarlet, his eyes filled with tears, he had assumed an expression of extreme interest and was gazing intently at a reproduction of a Byzantine mosaic.

'He's going on reading, he's got a nerve,' the lady said, looking at the Corsican.

The latter was undecided as to what to do. At the same time, the assistant librarian, a timid, respectable young man who was terrorized by the Corsican, slowly raised himself above his desk and called out: 'Paoli, what's the matter?' There was a moment of hesitation and I hoped that the affair was going to end there. But the Corsican must have thought about it and felt that he was ridiculous. With his nerves on edge, no longer knowing what to say to that silent victim, he drew himself up to his full height and swung his fist into thin air. The Autodidact turned round in alarm. He looked at the Corsican open-mouthed; there was a horrible fear in his eyes.

'If you strike me, I shall report you,' he mumbled. 'I wish to leave of my own free will.'

I got up in my turn, but it was too late: the Corsican gave a little whine of pleasure and suddenly crashed his fist into the Autodidact's nose. For a second I could see nothing but the latter's eyes, his magnificent eyes, wide with shame and horror above a sleeve and a swarthy fist. When the Corsican drew his fist back the Autodidact's nose was beginning to piss blood. He tried to put his hand to his face, but the Corsican struck him again on the corner of his mouth. The Autodidact collapsed on to his chair and stared in front of him with gentle, timid eyes. The blood was pouring from his nose on to his clothes. He groped about with his right hand, trying to find his pocket, while his left hand was stubbornly trying to wipe his streaming nostrils.

'I'm going,' he said, as if speaking to himself.

The woman beside me was pale and her eyes were shining.

'Filthy rotter,' she said, 'serves him right.'

I was shaking with anger. I went round the table. I grabbed the little Corsican by the neck, and I lifted him up, with his arms and legs waving in the air: I should have liked to smash him on the table. He had turned blue in the face and was struggling, trying to scratch me; but his short arms didn't reach my face. I didn't say a word, but I wanted to hit him on the nose and disfigure him. He realized this, he raised his elbow to protect his face: I was glad because I saw he was afraid. Suddenly he started gasping:

'Let go of me, you brute. Are you a fairy too?'

I still wonder why I let him go. Was I afraid of complications? Have these lazy years at Bouville rusted me? In the old days I wouldn't have let go of him without knocking out his teeth. I turned to the Autodidact, who had finally got up. But he avoided my eyes; his head bowed, he went and got his coat. He kept passing his left hand under his nose as if to stop the bleeding. But the blood was still flowing and I was afraid that he might faint. Without looking at anybody, he muttered:

'I've been coming here for years . . .'

But the little man had hardly got back on his feet before he had taken command of the situation once more. . . .

'Get the hell out of here,' he told the Autodidact, 'and don't ever set foot in here again or I'll have the police on you.' I caught up with the Autodidact at the foot of the stairs. I was embarrassed, ashamed of his shame, I didn't know what to say to him. He didn't seem to notice I was there. He had finally taken out his handkerchief and was spitting something out. His nose was bleeding a little less.

'Come to the chemist's with me,' I said to him awkwardly.

He didn't reply. A loud murmur was coming from the reading room. Everybody in there must have been talking at once. The woman gave a shrill burst of laughter.

'I can never come back here,' said the Autodidact. He turned round and looked with a puzzled expression at the staircase, at the entrance to the reading room. This movement made some blood run between his collar and his neck. His mouth and cheeks were smeared with blood.

'Come along,' I said, taking him by the arm.

He gave a shudder and pulled away violently.

'Leave me alone!'

'But you can't stay by yourself. You need somebody to wash your face and fix you up.'

He repeated:

'Leave me alone, please, Monsieur, leave me alone.'

He was on the verge of hysterics: I let him walk away. The setting sun lit up his bent back for a moment, then he disappeared. On the threshold there was a bloodstain in the shape of a star.

One hour later

The sky is grey, the sun is setting: the train leaves in two hours from now. I have crossed the municipal park for the last time and I am walking along the rue Boulibet. I *know* that it is the rue Boulibet, but I don't recognize it. Usually, when I turned into it, I felt as if I were going through a thick layer of common sense; clumsy and square, with its solemn ugliness, its curved, tarred roadway, the rue Boulibet looked like a national highway when it passes through rich country towns and is lined with big three-storey houses for nearly a mile; I used to call it a country road and it delighted me because it was so out of place, so paradoxical in a commercial port. Today the houses are there, but they have lost their rural appearance: they are buildings and nothing more. I had the same sort of feeling in the municipal park just now: the plants, the lawns, the Olivier Masqueret Fountain were so expressionless they looked positively stubborn. I understand: the town is abandoning me first. I haven't left Bouville and already I am no longer here. Bouville is silent. I find it strange that I have to stay another two hours in this town which, without bothering about me any more, has put away its furniture and covered it with dust sheets so as to be able to uncover it in all its freshness for new arrivals, this evening or tomorrow. I feel more forgotten than ever.

I take a few steps and I stop. I savour this total oblivion into which I have fallen. I am between two towns. One knows nothing of me, the other knows me no longer. Who remembers me? Perhaps a plump young woman in London ... and even then, is it really about *me* that she thinks? Besides, there is that fellow, that Egyptian. Perhaps he has just gone into her room, perhaps he has taken her in his arms. I am not jealous; I know perfectly well that she is outliving herself. Even if she loved him with all her heart, it would still be the love of a dead woman. I had her last living love. But all the same there is something he can give her: pleasure. And if she is fainting and sinking into ecstasy, then there is no longer anything in her which links her with me. She is having her orgasm and I am no more to her than if I had never met her; she has suddenly emptied herself of me and all the other consciousnesses in the world are also empty of me. That seems funny. Yet I know perfectly well that I exist, that *I* am here.

Now when I say 'I', it seems hollow to me. I can no longer manage to feel myself, I am so forgotten. The only real thing left in me is some existence which can feel itself existing. I give a long, voluptuous yawn. Nobody. Antoine Roquentin exists for Nobody. That amuses me. And exactly what is Antoine Roquentin? An abstraction. A pale little memory of myself wavers in my consciousness. Antoine Roquentin . . . And suddenly the I pales, pales and finally goes out.

Lucid, motionless, empty, the consciousness is situated between the walls; it perpetuates itself. Nobody inhabits it any more. A little while ago somebody still said *me*, said *my* consciousness. Who? Outside there were talking streets, with familiar colours and smells. There remain anonymous walls, and anonymous consciousness. This is what there is: walls, and between the walls, a small living and impersonal transparency. The consciousness exists like a tree, like a blade of grass. It dozes, it feels bored. Little ephemeral existences populate it like birds in branches. Populate it and disappear. Forgotten consciousness, forsaken between these walls, under the grey sky. And this is the meaning of its existence: it is that it is a consciousness of being superfluous. It dilutes itself, it scatters itself, it tries to lose itself on the brown wall, up the lamp-post, or over there in the evening mist. But it *never* forgets itself; it is a consciousness of being a consciousness which forgets itself. That is its lot. There is a muffled voice which says: 'The train leaves in two hours' and there is a consciousness of that voice. There is also a consciousness of a face. It passes by slowly, covered with blood, smeared, and its big eyes weep. It is not between the walls, it is nowhere. It disappears, a bent body with a bleeding head replaces it, walks slowly away, seems to stop at every step, never stops. There is a consciousness of this body walking slowly along a dark street. It walks, but it gets no further away. The dark street does not come to an end, it loses itself in nothingness. It is not between the walls, it is nowhere. And there is a consciousness of a muffled voice which says: 'The Autodidact is wandering through the town.'

Not through the same town, no! Between those toneless walls, the Autodidact is walking in a ferocious town which hasn't forgotten him. There are people who are thinking about him – the Corsican, the fat lady, perhaps everybody in the town. He has not yet lost, cannot lose his identity, that tortured, bleeding identity which they refused to kill. His lips, his nostrils hurt; he thinks: 'I'm hurt.' He walks, he must walk. If he stopped for a single moment, the high walls of the library would suddenly rise around him and shut him in; the Corsican would spring up beside him and the scene would begin again, exactly the same in all its details, and the woman would snigger: 'Rotters like that ought to be in jail.' He walks, he doesn't want to go home: the Corsican is still waiting for him in his room and the woman and the two boys: 'Don't try and deny it, I saw you.' And the scene would begin again. He thinks: 'Oh, God, if only I hadn't done that, if only I could not have done that, if only it could not be true!'

The tormented face passes back and forth before the consciousness: 'Perhaps he is going to kill himself.' No: that gentle, hunted soul cannot think of death.

There is knowledge of the consciousness. It sees right through itself, peaceful and empty between the walls, freed from the man who inhabited it, monstrous because it is nobody. The voice says: 'The trunks are registered. The train leaves in two hours.' The walls glide past to right and left. There is consciousness of macadam, consciousness of the ironmonger's, of the loop-holes in the barracks and the voice says: 'For the last time.'

Consciousness of Anny, of fat Anny, of old Anny, in her hotel room, there is consciousness of suffering, suffering is conscious between the long walls which are going away and will never return: 'Will there never be an end to it?' the voice sings a jazz tune between the walls, 'Some of these days'; will there never be an end to it? and the tune comes back softly, from behind, insidiously, to pick up the voice, and the voice sings without being able to stop and the body walks and there is consciousness of all that and consciousness, alas, of the consciousness. But nobody is there to suffer and wring his hands and take pity on himself. Nobody. It is a pure suffering of the crossroads, a forgotten suffering – which cannot forget itself. And the voice says: 'There is the Rendez-vous des Cheminots' and the I surges into the consciousness, it is *I*, Antoine Roquentin, I am leaving for Paris in a little while; I have come to say good-bye to the *patronne*.

'I've come to say good-bye to you.'

'You're leaving, Monsieur Antoine?'

'I'm going to live in Paris, just for a change.'

'You lucky man!'

How can I have pressed my lips on this moonlike face? Her body no longer belongs to me. Yesterday I would still have been able to imagine it under the black woollen dress. Today the dress is impenetrable. That white body with the veins on the surface of the skin, was it a dream?

'We'll miss you,' says the *patronne*. 'Won't you have something to drink? It's on the house.'

We sit down, we clink glasses. She lowers her voice a little.

'I'd got really used to you,' she says with polite regret, 'we got on well together.'

'I'll come back to see you.'

'That's right, Monsieur Antoine. The next time you're

243

passing through Bouville, you drop in and say hullo to us. You just say to yourself: "I'll go and say hullo to Madame Jeanne, she'll like that." I mean that, it's always nice to know what's happened to other people. Besides, people always come back here to see us. We have sailors, you know, serving with the Transat: sometimes I go two years without seeing them, because they're either in Brazil or New York or else working on a transport at Bordeaux. And then one fine day I see them again. "Hullo, Madame Jeanne." We have a drink together. Believe it or not I always remember what each one likes. From two years back! I say to Madeleine: "Give Monsieur Pierre a dry vermouth, and Monsieur Léon a Noilly Cinzano." They ask me: "How do you remember that?" "It's my business," I tell them.'

At the back of the room there is a burly man who has been sleeping with her lately. He calls her:

'*Patronne!*'

She gets up:

'Excuse me, Monsieur Antoine.'

The waitress comes over to me:

'So you're leaving us just like that?'

'I'm going to Paris.'

'I've lived in Paris,' she says proudly. 'For two years. I was working at Siméon's. But I was homesick.'

She hesitates for a second, then realizes she has nothing more to say to me:

'Well, good-bye, Monsieur Antoine.'

She wipes her hand on her apron and holds it out to me:

'Good-bye, Madeleine.'

She goes off. I pull the *Journal de Bouville* over to me, and then I push it away again: I read it a little while ago at the library, from the first line to the last.

The *patronne* doesn't come back: she abandons her dumpy hands to her friend, who kneads them passionately.

The train leaves in three quarters of an hour.

I work out my finances to pass the time.

Twelve hundred francs a month isn't a fortune. But if I economize a little it should be enough. A room for three hundred francs, fifteen francs a day for food: that leaves four hundred and fifty francs for laundry, incidentals, and the cinema. I won't need any new clothes for a long time. Both my suits are clean, even if they're a little shiny at the elbows: they'll last me another three or four years if I take care of them.

Good lord! Is it I who is going to lead that mushroom existence? What am I going to do all day long? I'll go for walks. I'll go and sit in the Tuileries Gardens on an iron chair – or rather on a bench, to save money. I'll go and read in the libraries. And then what? Once a week the cinema. And then what? Shall I treat myself to a Voltigeur on Sunday? Shall I go and play croquet with the pensioners in the Luxembourg Gardens? At the age of thirty! I feel sorry for myself. There are times when I wonder if I wouldn't do best to spend in one year the three hundred thousand francs I have left – and afterwards . . . But what would that give me? New suits? Women? Travel? I've had all that, and now it's over, I don't feel like it any more: not for what I'd get out of it! A year from now I'd find myself as empty as I am today, without even a memory and afraid to face death.

Thirty years old! And an annual income of 14,400 francs. Dividend coupons to cash every month. Yet I'm not an old man! Let them give me something to do, no matter what. . . . I'd better think about something else, because at this moment I'm putting on an act for my own benefit. I know perfectly well that I don't want to do anything; to do something is to create existence – and there's quite enough existence as it is. The fact is that I can't put down my pen: I think I'm going to have the Nausea and I have the impression that I put it off by writing. So I write down whatever comes into my head.

Madeleine, who wants to please me, calls to me from a distance, showing me a record:

'Your record, Monsieur Antoine, the one you like, do you want to hear it for the last time?'

'Please.'

I said that out of politeness, but I don't really feel in the mood for listening to a jazz tune. All the same, I'm going to pay attention, because, as Madeleine says, I'm hearing this record for the last time: it's a very old record; too old, even for the provinces; I shall look for it in vain in Paris. Madeleine is going to put it on the turn-table of the gramophone, it is going to spin; in the grooves, the steel needle is going to start jumping and grating and then, when they have spiralled it into the centre of the record, it will be finished, the hoarse voice which sings *Some of These Days* will fall silent forever.

It begins.

To think that there are idiots who derive consolation from the fine arts. Like my Aunt Bigeois: 'Chopin's *Preludes* were such a help to me when your poor uncle died.' And the concert halls are full to overflowing with humiliated, injured people who close their eyes and try to turn their pale faces into receiving aerials. They imagine that the sounds they receive flow into them, sweet and nourishing, and that their sufferings become music, like those of young Werther; they think that beauty is compassionate towards them. The mugs.

I'd like them to tell me whether they find this music compassionate. Just now, I was certainly a long way from swimming in bliss. On the surface I was doing my accounts, automatically. Underneath were stagnating all those unpleasant thoughts which have taken the shape of unformulated questions, of mute astonishments which no longer leave me either by day or by night. Thoughts about Anny, about my wasted life. And then, still further down, the Nausea, as timid as a dawn. But at that particular moment there was no music, I was morose and calm. All the objects around me were made of the same material as I, a sort of shoddy suffering. The world was so ugly, outside me, these dirty glasses on the table were so ugly, and the brown stains on the mirror and Madeleine's apron and the kindly look of the *patronne*'s burly lover were so ugly, the very existence of the world was so ugly, that I felt completely at ease, at home.

Now there is this tune on the saxophone. And I am ashamed. A conceited little suffering has just been born, an exemplary suffering. Four notes on the saxophone. They come and go, they seem to say: 'You must do like us, suffer in strict time.' Well, yes! Of course I'd be glad to suffer that way, in strict time, without any complacency, without any self-pity, with an arid purity. But is it my fault if the beer at the bottom of my glass is warm, if there are brown stains on the mirror, if I am superfluous, if the sincerest and driest of my sufferings trails along heavily, with too much flesh and its skin too loose, like the sea-elephant, with bulging eyes which are wet and touching yet so ugly? No, they certainly can't say it's compassionate, this little diamond pain which is spinning around above the record and dazzling me. It isn't even ironic: it spins gaily, completely absorbed in itself; it has cut like a scythe through the insipid intimacy of the world and now it spins and all of us, Madeleine, the burly man, the *patronne,* I myself and the tables, the benches, the stained mirror, the glasses, all of us who were abandoning ourselves to existence, because we were between ourselves, just between ourselves – it has caught us in our untidy, everyday condition: I am ashamed for myself and for what exists *in front of it.*

It does not exist. It is even irritating in its non-existence; if I were to get up, if I were to snatch that record from the turn-table which is holding it and if I were to break it in two, I wouldn't reach *it*. It is beyond – always beyond something, beyond a voice, beyond a violin note. Through layers and layers of existence, it unveils itself, slim and firm, and when you try to seize it you meet nothing but existents, you run up against existents devoid of meaning. It is behind them: I can't even hear it, I hear sounds, vibrations in the air which unveil it. It does not exist, since it has nothing superfluous: it is all the rest which is superfluous in relation to it. It *is*.

And I too have wanted to *be*. Indeed I have never wanted anything else; that's what lay at the bottom of my life: behind all these attempts which seemed unconnected, I find the same desire: to drive existence out of me, to empty the moments of their fat, to wring them, to dry them, to purify myself, to harden myself, to produce in short the sharp, precise sound of a saxophone note. That could even serve as a fable: there was a poor fellow who had got into the wrong world. He existed, like other people, in the world of municipal parks, of *bistros*, of ports and he wanted to convince himself that he was living somewhere else, behind the canvas of paintings, with the doges of Tintoretto, with Gozzoli's worthy Florentines, behind the pages of books, with Fabrice del Dongo and Julien Sorel, behind gramophone records, with the long dry laments of jazz music. And then, after making a complete fool of himself, he understood, he opened his eyes, he saw that there had been a mistake: he was in a *bistro*, in fact, in front of a glass of warm beer. He sat there on the bench, utterly depressed; he thought: I am a fool. And at that very moment, on the other side of existence, in that other world which you can see from a distance, but without ever approaching it, a little melody started dancing, started singing: 'You must be like me; you must suffer in strict time.'

The voice sings:

> Some of these days
> You'll miss me honey

Somebody must have scratched the record at that spot, because it makes a peculiar noise. And there is something that wrings the heart: it is that the melody is absolutely untouched by this little stuttering of the needle on the record. It is so far away – so far behind. I understand that too: the record is getting scratched and worn, the singer may be dead; I myself am going to leave, I am going to catch my train. But behind the existence which falls from one present to the next, without a past, without a future, behind these sounds which decompose from day to day, peels away and slips towards death, the melody stays the same, young and firm, like a pitiless witness.

The voice has fallen silent. The disc scrapes a little then stops. Delivered from a troublesome dream, the café ruminates, chews on the pleasure of existing. The *patronne*'s face is flushed, she slaps the fat white cheeks of her new friend, but without succeeding in bringing any colour to them. A dead man's cheeks. I stagnate, I fall half-asleep. In a quarter of an hour I will be on the train, but I don't think about it. I think about a clean-shaven American, with thick black eyebrows, who is suffocating with the heat, on the twentieth floor of a New York skyscraper. Over New York the sky is burning, the blue of the sky has caught fire, huge yellow flames are licking the roofs; the Brooklyn children are going to stand in bathing-trunks under the jets of hose-pipes. The dark room on the twentieth floor is baking hot. The American with the black eyebrows sighs, pants and the sweat rolls down his cheeks. He is sitting in shirt-sleeves at his piano:

he has a taste of smoke in his mouth and, vaguely, a ghost of a tune in his head. 'Some of these days'. Tom will come along in an hour with his hip-flask; then the two of them will flop into leather armchairs and drink great draughts of spirits and the fire in the sky will come and burn their throats, they will feel the weight of an immense torrid slumber. But first of all that tune must be noted down. 'Some of these days'. The moist hand picks up the pencil on the piano. 'Some of these days, you'll miss me honey.'

It happened like that. Like that or some other way, it doesn't matter. That is how it was born. It was the worn body of that Jew with coal-black eye-brows which it chose to give it birth. He held his pencil limply and drops of sweat fell from his ringed fingers on to the paper. And why not me? Why had it to be that fat lout full of stale beer and spirits who was chosen so that the miracle could be performed?

'Madeleine, will you put the record on again? Just once, before I leave.'

Madeleine starts laughing. She turns the handle and it begins again. But I am no longer thinking about myself. I am thinking about that fellow out there who composed this tune, one day in July, in the black heat of his room. I try to think about him *through* the melody, through the white, acid sounds of the saxophone. He made that. He had troubles, everything wasn't working out for him as it should have: bills to pay – and then there must have been a woman somewhere who wasn't thinking about him the way he would have liked her to – and then there was this terrible heatwave which was turning men into pools of melting fat. There is nothing very pretty or very glorious about all that. But when I hear the song and I think that it was that fellow who made it, I find his suffering and his sweat . . . moving. He was lucky. He can't have realized that, of course. He must have thought: with a little luck, this thing ought to bring in fifty dollars. Well, this is the first time for years that a man has struck me as moving. I should like to know something about that fellow. I should be interested to find out what sort of troubles he had, whether he had a woman or whether he lived alone. Not at all out of humanism; far from it, but because he made that. I've no desire to know him – besides, he may be dead. Just to get a little information about him and to be able to think about him, now and then, when listening to this record. I don't suppose it would make the slightest difference to the fellow if he were told that in the seventh largest town in France, in the vicinity of the station, somebody is thinking about him. But I would be happy if I were in his place; I envy him. I have to go. I get up, but I hesitate for a moment, I should like to hear the Negress sing. For the last time.

She sings. That makes two people who are saved: the Jew and the Negress. Saved. Perhaps they thought they were lost right until the very end, drowned in existence. Yet nobody could think about me as I think about them, with this gentle feeling. Nobody, not even Anny. For me they are a little like dead people, a little like heroes of novels; they have cleansed themselves of the sin of existing. Not completely, of course – but as much as any man can. This idea suddenly bowls me over, because I didn't even hope for that any more. I feel something timidly brushing against me and I dare not move because I am afraid it might go away. Something I didn't know any more: a sort of joy.

The Negress sings. So you can justify your existence? Just a little? I feel extraordinarily intimidated. It isn't that I have much hope. But I am like a man who is completely frozen after a journey through the snow and who suddenly comes into a warm room. I imagine he would remain motionless

251

near the door, still feeling cold, and that slow shivers would run over the whole of his body.

Some of these days
You'll miss me honey

Couldn't I try ... Naturally, it wouldn't be a question of a tune ... But couldn't I in another medium? ... It would have to be a book: I don't know how to do anything else. But not a history book: history talks about what has existed – an existent can never justify the existence of another existent. My mistake was to try to resuscitate Monsieur de Rollebon. Another kind of book. I don't quite know which kind – but you would have to guess, behind the printed words, behind the pages, something which didn't exist, which was above existence. The sort of story, for example, which could never happen, an adventure. It would have to be beautiful and hard as steel and make people ashamed of their existence.

I am going, I feel irresolute. I dare not make a decision. If I were sure that I had talent ... but I have never, never written anything of that sort; historical articles, yes – if you could call them that. A book. A novel. And there would be people who would read this novel and who would say: 'It was Antoine Roquentin who wrote it, he was a red-headed fellow who hung about in cafés', and they would think about my life as I think about the life of that Negress: as about something precious and almost legendary. A book. Naturally, at first it would only be a tedious, tiring job, it wouldn't prevent me from existing or from feeling that I exist. But a time would have to come when the book would be written, would be behind me, and I think that a little of its light would fall over my past. Then, through it, I might be able to recall my life without repugnance. Perhaps one day, thinking about this very moment, about this dismal moment at which I am waiting, round-shouldered, for it to be time to get on the train, perhaps I might feel my heart beat faster and say to myself: 'It was on that day, at that moment that it all started.' And I might succeed – in the past, simply in the past – in accepting myself.

Night is falling. On the first floor of the Hôtel Printania two windows have just lighted up. The yard of the New Station smells strongly of damp wood: tomorrow it will rain over Bouville.

READ MORE IN PENGUIN

In every corner of the world, on every subject under the sun, Penguin represents quality and variety – the very best in publishing today.

For complete information about books available from Penguin – including Puffins, Penguin Classics and Arkana – and how to order them, write to us at the appropriate address below. Please note that for copyright reasons the selection of books varies from country to country.

In the United Kingdom: Please write to *Dept. EP, Penguin Books Ltd, Bath Road, Harmondsworth, West Drayton, Middlesex UB7 ODA*

In the United States: Please write to *Consumer Sales, Penguin Putnam Inc., P.O. Box 999, Dept. 17109, Bergenfield, New Jersey 07621-0120*. VISA and MasterCard holders call 1-800-253-6476 to order Penguin titles

In Canada: Please write to *Penguin Books Canada Ltd, 10 Alcorn Avenue, Suite 300, Toronto, Ontario M4V 3B2*

In Australia: Please write to *Penguin Books Australia Ltd, P.O. Box 257, Ringwood, Victoria 3134*

In New Zealand: Please write to *Penguin Books (NZ) Ltd, Private Bag 102902, North Shore Mail Centre, Auckland 10*

In India: Please write to *Penguin Books India Pvt Ltd, 210 Chiranjiv Tower, 43 Nehru Place, New Delhi 110 019*

In the Netherlands: Please write to *Penguin Books Netherlands bv, Postbus 3507, NL-1001 AH Amsterdam*

In Germany: Please write to *Penguin Books Deutschland GmbH, Metzlerstrasse 26, 60594 Frankfurt am Main*

In Spain: Please write to *Penguin Books S. A., Bravo Murillo 19, 1° B, 28015 Madrid*

In Italy: Please write to *Penguin Italia s.r.l., Via Benedetto Croce 2, 20094 Corsico, Milano*

In France: Please write to *Penguin France, Le Carré Wilson, 62 rue Benjamin Baillaud, 31500 Toulouse*

In Japan: Please write to *Penguin Books Japan Ltd, Kaneko Building, 2-3-25 Koraku, Bunkyo-Ku, Tokyo 112*

In South Africa: Please write to *Penguin Books South Africa (Pty) Ltd, Private Bag X14, Parkview, 2122 Johannesburg*

BY THE SAME AUTHOR

The Age of Reason

Set in the volatile Paris summer of 1938, *The Age of Reason* follows two days in the life of Mathieu Delarue, a philosophy teacher, and his circle in the cafes and bars of Montparnasse. Mathieu has so far managed to contain sex and personal freedom in conveniently separate compartments. But now he is in trouble, urgently trying to raise 4,000 francs to procure a safe abortion for his mistress, Marcelle. Beyond all this, filtering an uneasy light on his predicament, rises the distant threat of the coming of the Second World War.

The Reprieve

September 1938: in a heat wave Europe tensely awaits the outcome of the Munich conference. In Paris people are waiting too, among them Mathieu, Jacques and Philippe – not one of them ready to fight.

Cutting from one scene to the next, Sartre depicts the hopes, fears and self-deceptions of Munich, building a powerful montage of that critical week when Europe, in its pathetic longing for a reprieve, blinkered itself against the threat of war.

Iron in the Soul

June 1940: this was the summer of defeat. Day by day, hour by hour, *Iron in the Soul* unfolds what men thought and felt and did as France fell. Men who shrugged, men who ran, men who fought and tragic men like Mathieu, riven with remorse, who must somehow learn to kill.

also published:

Altona and Other Plays
In Camera and Other Plays
Words
Three Plays
Roads to Freedom